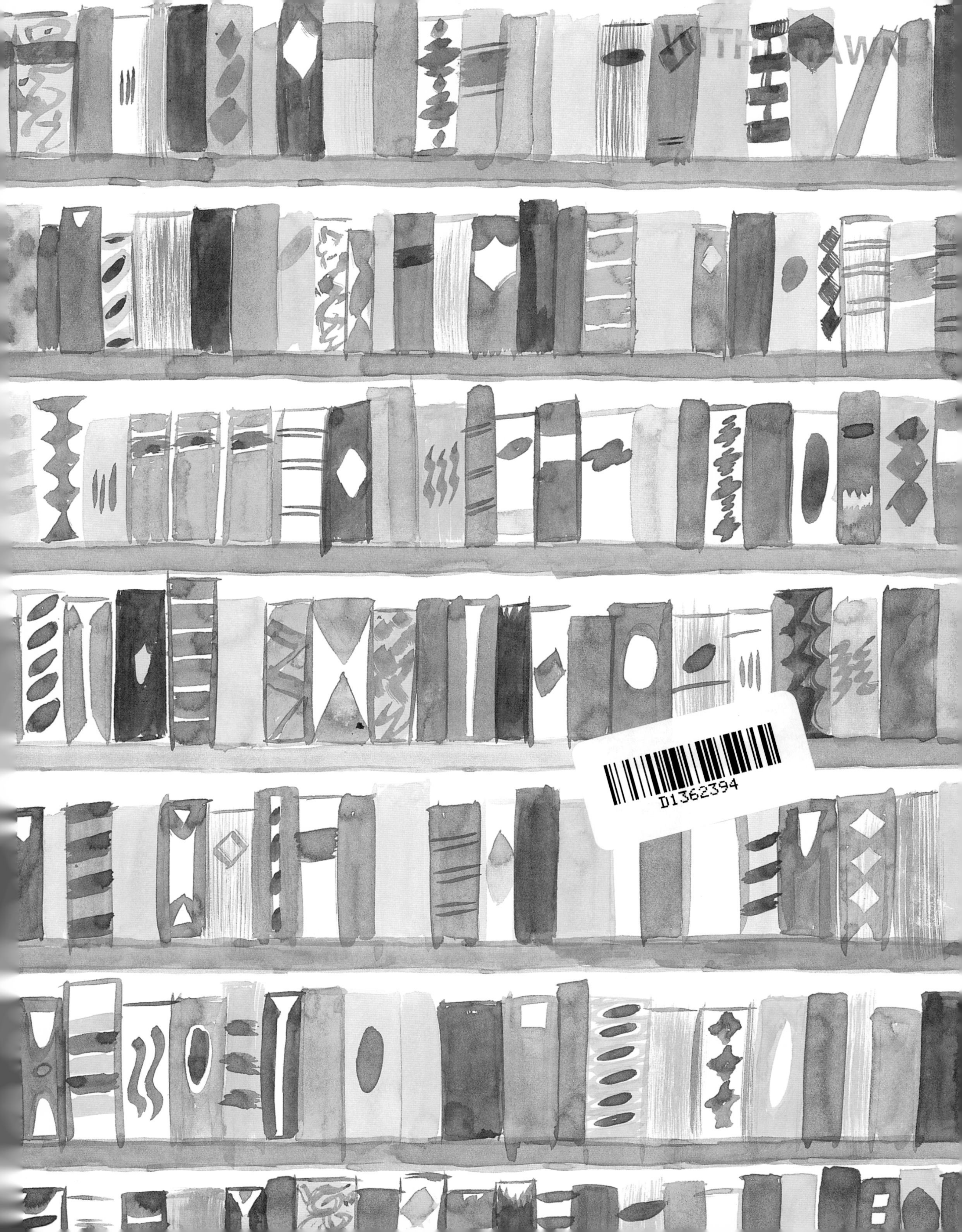

This book belongs to:

The Bind

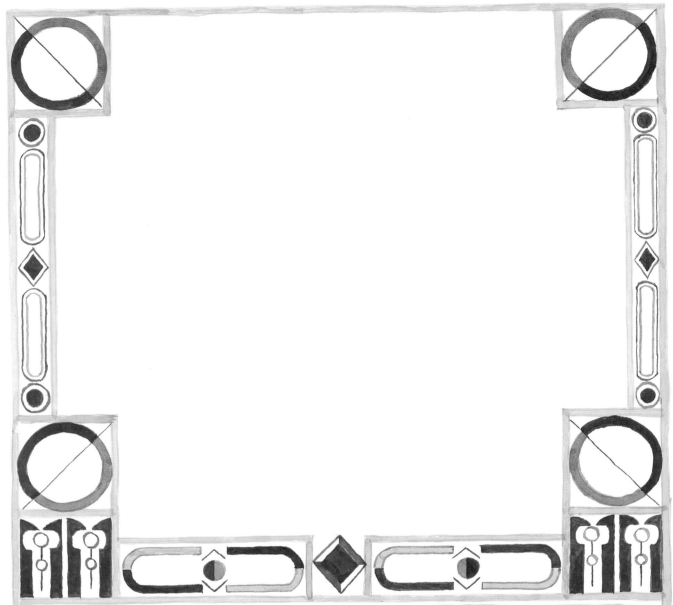

13579108642   JONATHAN CAPE, AN IMPRINT OF VINTAGE PUBLISHING, 20 VAUXHALL BRIDGE ROAD, LONDON, SW1V 2SA. JONATHAN CAPE IS PART OF THE PENGUIN RANDOM HOUSE GROUP OF COMPANIES WHOSE ADDRESSES CAN BE FOUND AT GLOBAL.PENGUINRANDOMHOUSE.COM.

FIRST PUBLISHED BY JONATHAN CAPE IN 2015.

WWW.VINTAGE-BOOKS.CO.UK

A CIP CATALOGUE RECORD FOR THIS BOOK IS AVAILABLE FROM THE BRITISH LIBRARY
ISBN 9780224097024 PRINTED AND BOUND IN CHINA BY C&C OFFSET PRINTING, LTD

THE AUTHOR WOULD LIKE TO THANK THE SOCIETY OF AUTHORS FOR THEIR GENEROSITY AND SUPPORT, AND DAN FRANKLIN, NEIL BRADFORD AND SUZANNE DEAN AT JONATHAN CAPE.
ALSO, THE FOLLOWING PEOPLE FOR THEIR THOUGHTS AND HELP WITH RESEARCH: JONATHAN SMITH, MARC BAINES, ROMILLY SAUMAREZ-SMITH, BERNARD MIDDLETON, ANDY CLARKE, CHARLES GLEDHILL, MARK WINSTANLEY AND STAFF AT THE WYVERN BINDERY, ALYSON STRACHAN AT SHEPHERD'S, KATHERINE JONES AT THE V&A AND RIBA, PHILIPPA MARKS AT THE BRITISH LIBRARY, EDWARD BAYNTUN-COWARD OF GEORGE BAYNTUN, AND JANET GOLLAN AT EDINBURGH LIBRARIES.

FOR MY FAMILY, WHO ARE NOTHING LIKE THE EGRETS.

"The Bind"

BY

William Goldsmith

JONATHAN CAPE LONDON

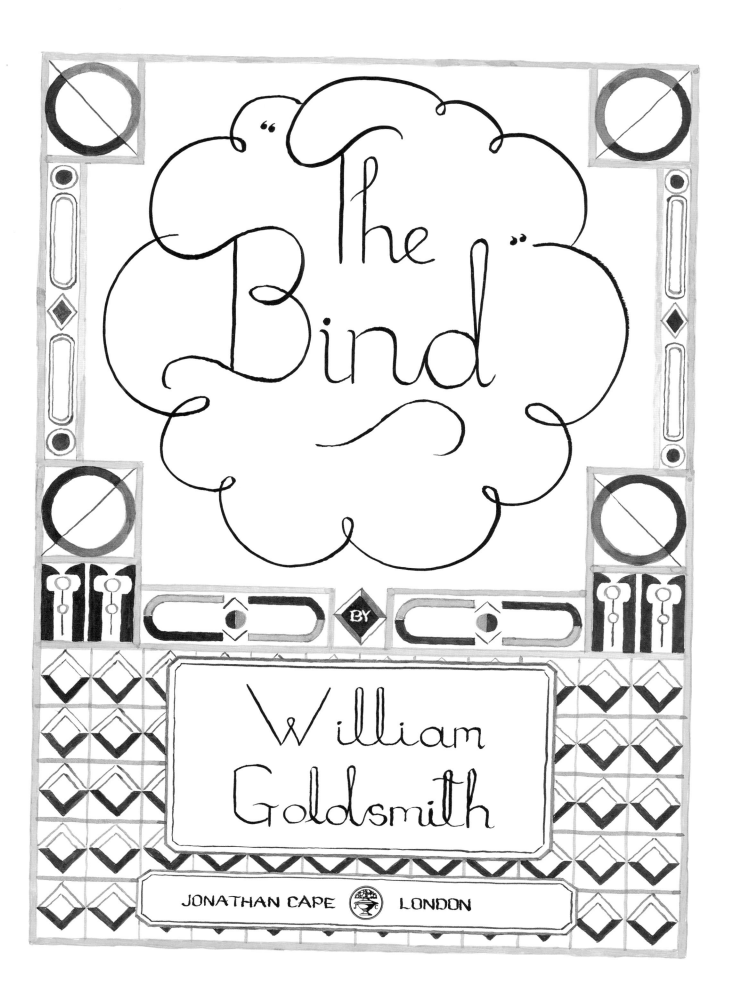

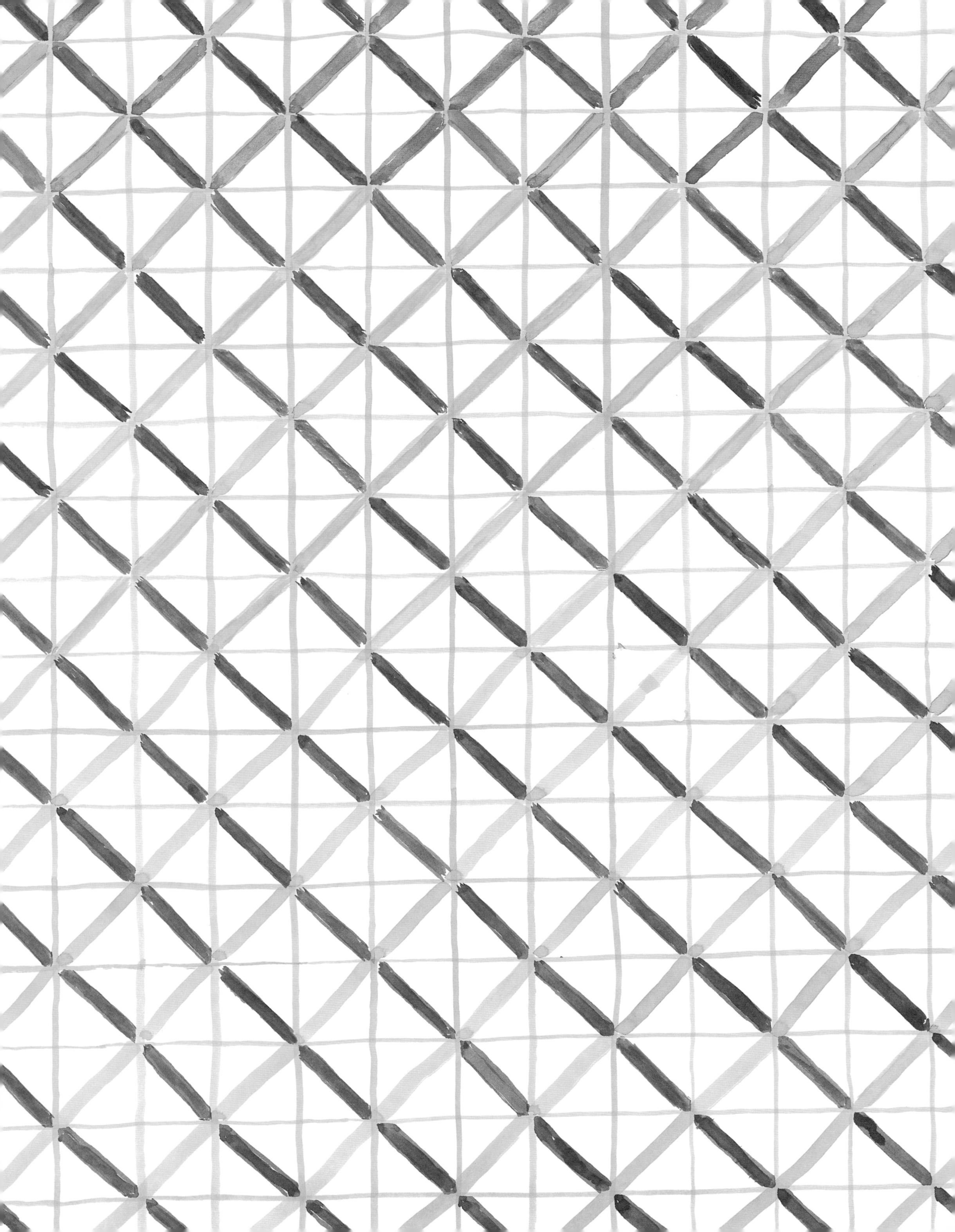

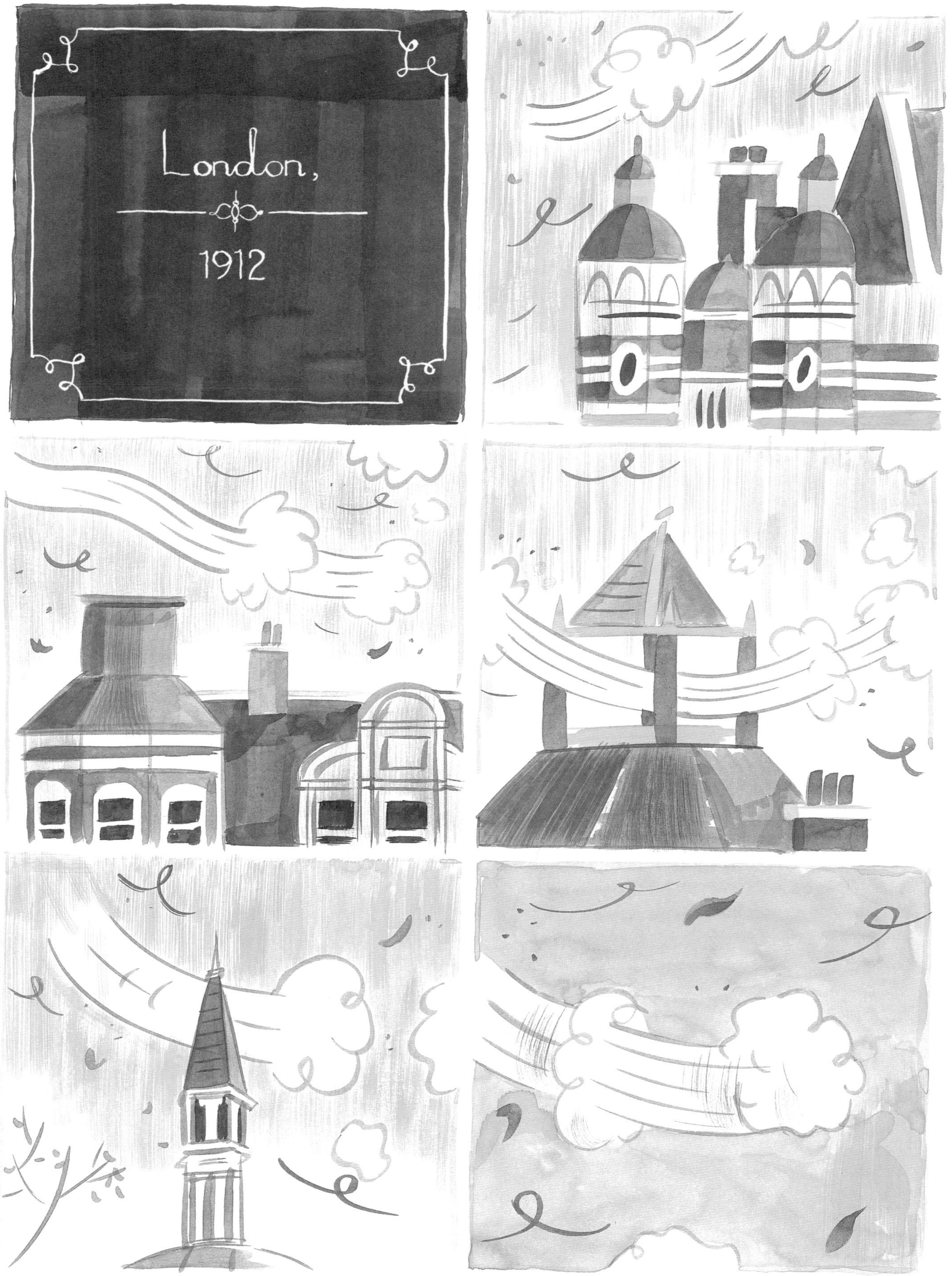
London,
1912

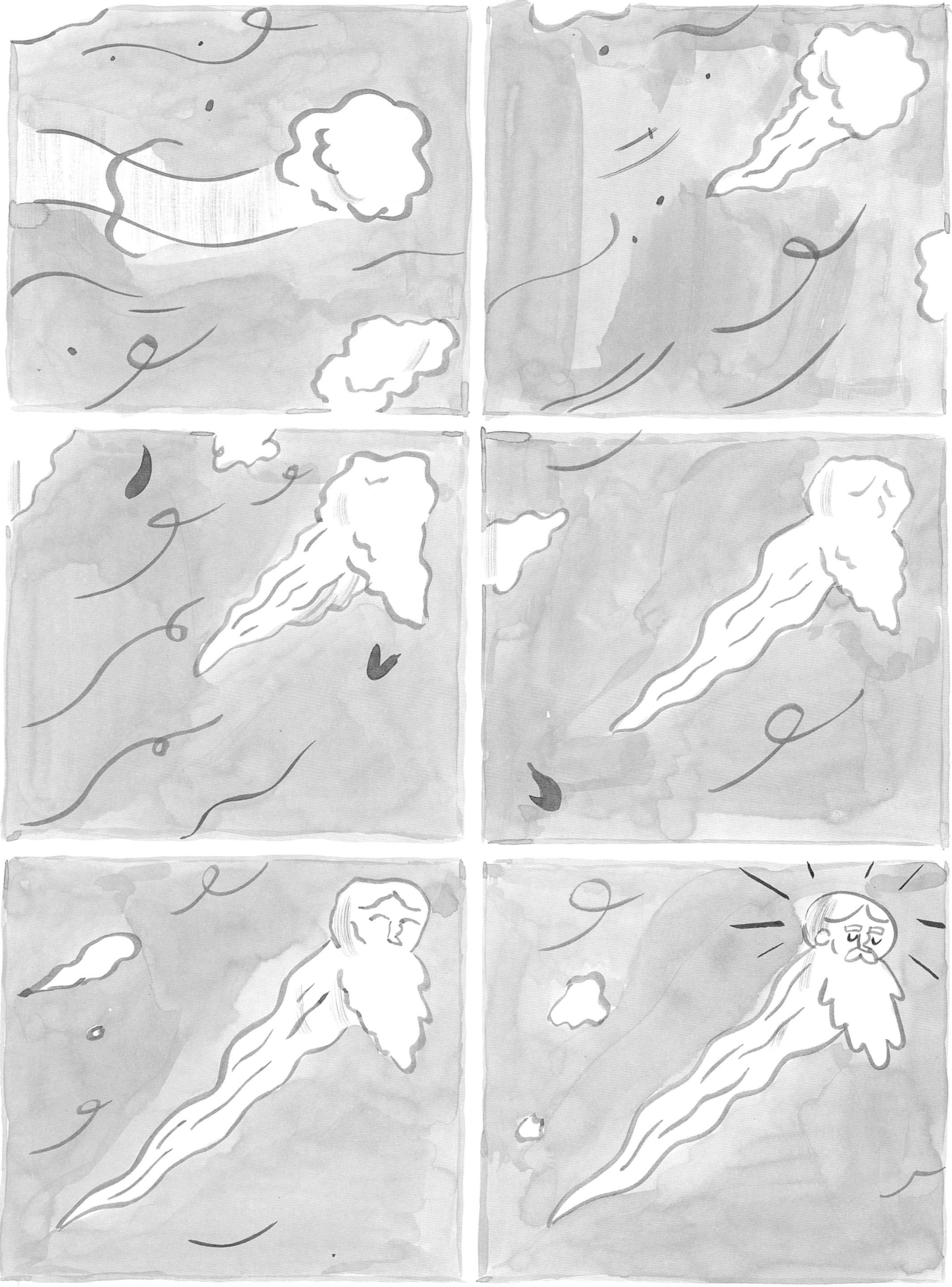

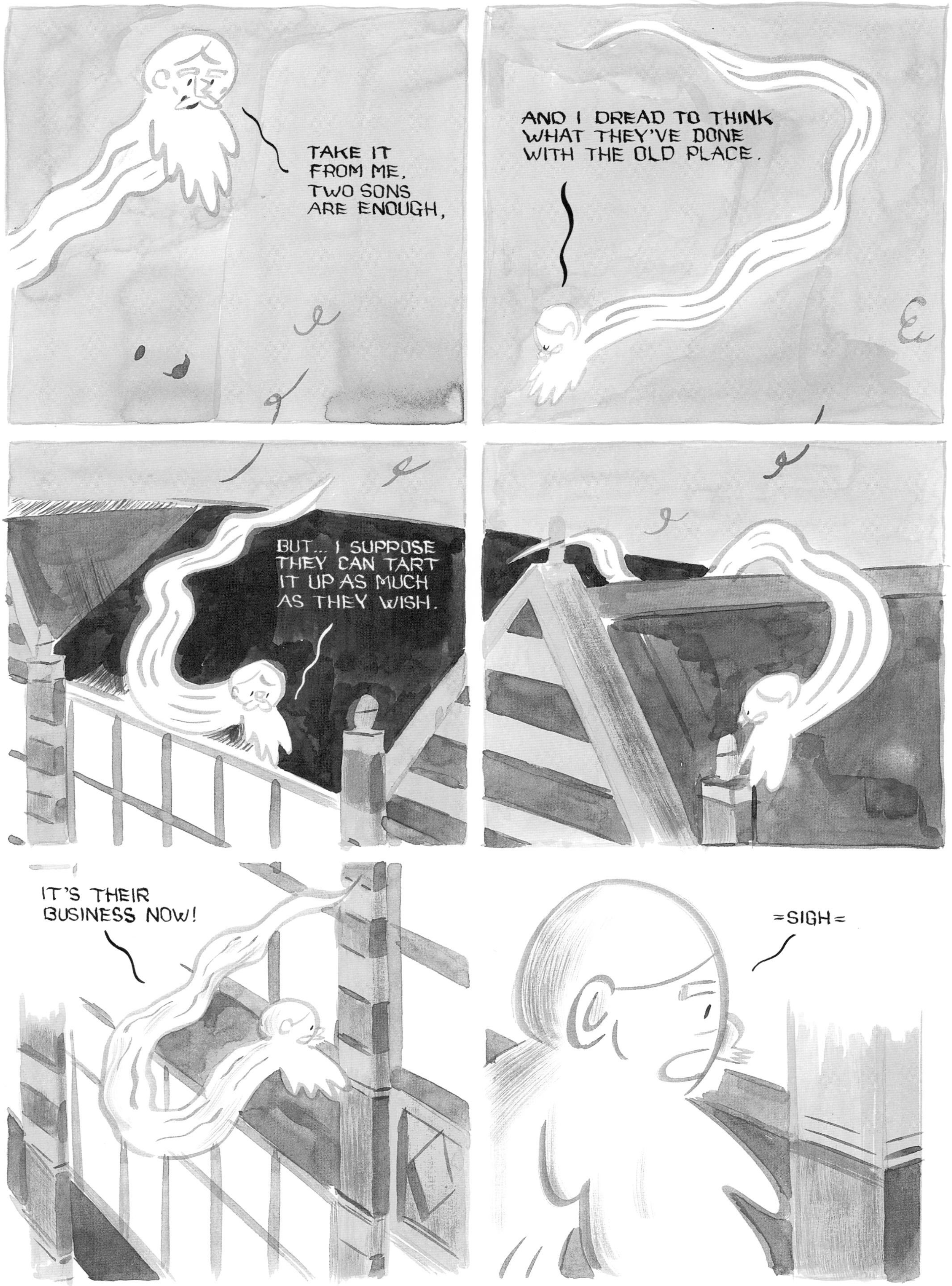
TAKE IT FROM ME, TWO SONS ARE ENOUGH,
AND I DREAD TO THINK WHAT THEY'VE DONE WITH THE OLD PLACE.
BUT... I SUPPOSE THEY CAN TART IT UP AS MUCH AS THEY WISH.
IT'S THEIR BUSINESS NOW!
=SIGH=

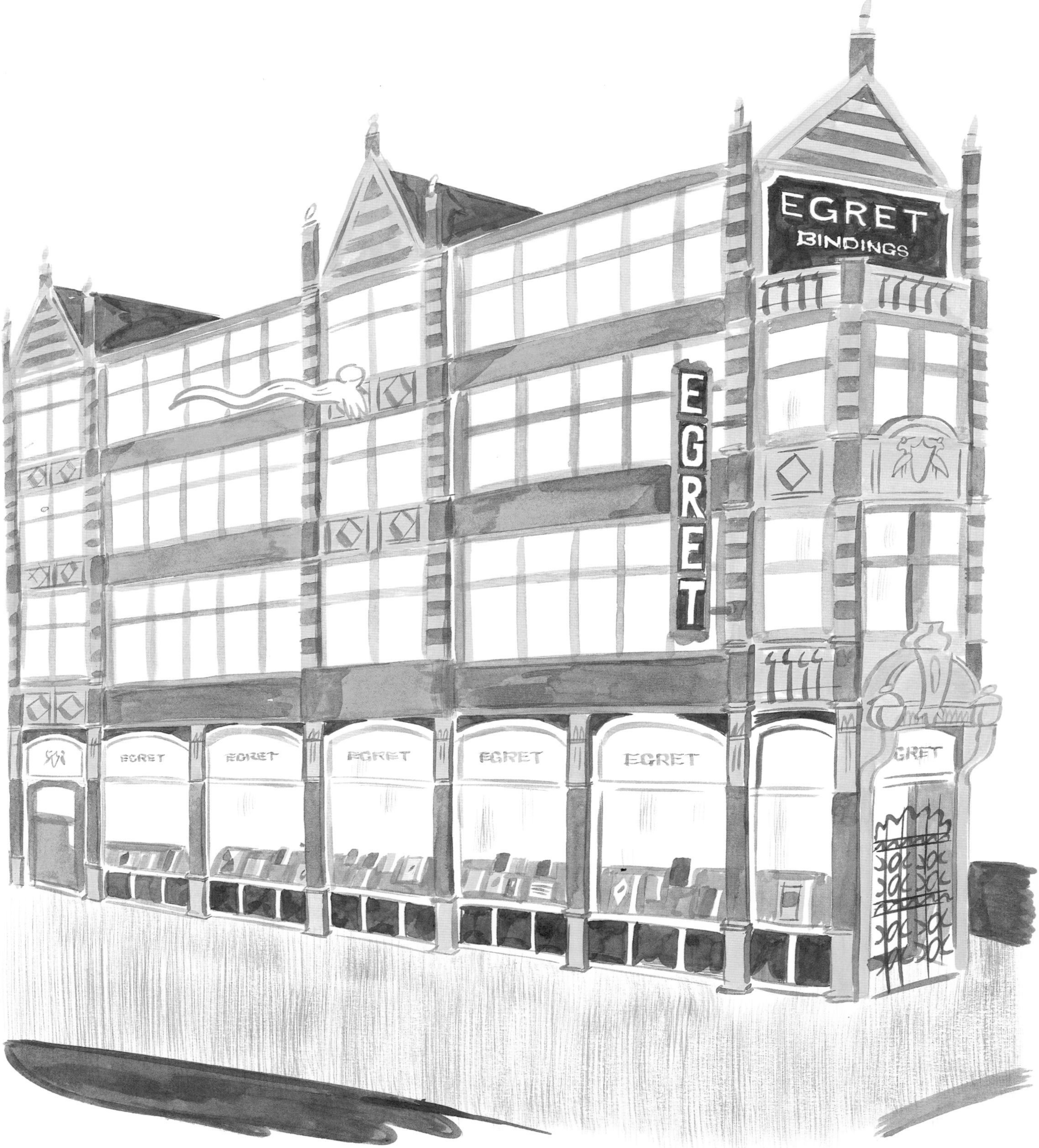
EGRET
BINDINGS
EGRET
EGRET
EGRET
EGRET
EGRET
EGRET
GRET

PART ONE:

The Spirit of a Bookbinder

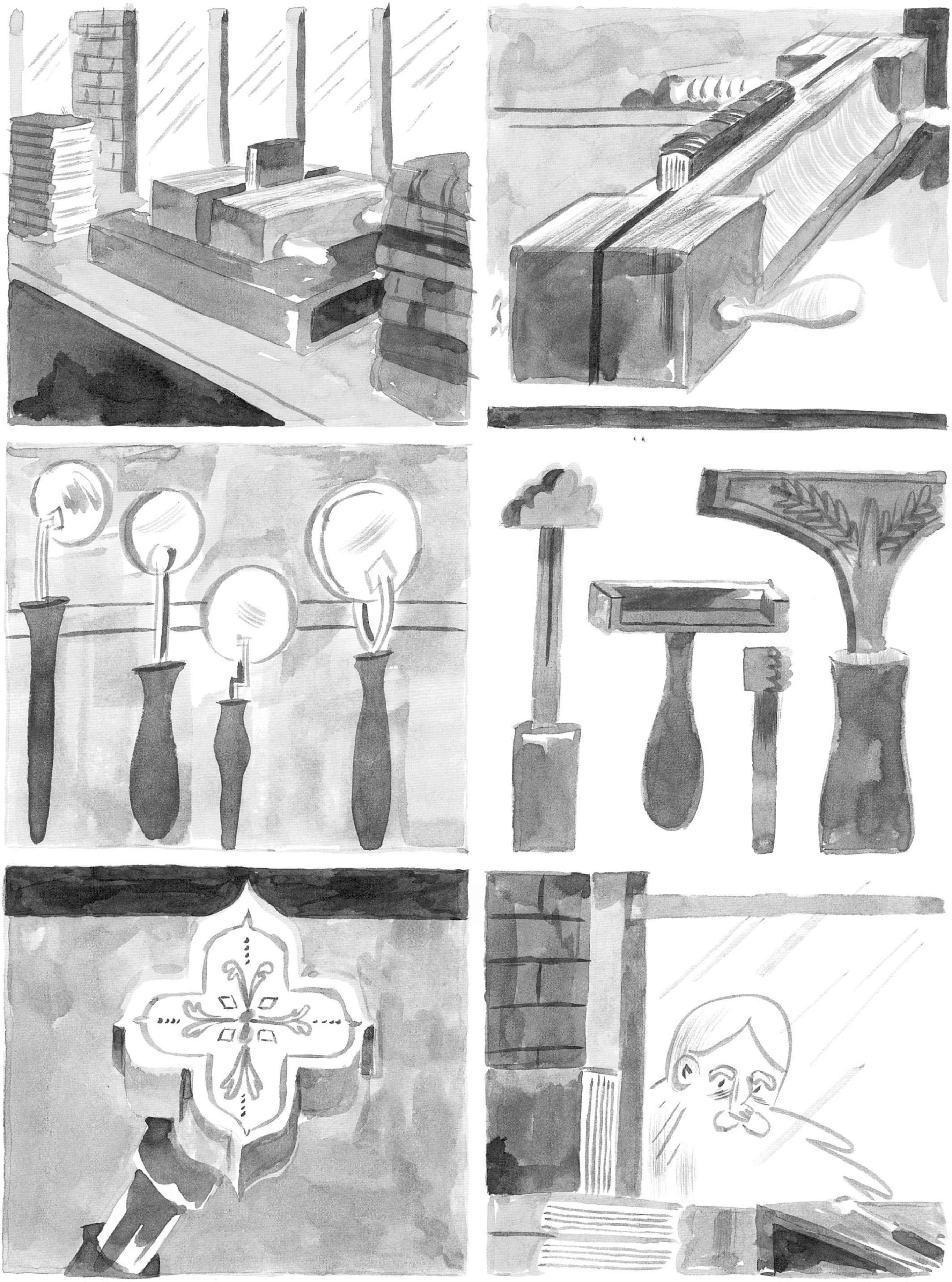

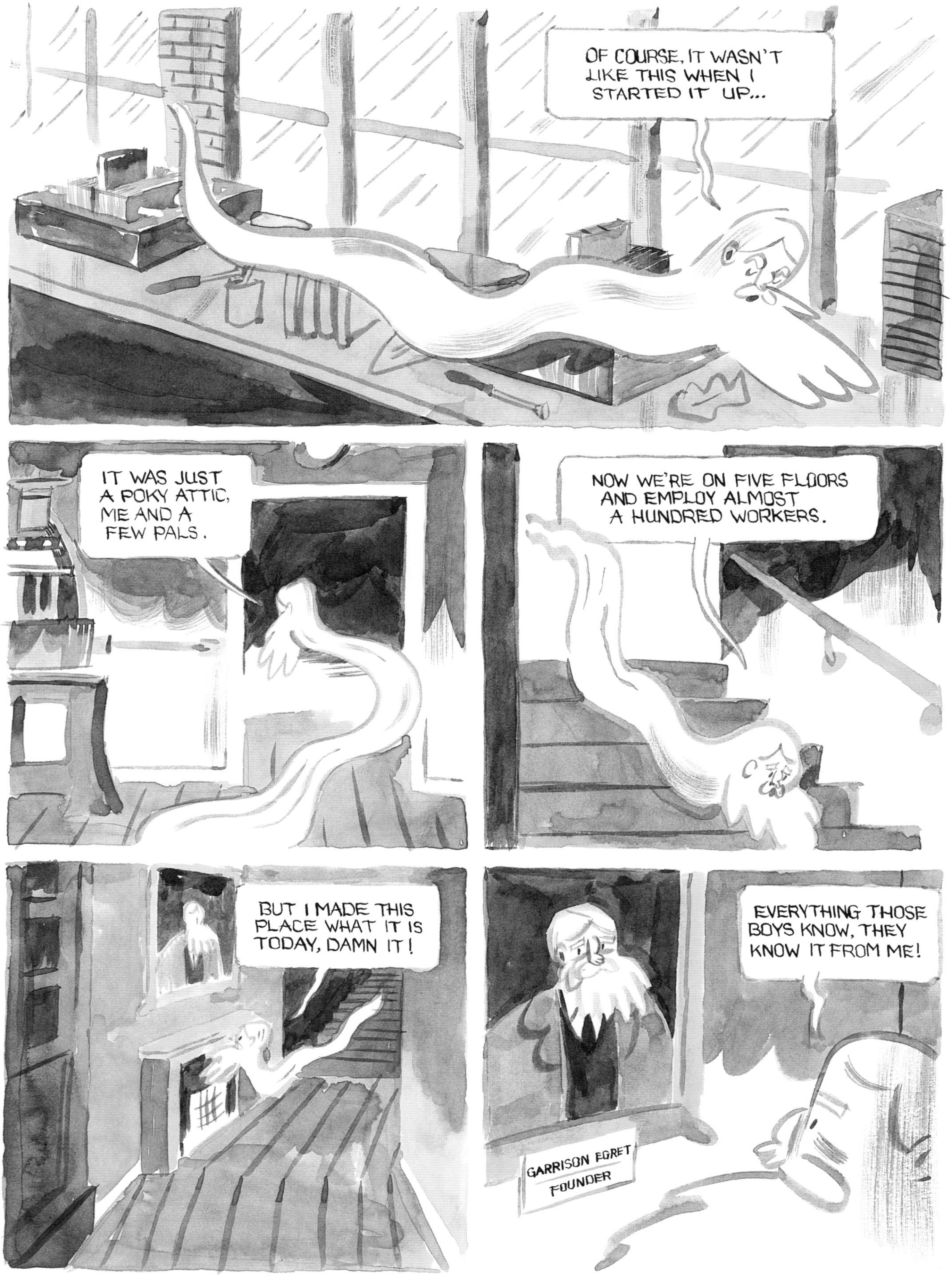
OF COURSE, IT WASN'T LIKE THIS WHEN I STARTED IT UP...
IT WAS JUST A POKY ATTIC, ME AND A FEW PALS.
NOW WE'RE ON FIVE FLOORS AND EMPLOY ALMOST A HUNDRED WORKERS.
BUT I MADE THIS PLACE WHAT IT IS TODAY, DAMN IT!
GARRISON EGRET
FOUNDER
EVERYTHING THOSE BOYS KNOW, THEY KNOW IT FROM ME!

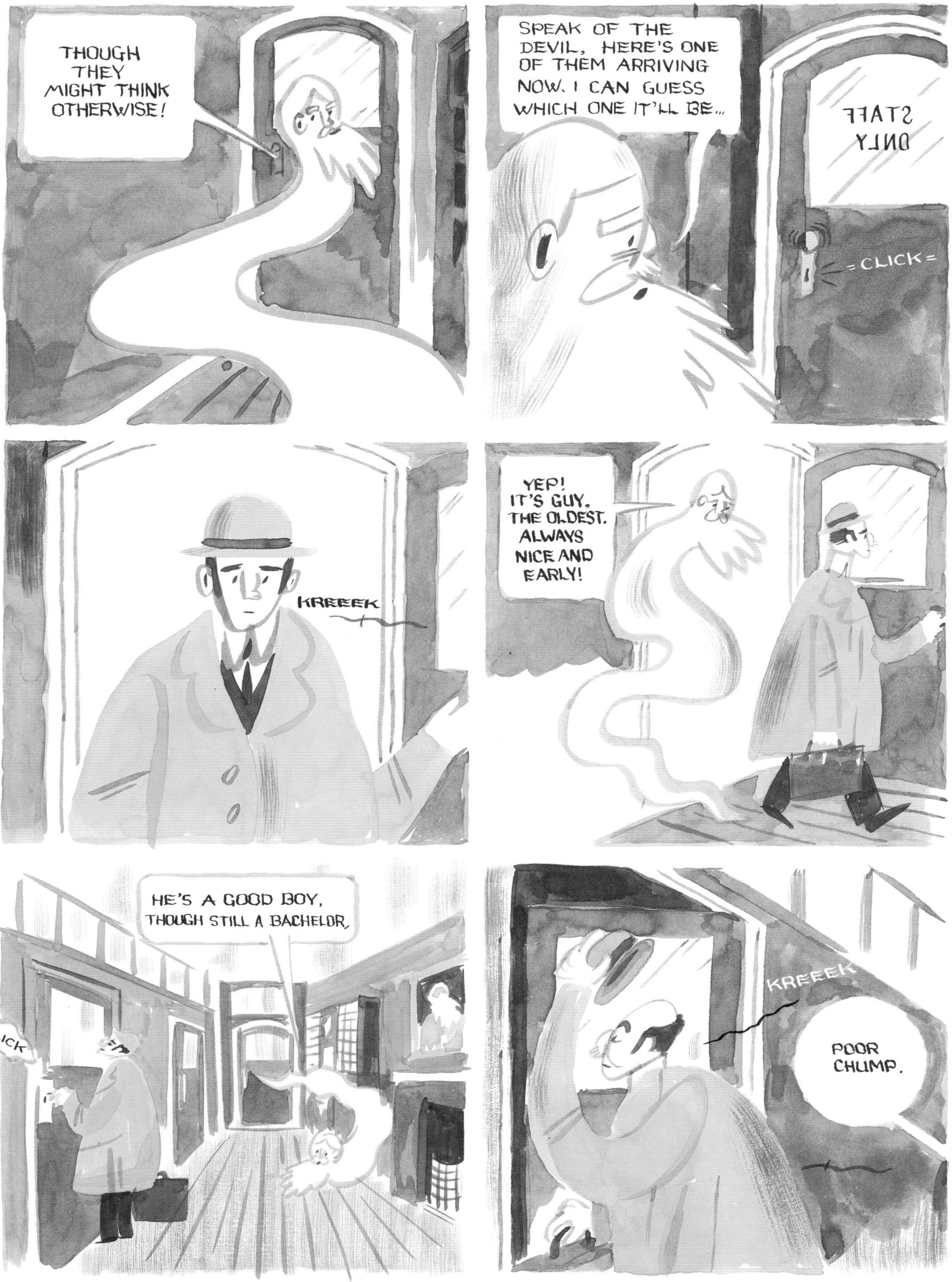
THOUGH THEY MIGHT THINK OTHERWISE!
SPEAK OF THE DEVIL, HERE'S ONE OF THEM ARRIVING NOW. I CAN GUESS WHICH ONE IT'LL BE...
STAFF ONLY
=CLICK=
KREEEK
YEP! IT'S GUY, THE OLDEST. ALWAYS NICE AND EARLY!
CLICK
HE'S A GOOD BOY, THOUGH STILL A BACHELOR,
KREEEK
POOR CHUMP.

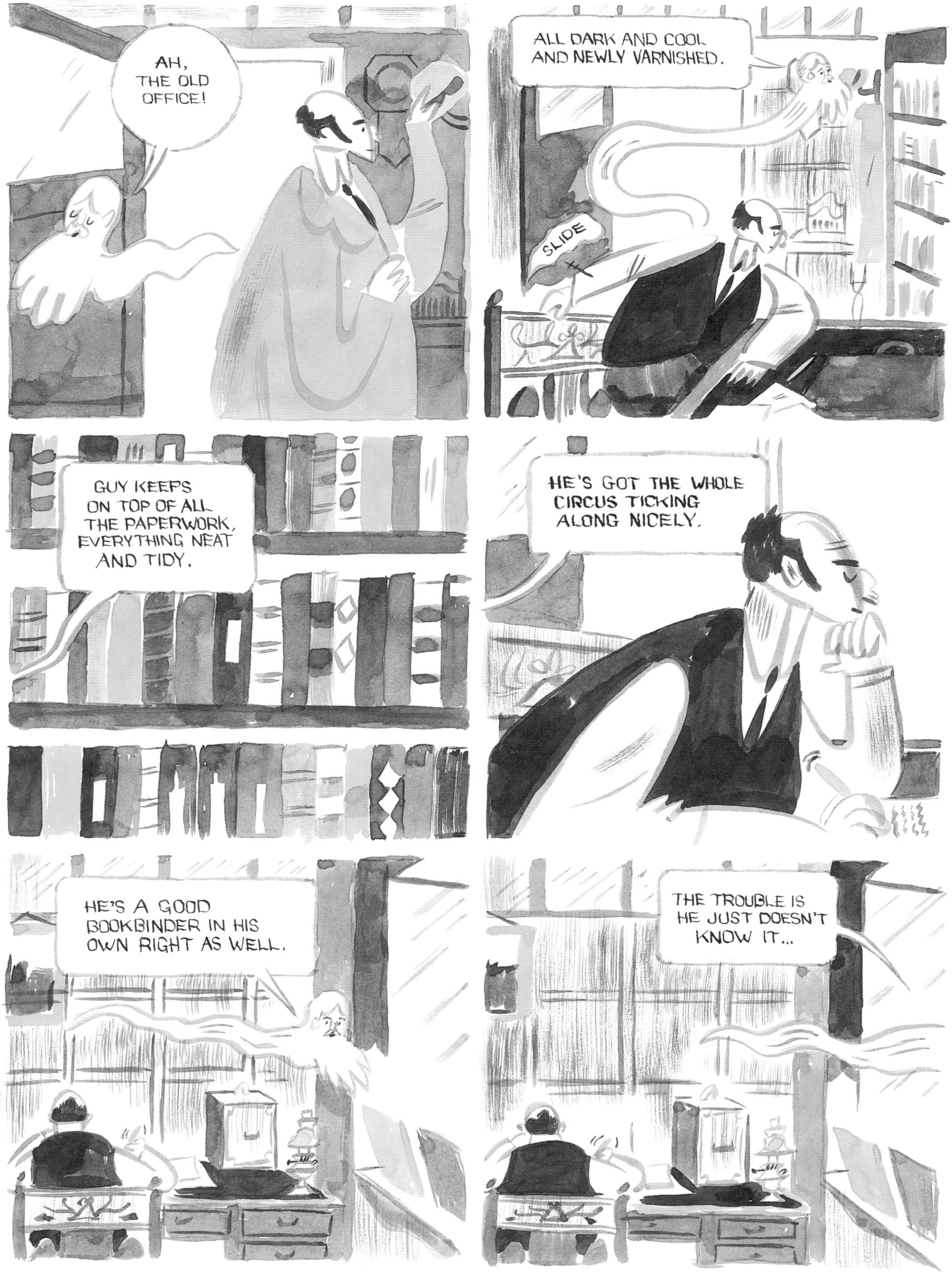
AH, THE OLD OFFICE!
ALL DARK AND COOL AND NEWLY VARNISHED.
SLIDE
GUY KEEPS ON TOP OF ALL THE PAPERWORK, EVERYTHING NEAT AND TIDY.
HE'S GOT THE WHOLE CIRCUS TICKING ALONG NICELY.
HE'S A GOOD BOOKBINDER IN HIS OWN RIGHT AS WELL.
THE TROUBLE IS HE JUST DOESN'T KNOW IT...

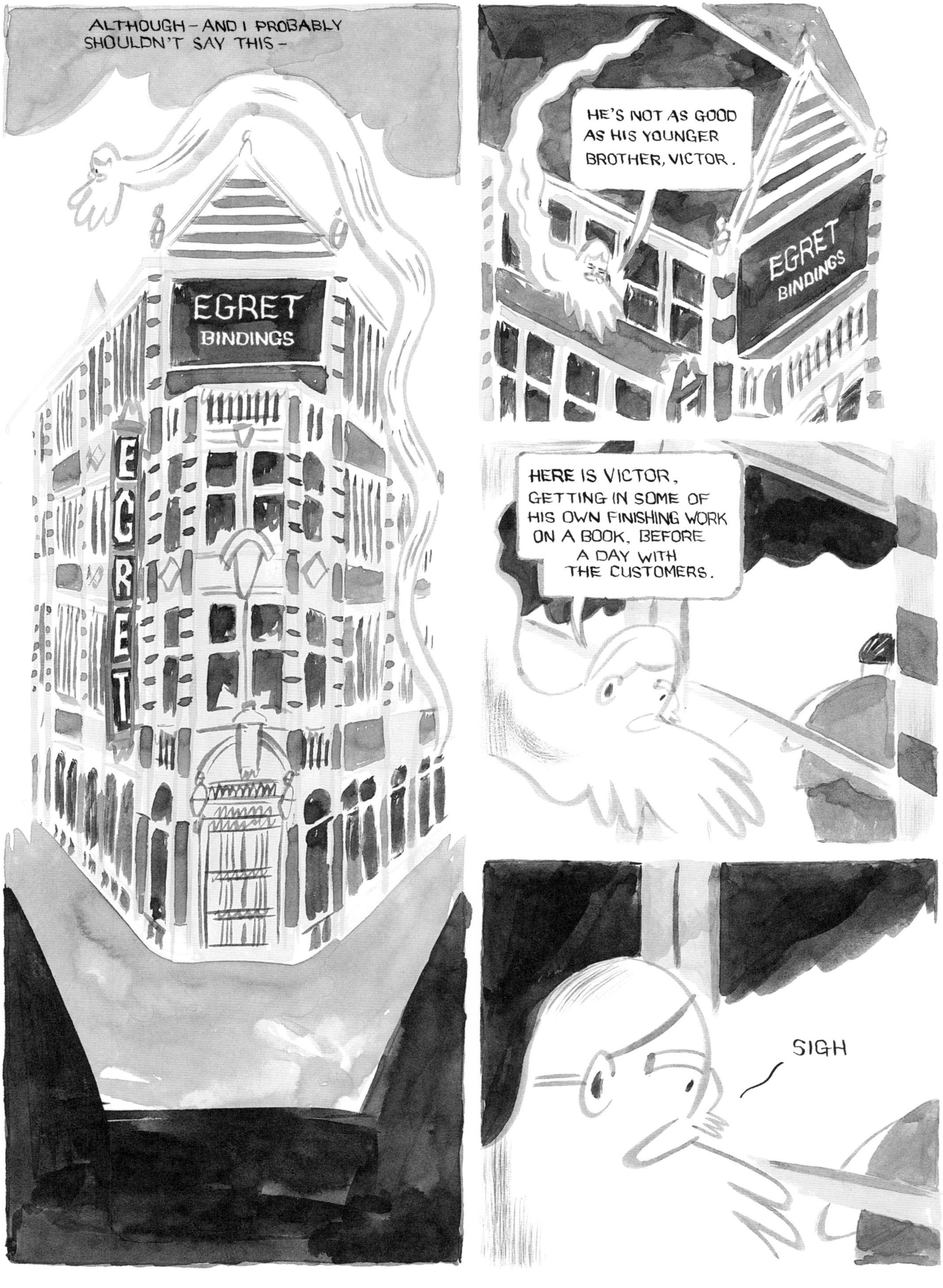
ALTHOUGH – AND I PROBABLY SHOULDN'T SAY THIS –
EGRET BINDINGS
EGRET
HE'S NOT AS GOOD AS HIS YOUNGER BROTHER, VICTOR.
EGRET BINDINGS
HERE IS VICTOR, GETTING IN SOME OF HIS OWN FINISHING WORK ON A BOOK, BEFORE A DAY WITH THE CUSTOMERS.
SIGH

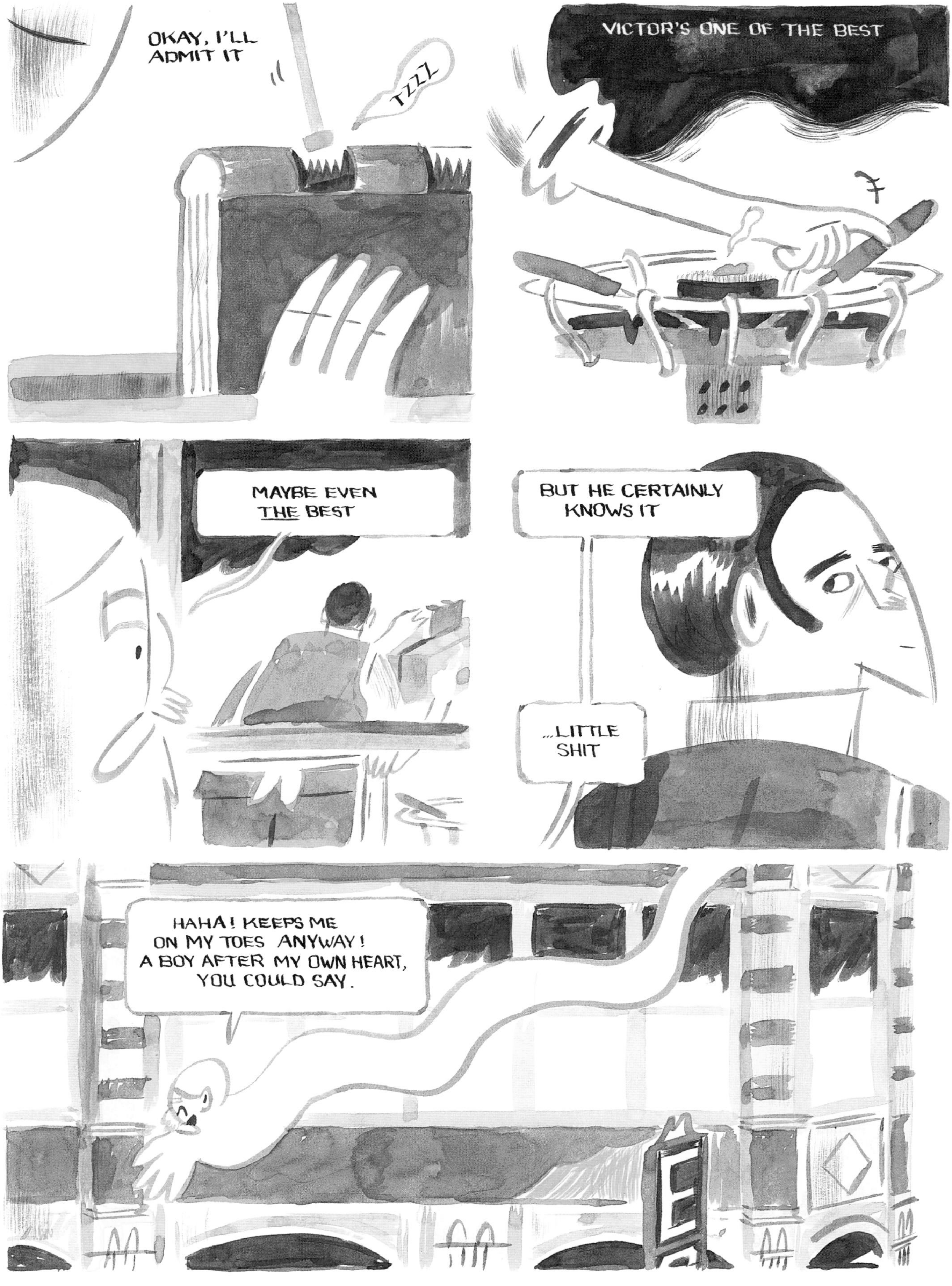
OKAY, I'LL ADMIT IT
TZZZ
VICTOR'S ONE OF THE BEST
MAYBE EVEN THE BEST
BUT HE CERTAINLY KNOWS IT
...LITTLE SHIT
HAHA! KEEPS ME ON MY TOES ANYWAY! A BOY AFTER MY OWN HEART, YOU COULD SAY.

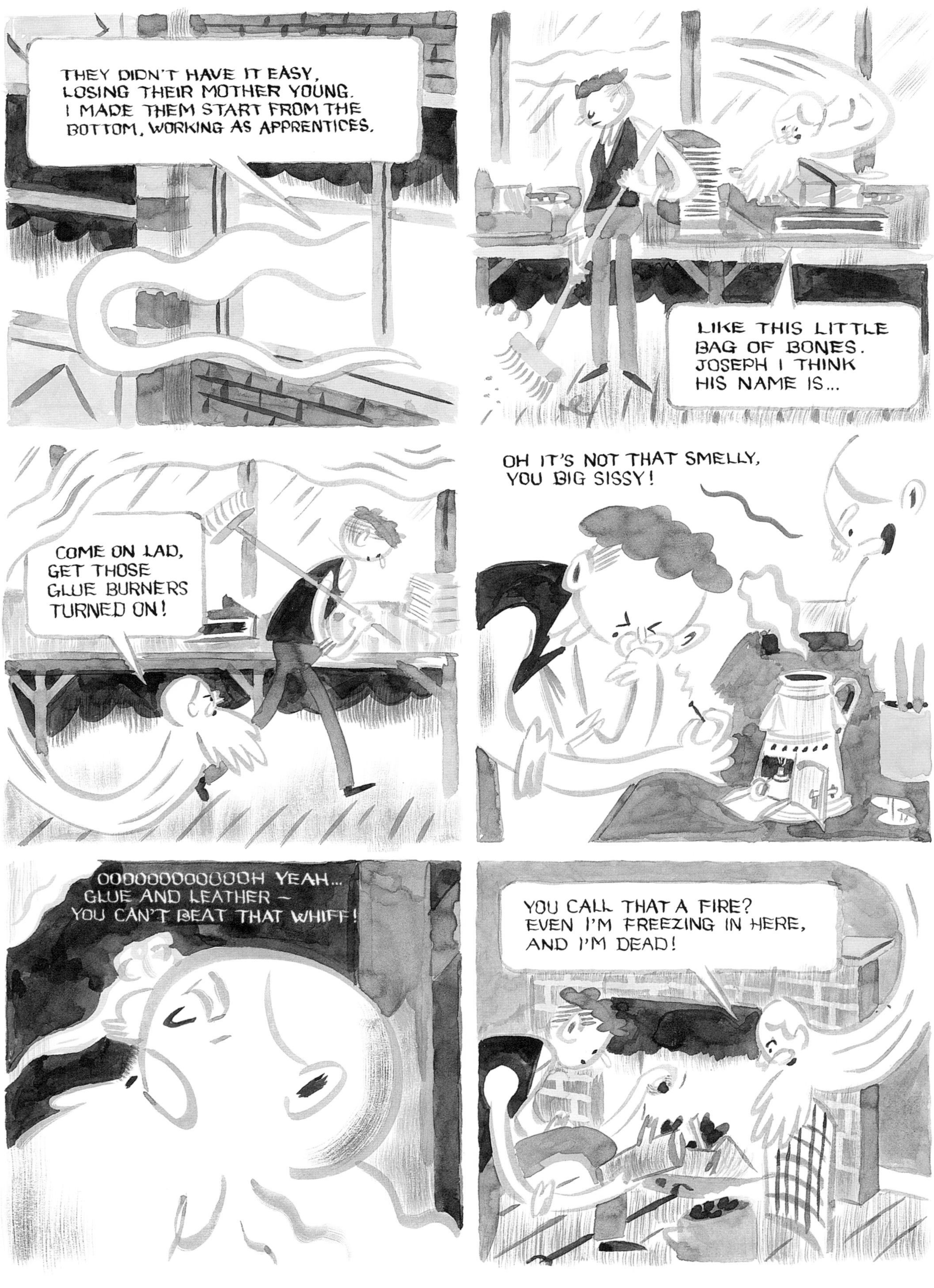
THEY DIDN'T HAVE IT EASY, LOSING THEIR MOTHER YOUNG. I MADE THEM START FROM THE BOTTOM, WORKING AS APPRENTICES.
LIKE THIS LITTLE BAG OF BONES. JOSEPH I THINK HIS NAME IS...
COME ON LAD, GET THOSE GLUE BURNERS TURNED ON!
OH IT'S NOT THAT SMELLY, YOU BIG SISSY!
OOOOOOOOOOOOOH YEAH... GLUE AND LEATHER – YOU CAN'T BEAT THAT WHIFF!
YOU CALL THAT A FIRE? EVEN I'M FREEZING IN HERE, AND I'M DEAD!

WHERE THE HELL ARE THEY FINDING THESE KIDS?

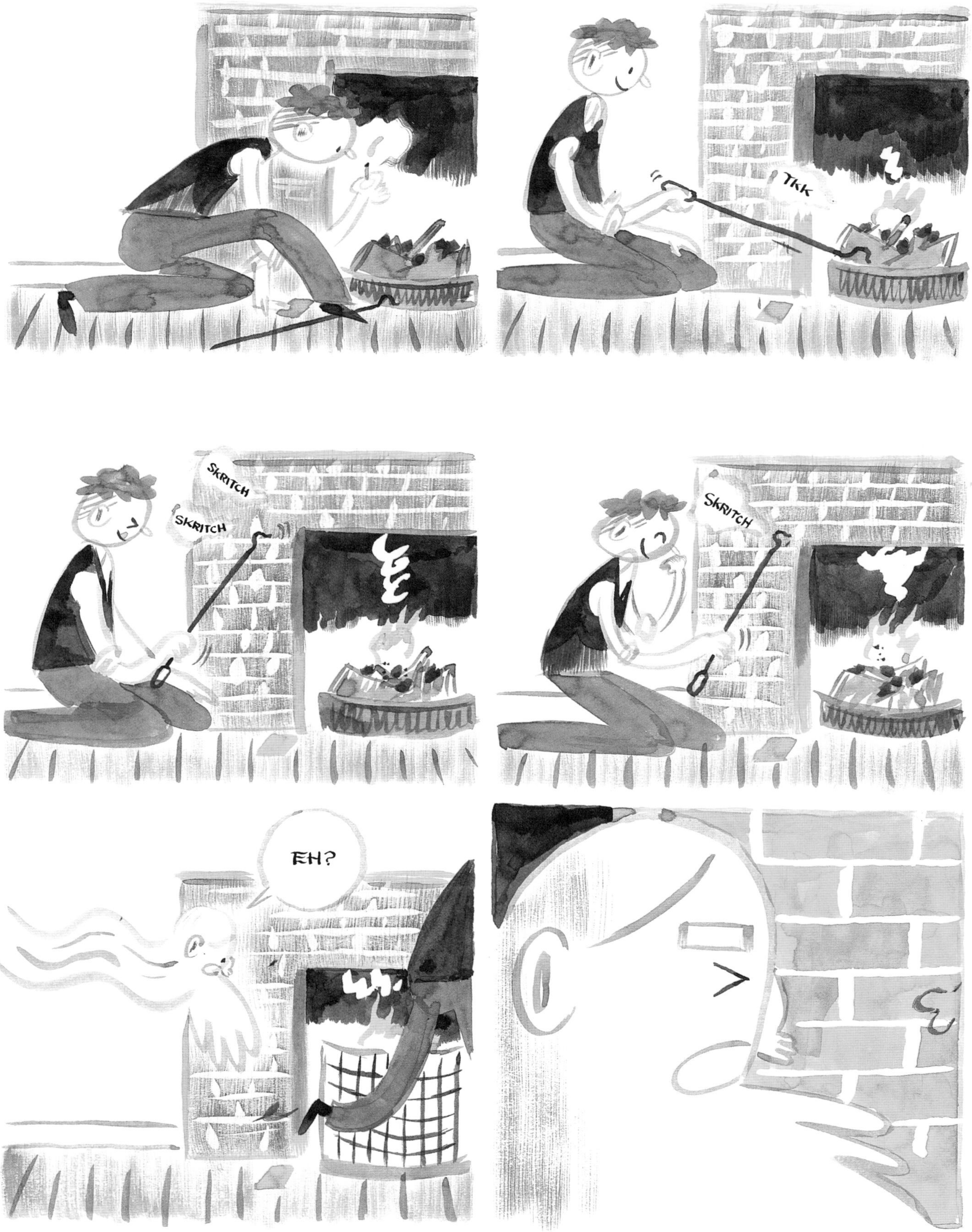
TKK
SKRITCH
SKRITCH
SKRITCH
EH?

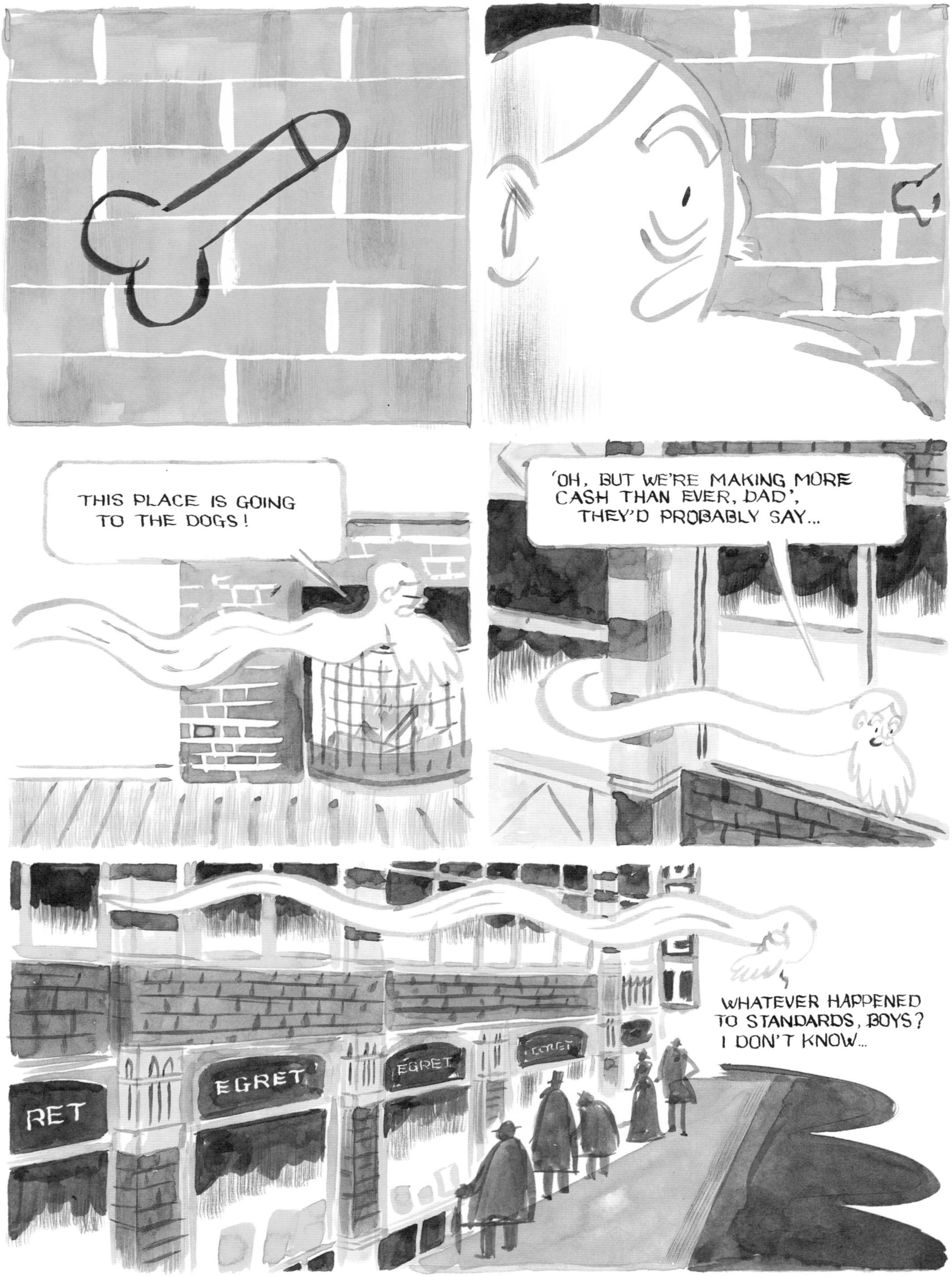
THIS PLACE IS GOING TO THE DOGS!
'OH, BUT WE'RE MAKING MORE CASH THAN EVER, DAD', THEY'D PROBABLY SAY...
RET
EGRET
EGRET
EGRET
WHATEVER HAPPENED TO STANDARDS, BOYS? I DON'T KNOW...

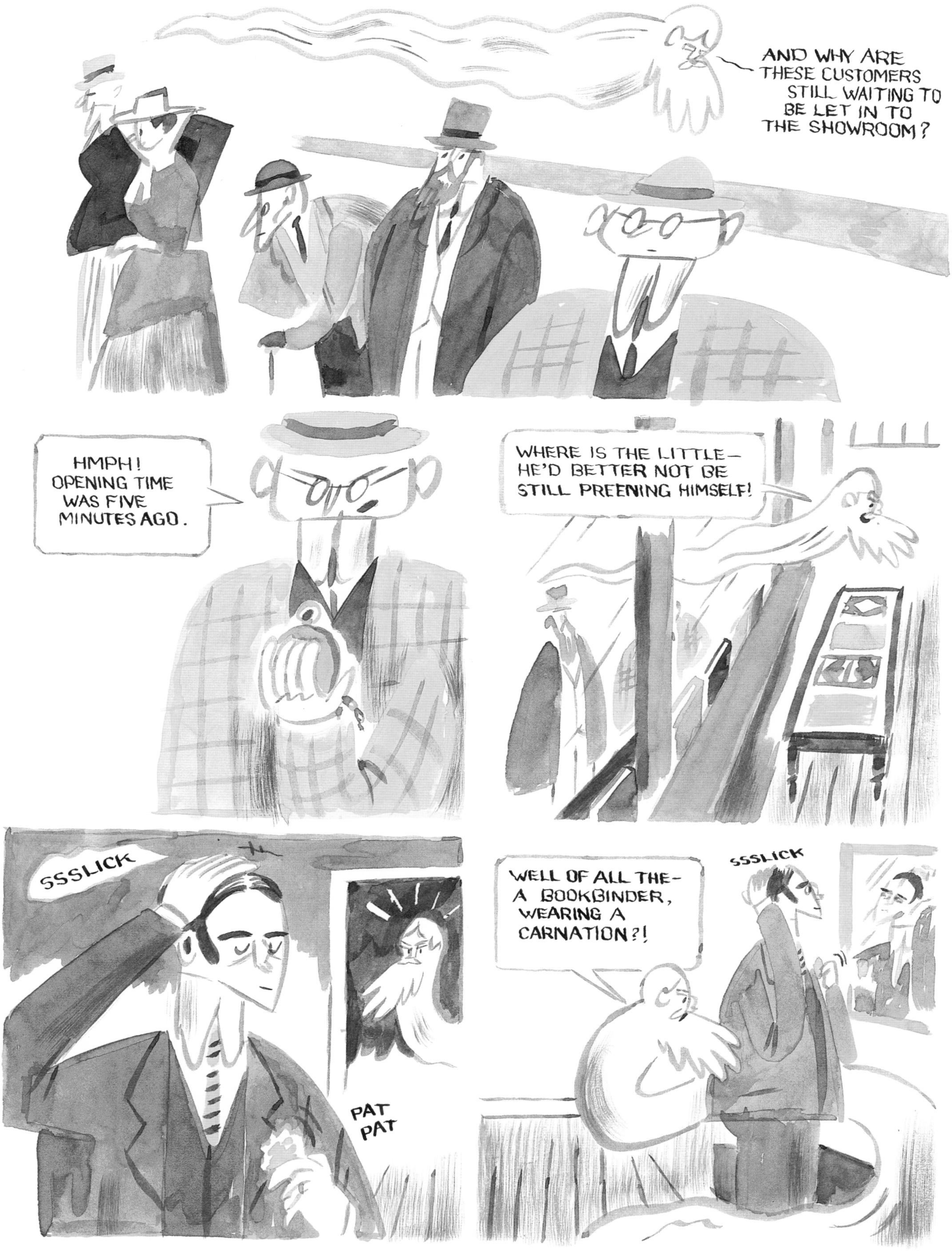
AND WHY ARE THESE CUSTOMERS STILL WAITING TO BE LET IN TO THE SHOWROOM?
HMPH! OPENING TIME WAS FIVE MINUTES AGO.
WHERE IS THE LITTLE— HE'D BETTER NOT BE STILL PREENING HIMSELF!
SSSLICK
PAT PAT
WELL OF ALL THE— A BOOKBINDER, WEARING A CARNATION?!
SSSLICK

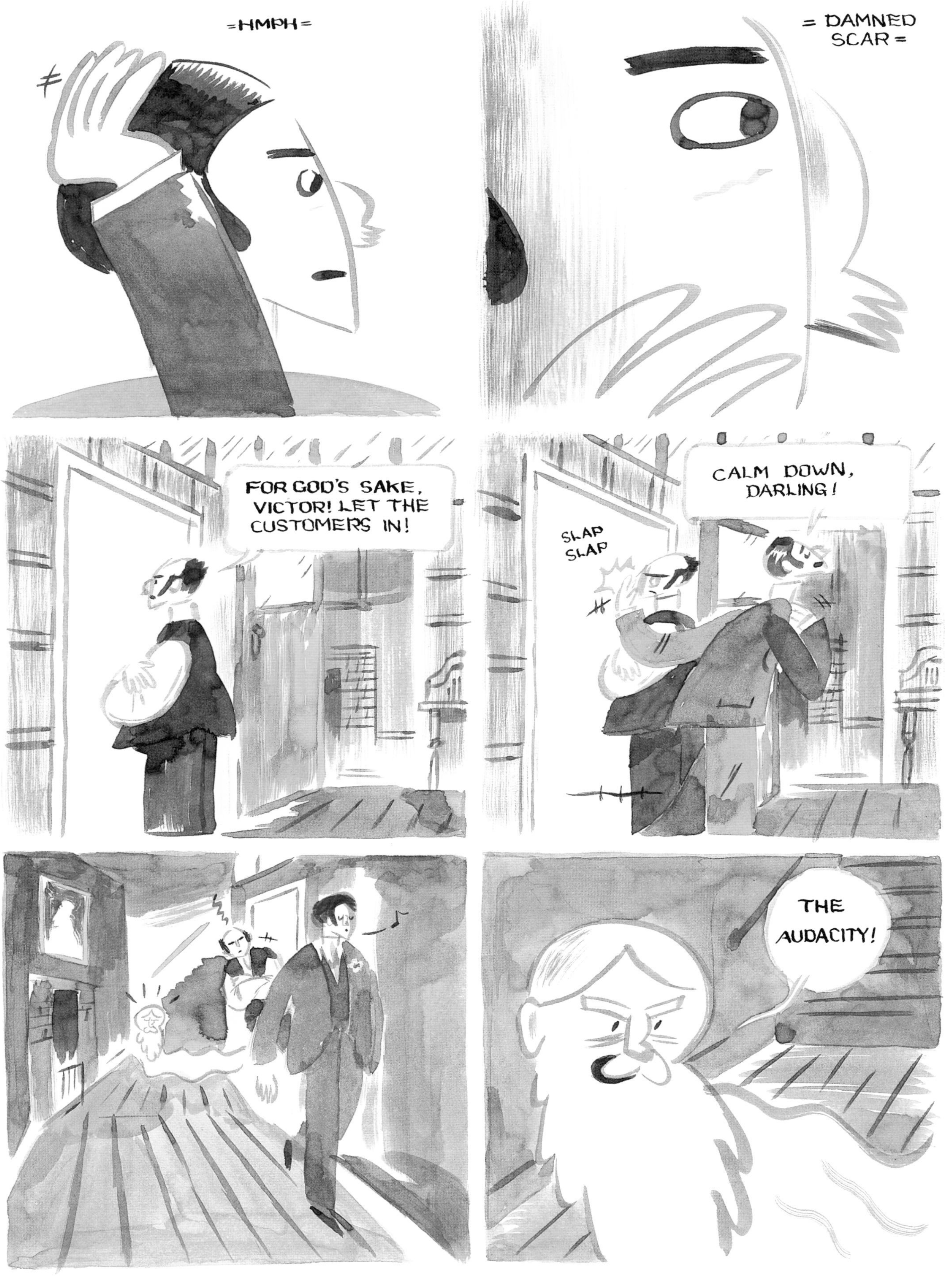
=HMPH=
= DAMNED SCAR =
FOR GOD'S SAKE, VICTOR! LET THE CUSTOMERS IN!
SLAP SLAP
CALM DOWN, DARLING!
THE AUDACITY!

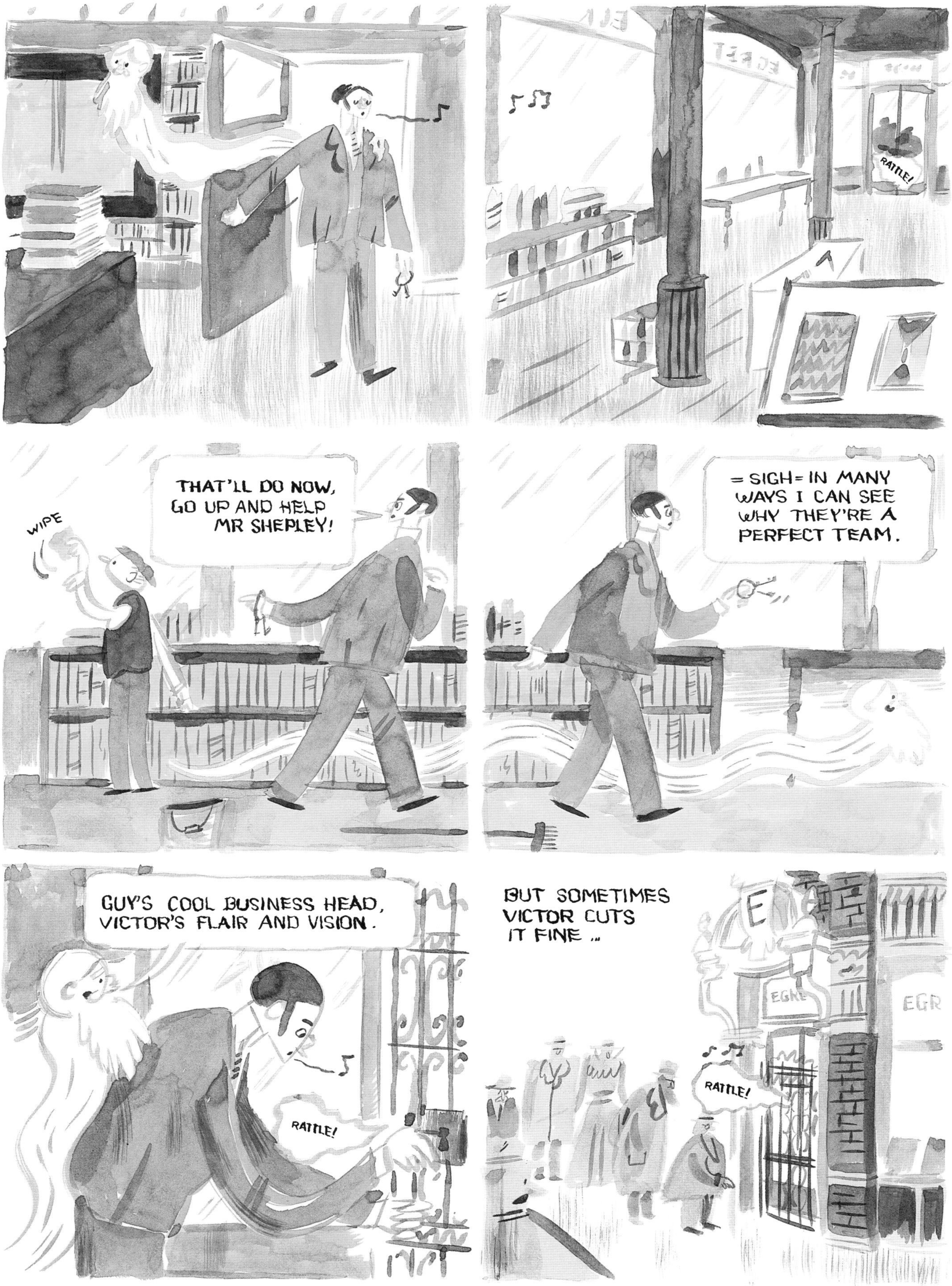
RATTLE!
WIPE
THAT'LL DO NOW, GO UP AND HELP MR SHEPLEY!
=SIGH= IN MANY WAYS I CAN SEE WHY THEY'RE A PERFECT TEAM.
GUY'S COOL BUSINESS HEAD, VICTOR'S FLAIR AND VISION.
RATTLE!
BUT SOMETIMES VICTOR CUTS IT FINE ...
E
EGRE
EGR
RATTLE!

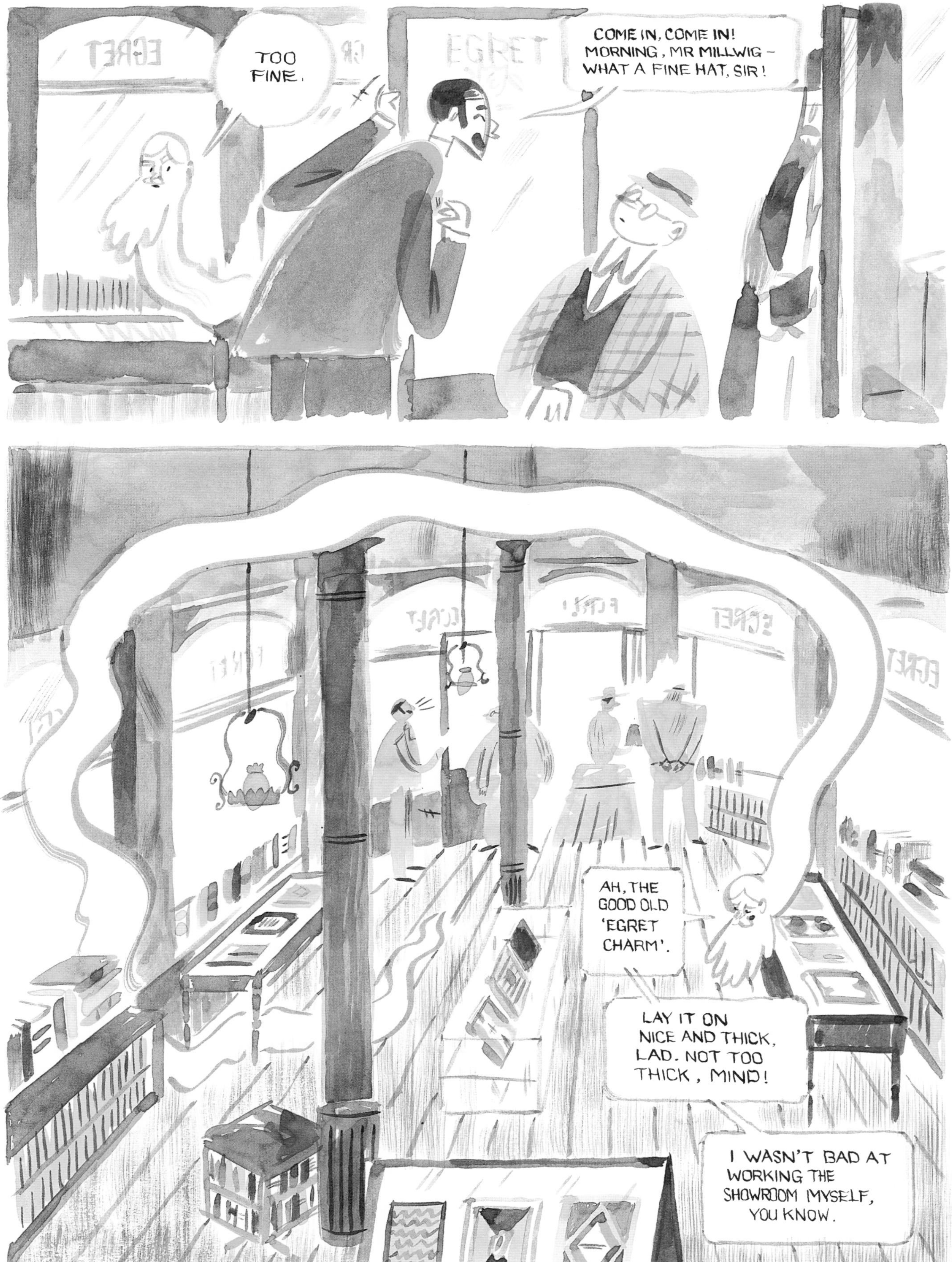
EGRET
COME IN, COME IN! MORNING, MR MILLWIG – WHAT A FINE HAT, SIR!
TOO FINE.
AH, THE GOOD OLD 'EGRET CHARM'.
LAY IT ON NICE AND THICK, LAD. NOT TOO THICK, MIND!
I WASN'T BAD AT WORKING THE SHOWROOM MYSELF, YOU KNOW.

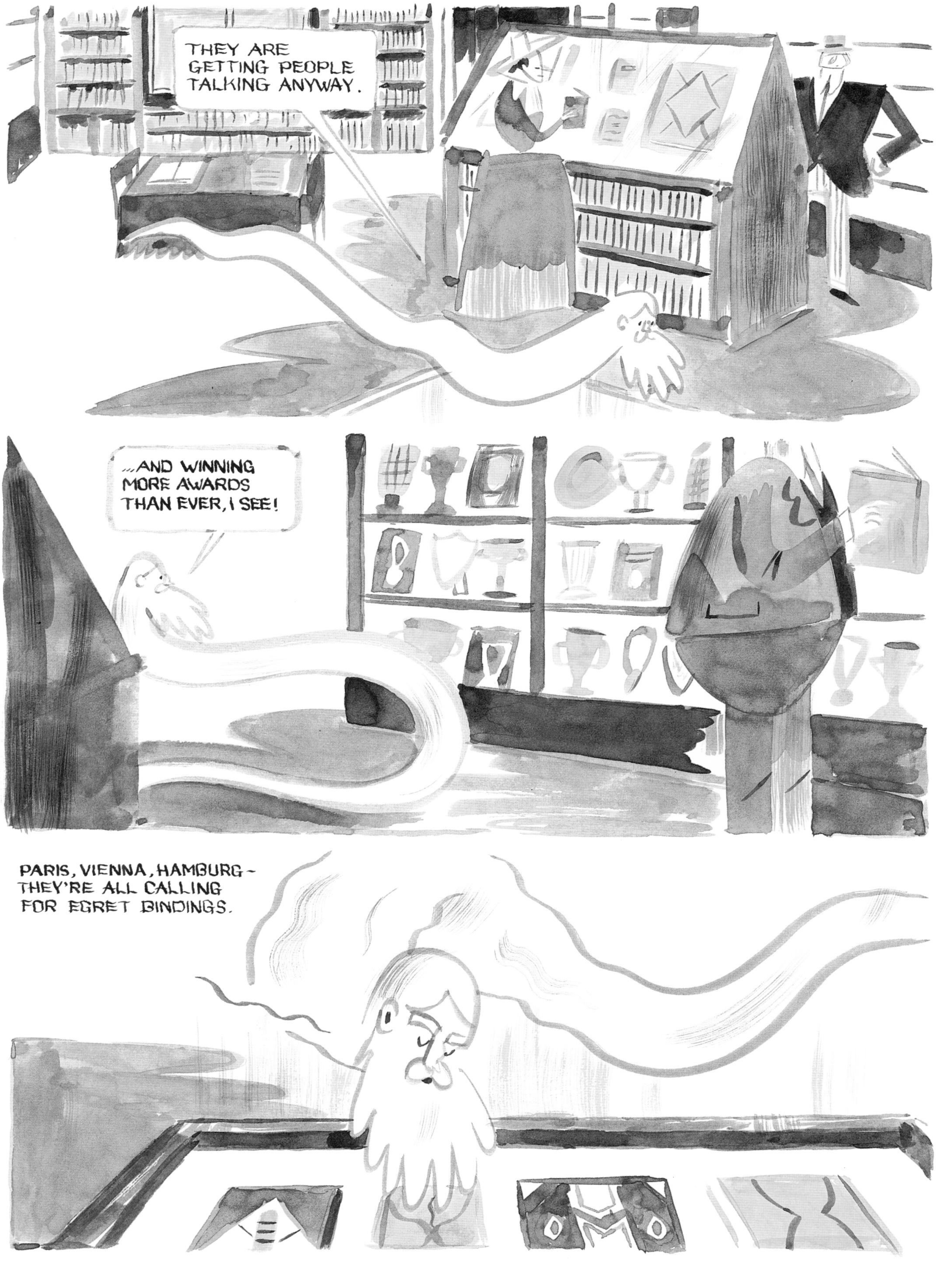
THEY ARE GETTING PEOPLE TALKING ANYWAY.
...AND WINNING MORE AWARDS THAN EVER, I SEE!
PARIS, VIENNA, HAMBURG - THEY'RE ALL CALLING FOR EGRET BINDINGS.

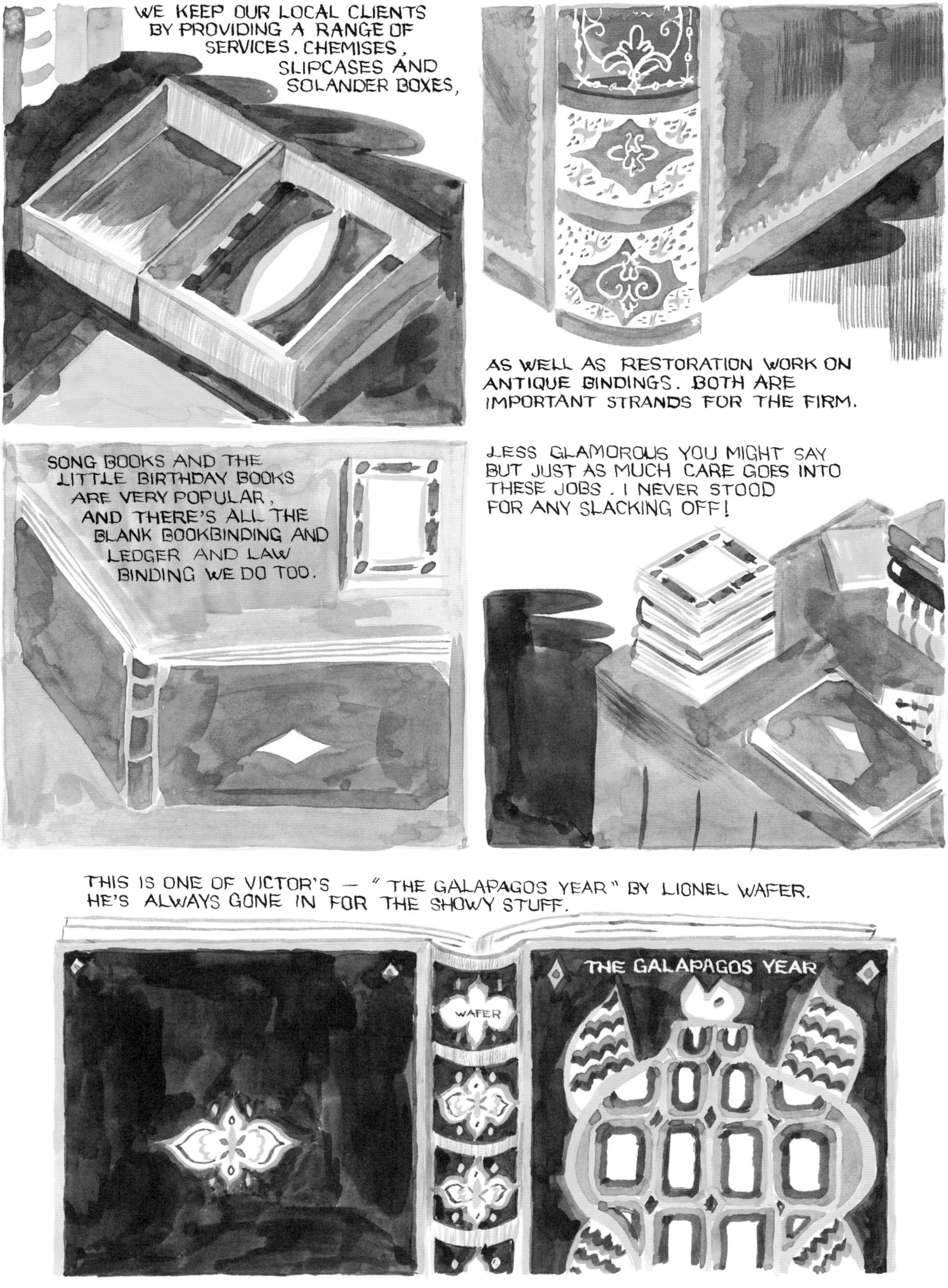
WE KEEP OUR LOCAL CLIENTS BY PROVIDING A RANGE OF SERVICES. CHEMISES, SLIPCASES AND SOLANDER BOXES,
AS WELL AS RESTORATION WORK ON ANTIQUE BINDINGS. BOTH ARE IMPORTANT STRANDS FOR THE FIRM.
SONG BOOKS AND THE LITTLE BIRTHDAY BOOKS ARE VERY POPULAR, AND THERE'S ALL THE BLANK BOOKBINDING AND LEDGER AND LAW BINDING WE DO TOO.
LESS GLAMOROUS YOU MIGHT SAY BUT JUST AS MUCH CARE GOES INTO THESE JOBS. I NEVER STOOD FOR ANY SLACKING OFF!
THIS IS ONE OF VICTOR'S — "THE GALAPAGOS YEAR" BY LIONEL WAFER. HE'S ALWAYS GONE IN FOR THE SHOWY STUFF.
WAFER
THE GALAPAGOS YEAR

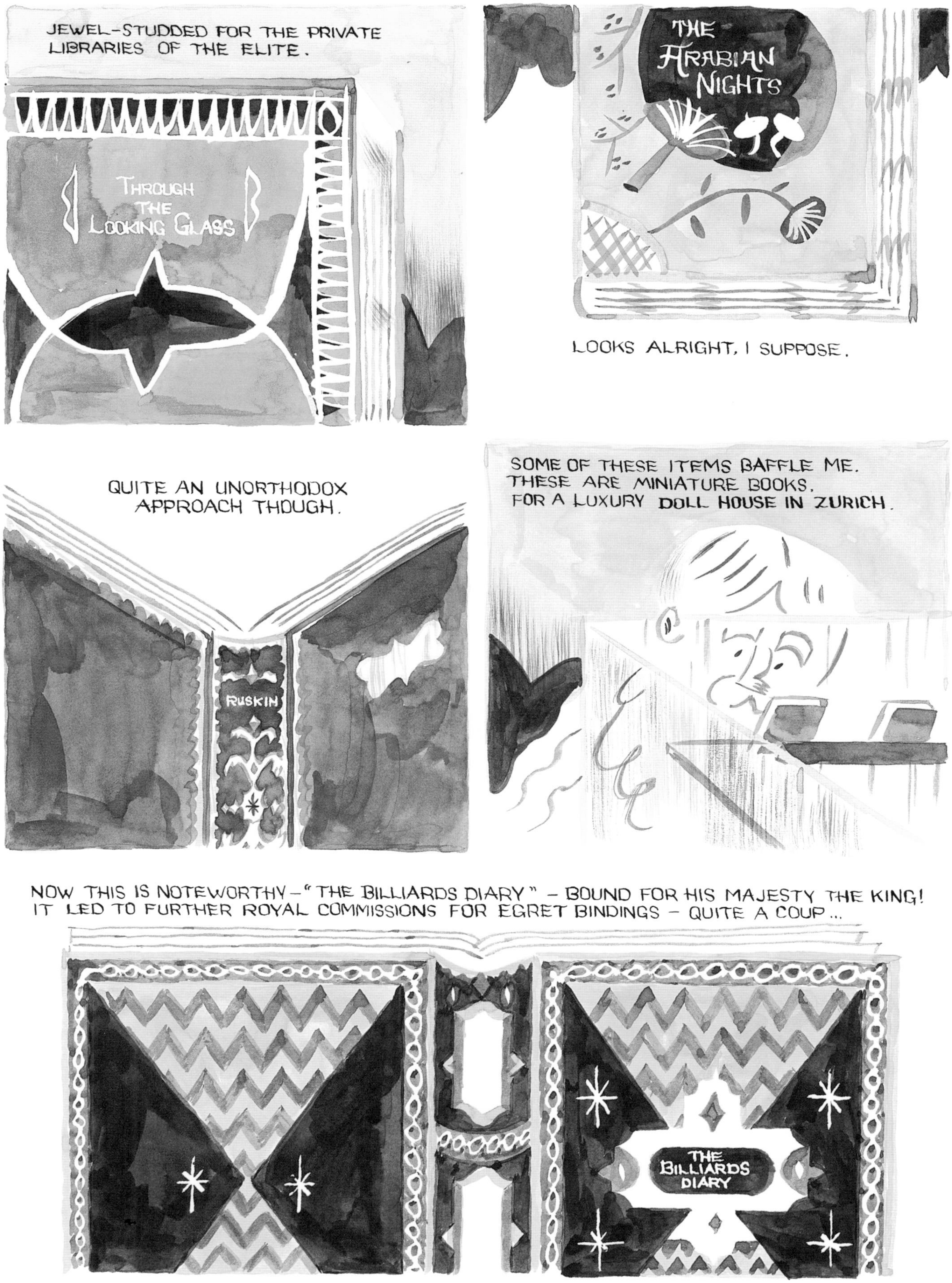
JEWEL-STUDDED FOR THE PRIVATE LIBRARIES OF THE ELITE.
THROUGH THE LOOKING GLASS
THE ARABIAN NIGHTS
LOOKS ALRIGHT, I SUPPOSE.
QUITE AN UNORTHODOX APPROACH THOUGH.
RUSKIN
SOME OF THESE ITEMS BAFFLE ME. THESE ARE MINIATURE BOOKS, FOR A LUXURY DOLL HOUSE IN ZURICH.
NOW THIS IS NOTEWORTHY – "THE BILLIARDS DIARY" – BOUND FOR HIS MAJESTY THE KING! IT LED TO FURTHER ROYAL COMMISSIONS FOR EGRET BINDINGS – QUITE A COUP...
THE BILLIARDS DIARY

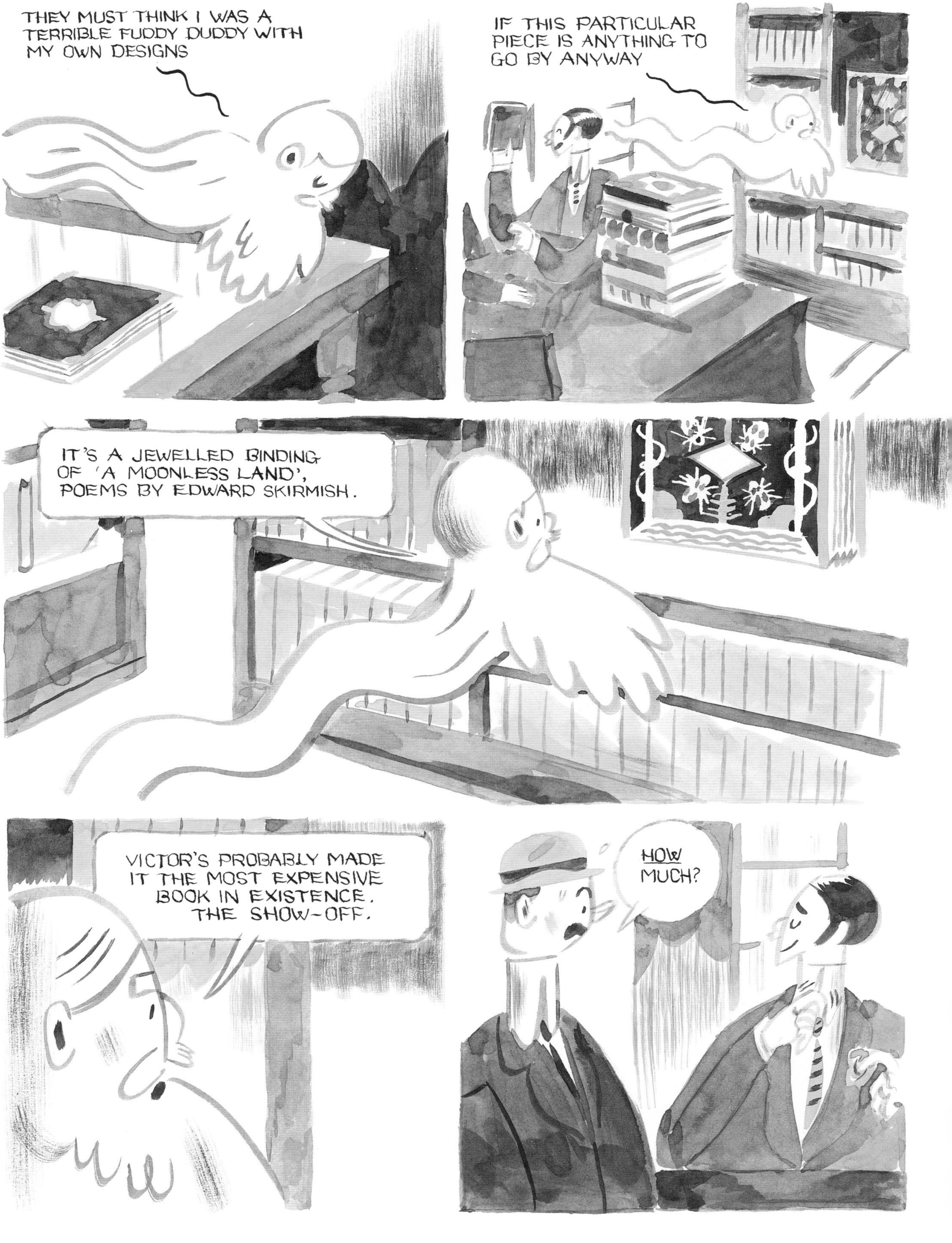
THEY MUST THINK I WAS A TERRIBLE FUDDY DUDDY WITH MY OWN DESIGNS
IF THIS PARTICULAR PIECE IS ANYTHING TO GO BY ANYWAY
IT'S A JEWELLED BINDING OF 'A MOONLESS LAND', POEMS BY EDWARD SKIRMISH.
VICTOR'S PROBABLY MADE IT THE MOST EXPENSIVE BOOK IN EXISTENCE. THE SHOW-OFF.
HOW MUCH?

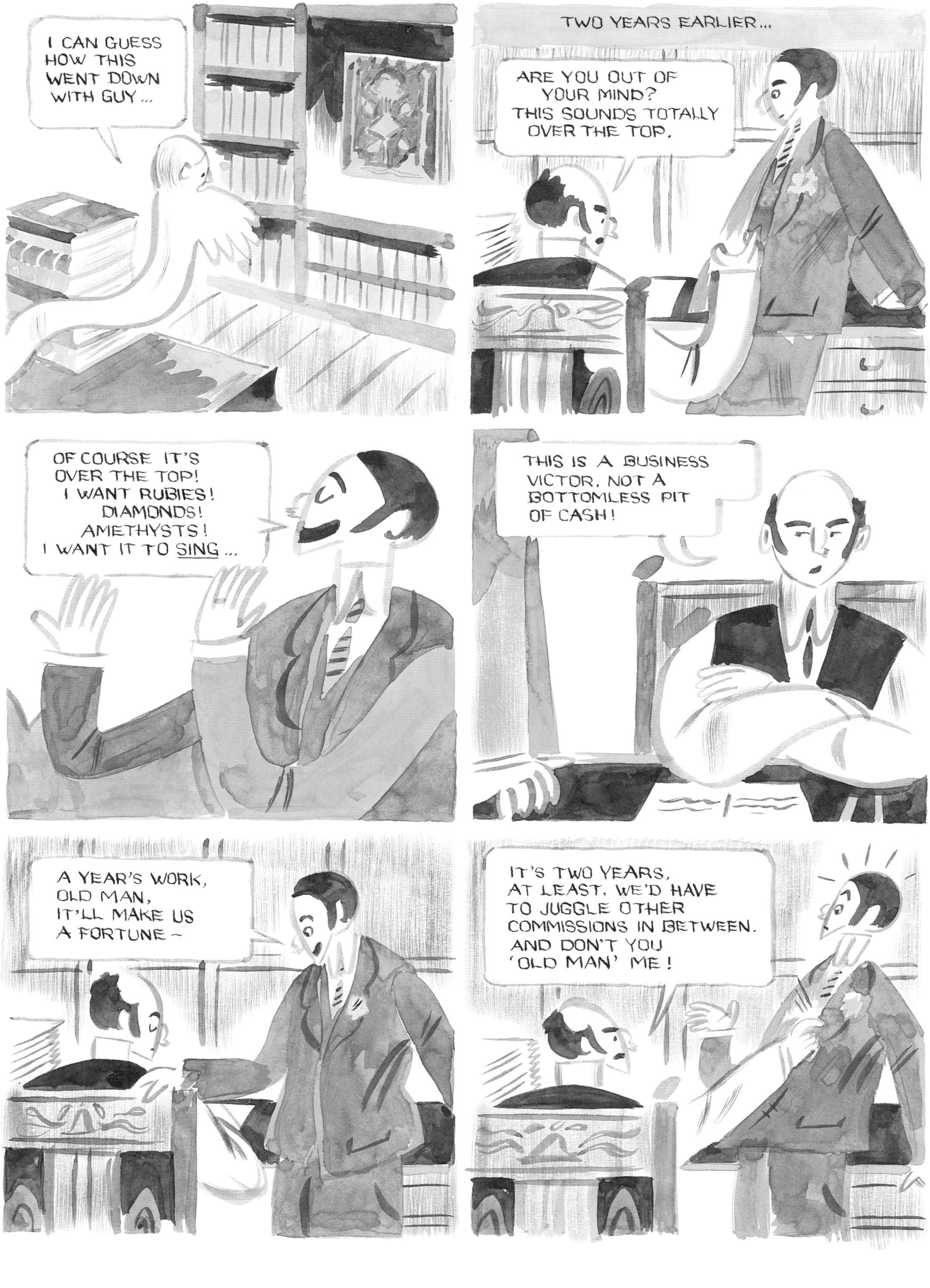
I CAN GUESS HOW THIS WENT DOWN WITH GUY...
TWO YEARS EARLIER...
ARE YOU OUT OF YOUR MIND? THIS SOUNDS TOTALLY OVER THE TOP.
OF COURSE IT'S OVER THE TOP! I WANT RUBIES! DIAMONDS! AMETHYSTS! I WANT IT TO SING...
THIS IS A BUSINESS VICTOR, NOT A BOTTOMLESS PIT OF CASH!
A YEAR'S WORK, OLD MAN, IT'LL MAKE US A FORTUNE –
IT'S TWO YEARS, AT LEAST. WE'D HAVE TO JUGGLE OTHER COMMISSIONS IN BETWEEN. AND DON'T YOU 'OLD MAN' ME!

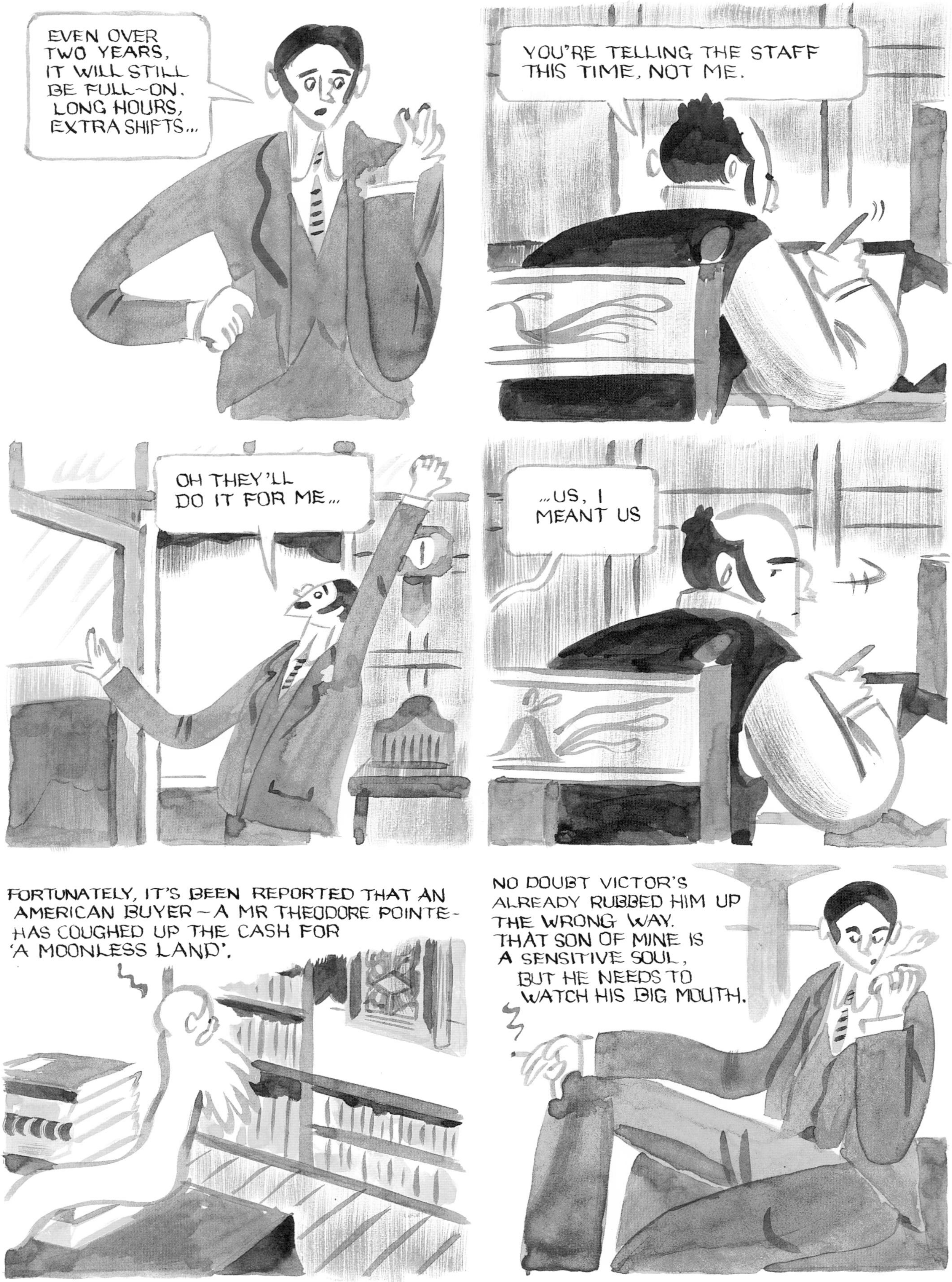
EVEN OVER TWO YEARS, IT WILL STILL BE FULL-ON. LONG HOURS, EXTRA SHIFTS...
YOU'RE TELLING THE STAFF THIS TIME, NOT ME.
OH THEY'LL DO IT FOR ME...
...US, I MEANT US
FORTUNATELY, IT'S BEEN REPORTED THAT AN AMERICAN BUYER – A MR THEODORE POINTE – HAS COUGHED UP THE CASH FOR 'A MOONLESS LAND'.
NO DOUBT VICTOR'S ALREADY RUBBED HIM UP THE WRONG WAY. THAT SON OF MINE IS A SENSITIVE SOUL, BUT HE NEEDS TO WATCH HIS BIG MOUTH.

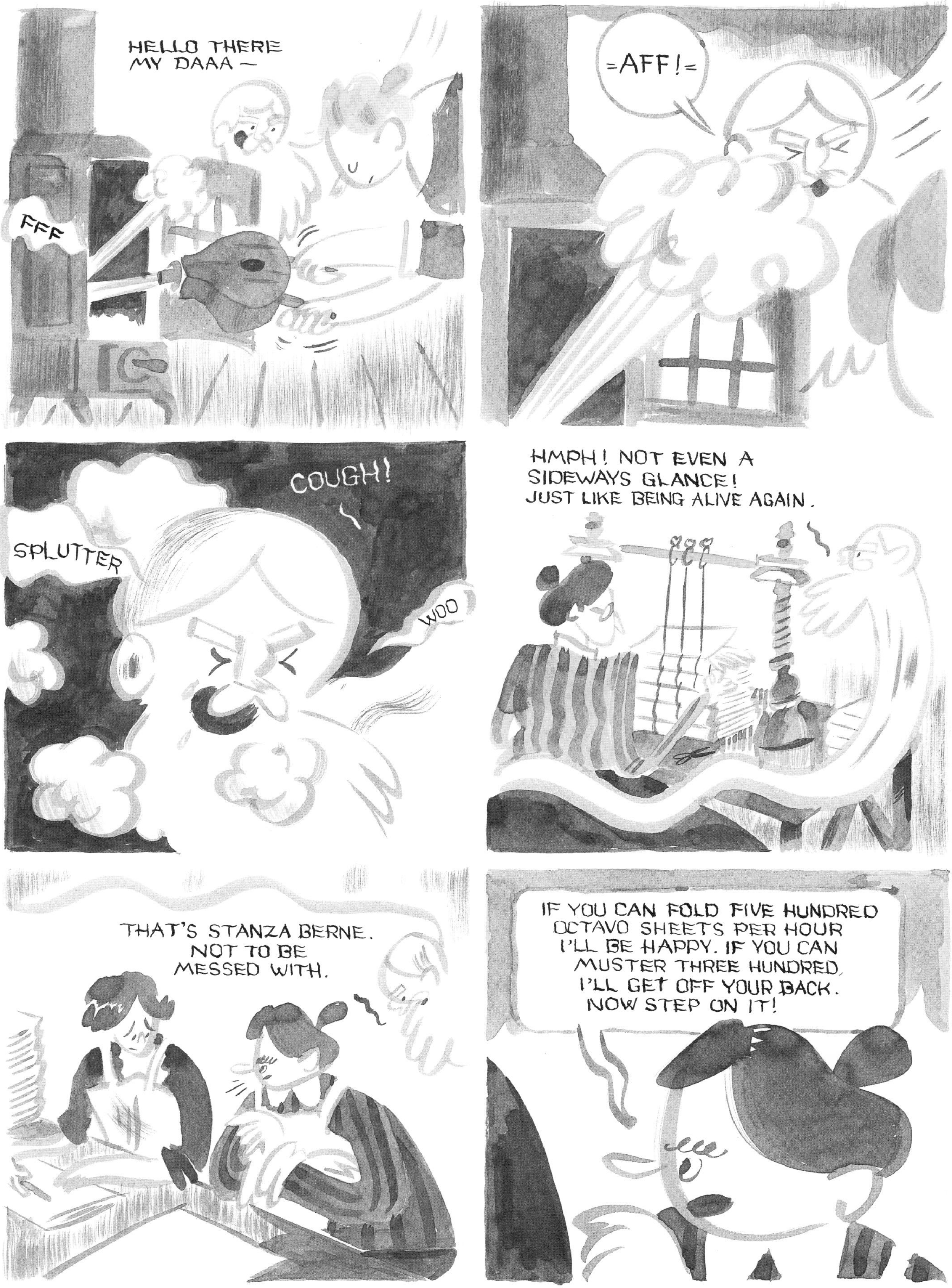
HELLO THERE MY DAAA —
FFF
=AFF!=
COUGH!
SPLUTTER
WOO
HMPH! NOT EVEN A SIDEWAYS GLANCE! JUST LIKE BEING ALIVE AGAIN.
THAT'S STANZA BERNE. NOT TO BE MESSED WITH.
IF YOU CAN FOLD FIVE HUNDRED OCTAVO SHEETS PER HOUR I'LL BE HAPPY. IF YOU CAN MUSTER THREE HUNDRED, I'LL GET OFF YOUR BACK. NOW STEP ON IT!

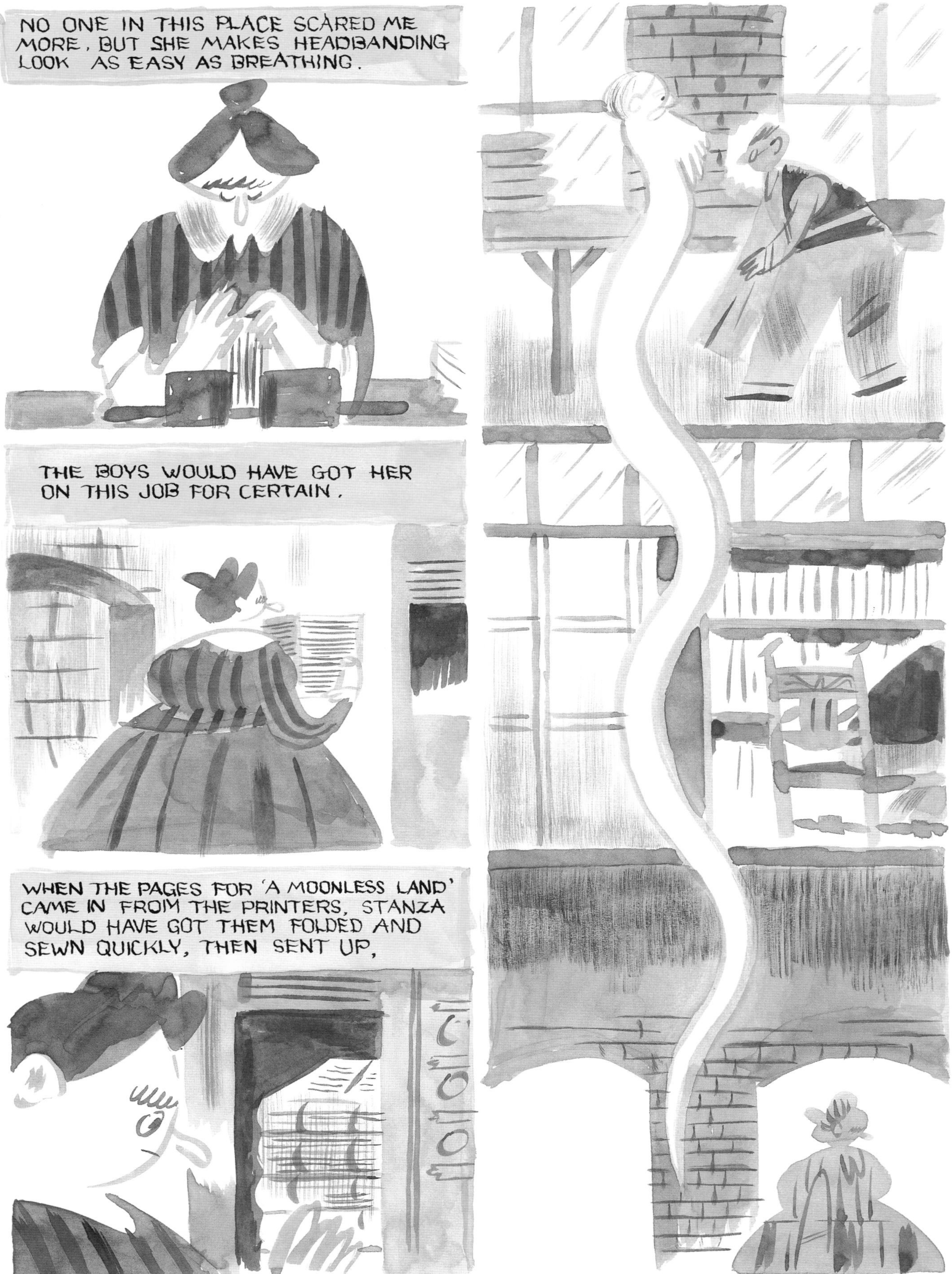
NO ONE IN THIS PLACE SCARED ME MORE, BUT SHE MAKES HEADBANDING LOOK AS EASY AS BREATHING.
THE BOYS WOULD HAVE GOT HER ON THIS JOB FOR CERTAIN.
WHEN THE PAGES FOR 'A MOONLESS LAND' CAME IN FROM THE PRINTERS, STANZA WOULD HAVE GOT THEM FOLDED AND SEWN QUICKLY, THEN SENT UP,

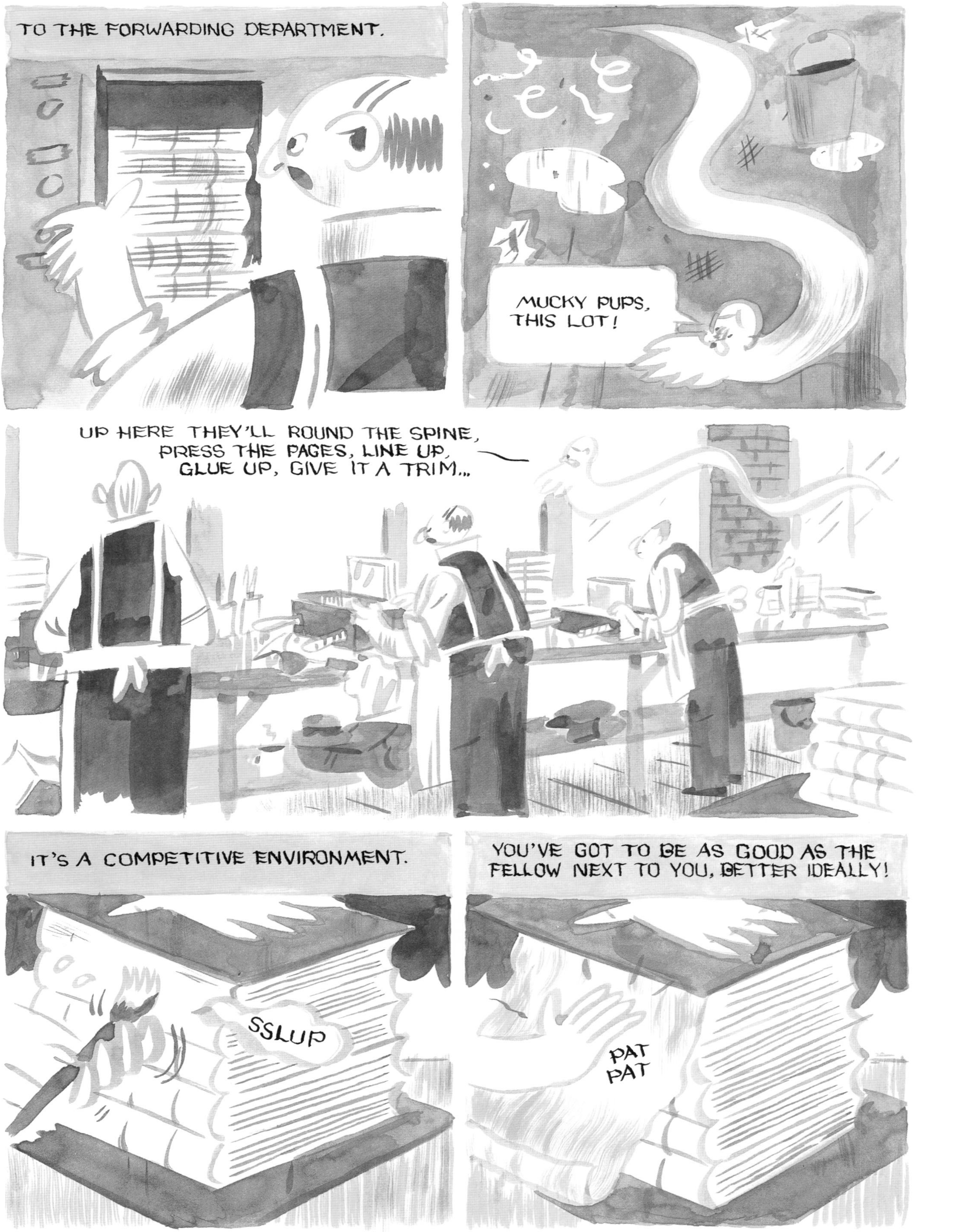
TO THE FORWARDING DEPARTMENT.
MUCKY PUPS, THIS LOT!
UP HERE THEY'LL ROUND THE SPINE, PRESS THE PAGES, LINE UP, GLUE UP, GIVE IT A TRIM...
IT'S A COMPETITIVE ENVIRONMENT.
SSLUP
YOU'VE GOT TO BE AS GOOD AS THE FELLOW NEXT TO YOU, BETTER IDEALLY!
PAT PAT

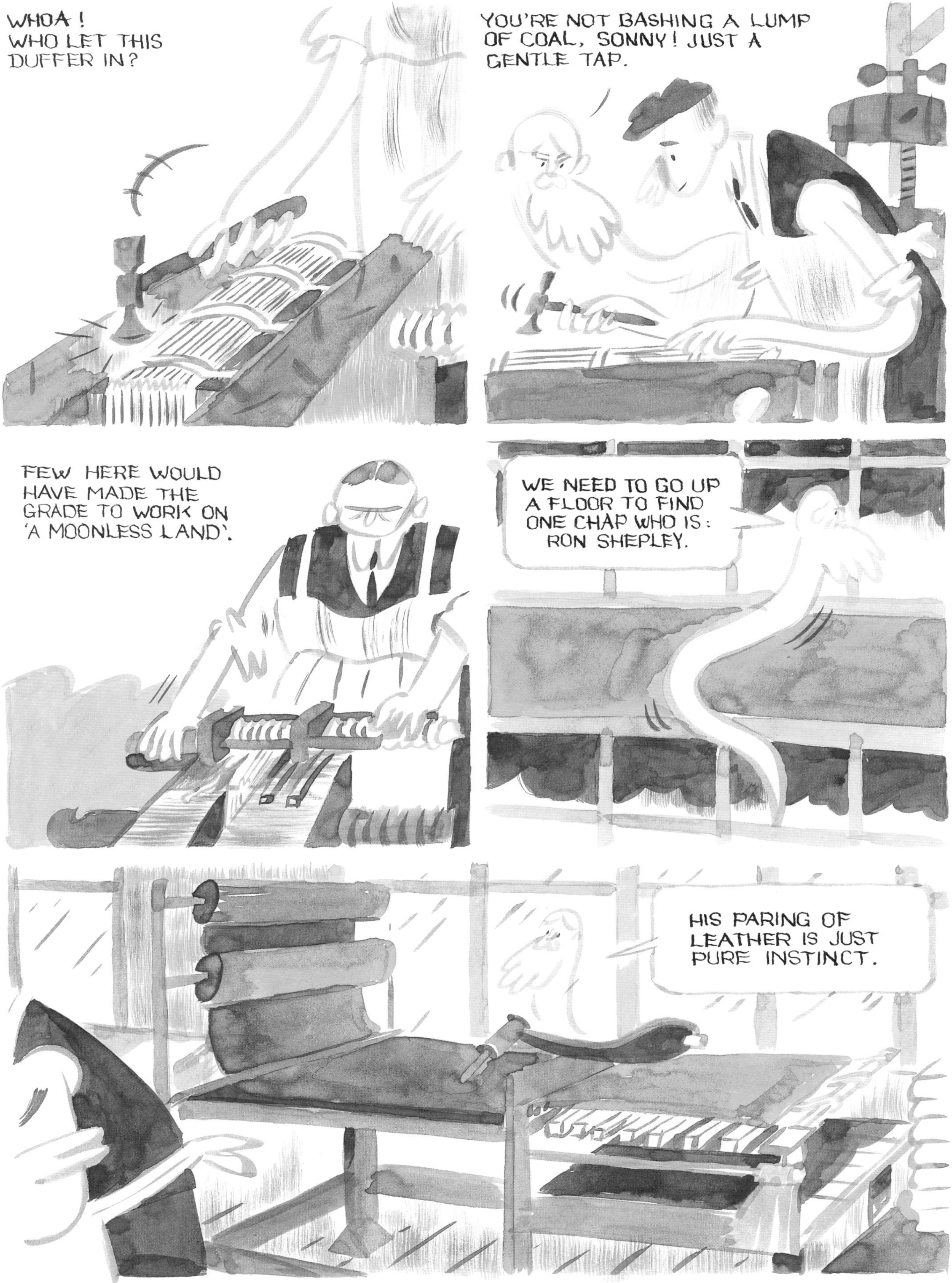

WHOA !
WHO LET THIS
DUFFER IN?
YOU'RE NOT BASHING A LUMP OF COAL, SONNY! JUST A GENTLE TAP.
FEW HERE WOULD HAVE MADE THE GRADE TO WORK ON 'A MOONLESS LAND'.
WE NEED TO GO UP A FLOOR TO FIND ONE CHAP WHO IS: RON SHEPLEY.
HIS PARING OF LEATHER IS JUST PURE INSTINCT.

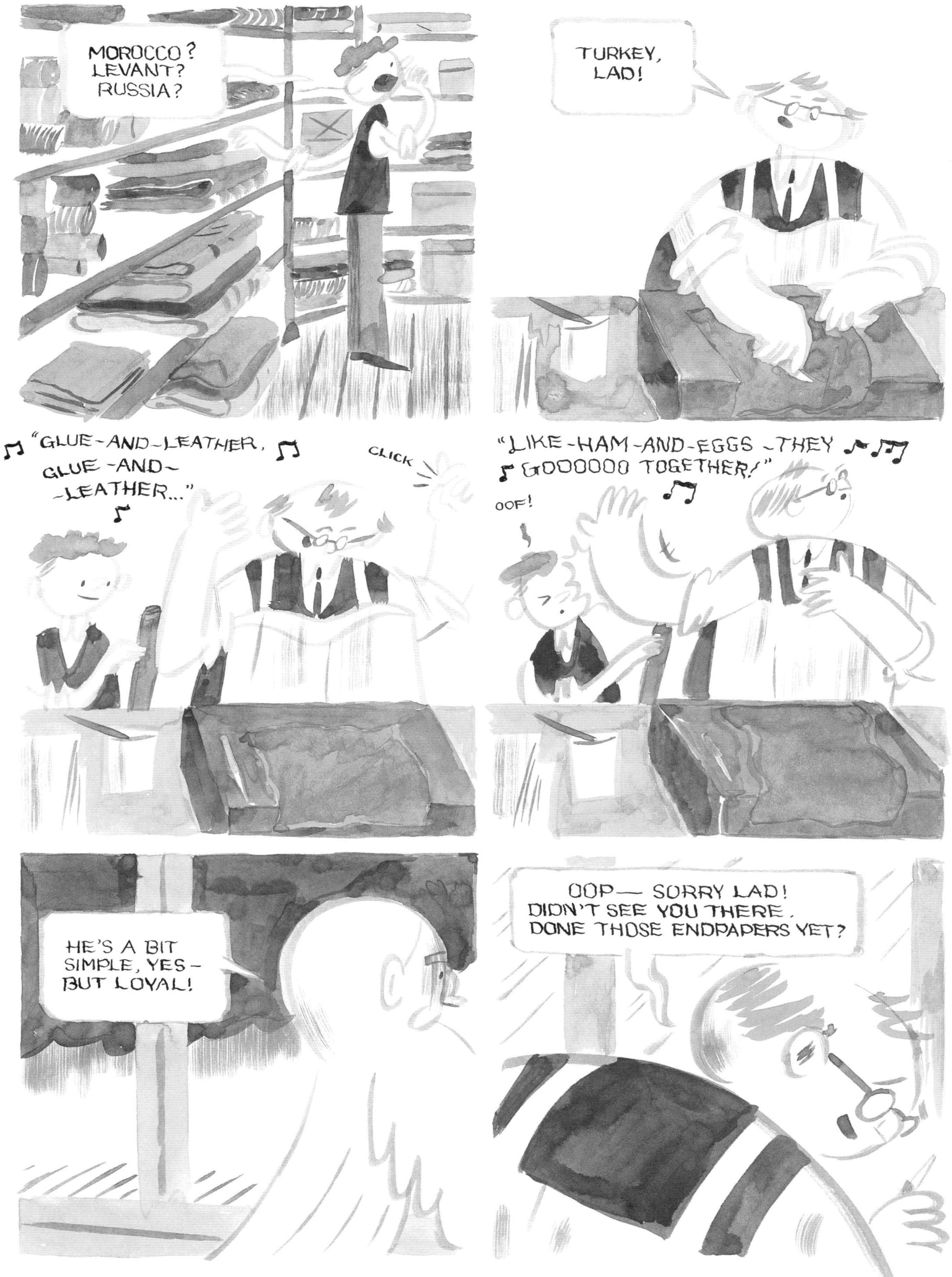
MOROCCO? LEVANT? RUSSIA?
TURKEY, LAD!
"GLUE-AND-LEATHER, GLUE-AND--LEATHER..."
CLICK
"LIKE-HAM-AND-EGGS-THEY GOOOOOO TOGETHER!"
OOF!
HE'S A BIT SIMPLE, YES-BUT LOYAL!
OOP— SORRY LAD! DIDN'T SEE YOU THERE. DONE THOSE ENDPAPERS YET?

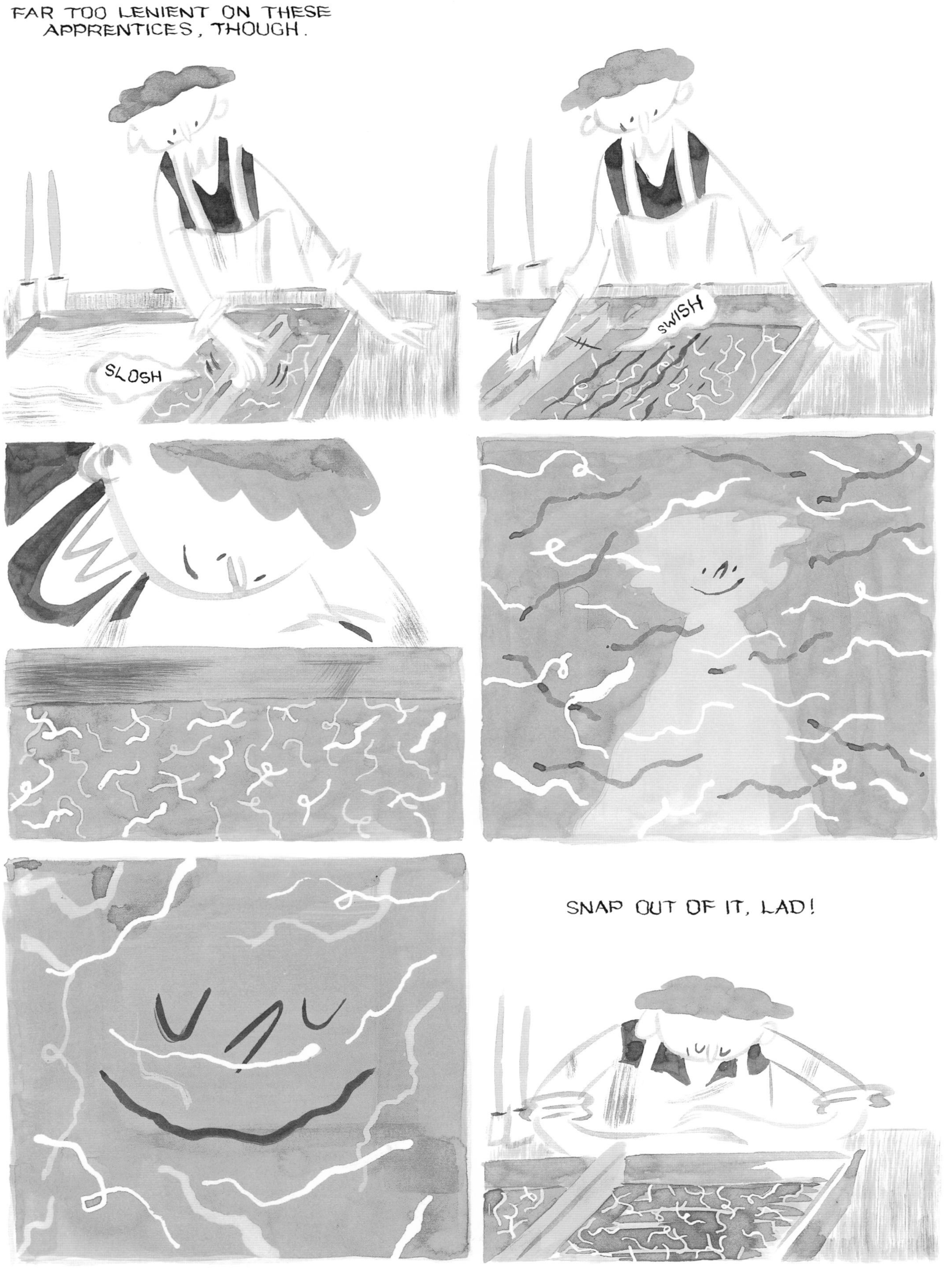
FAR TOO LENIENT ON THESE APPRENTICES, THOUGH.
SLOSH
SWISH
SNAP OUT OF IT, LAD!

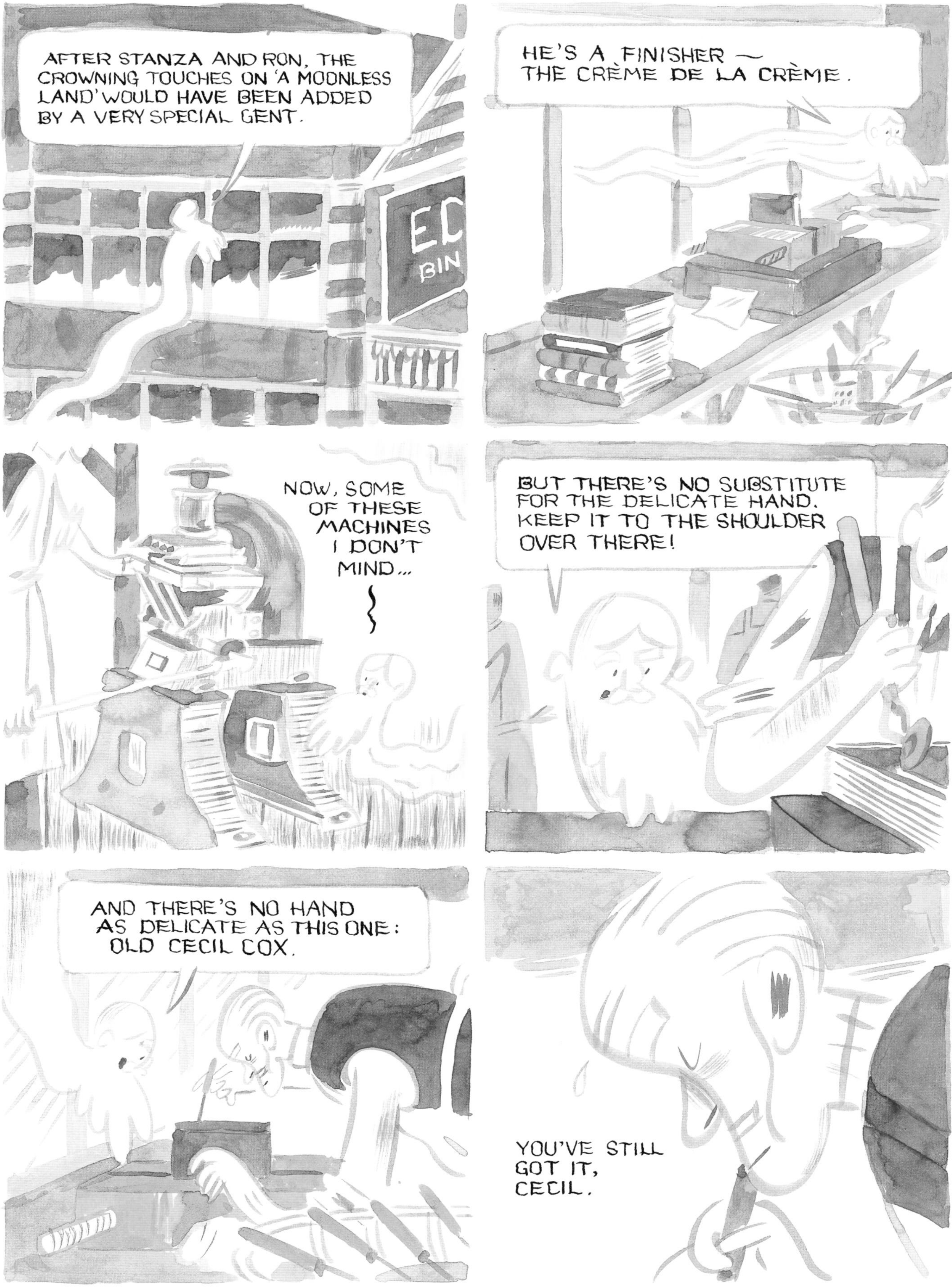
AFTER STANZA AND RON, THE CROWNING TOUCHES ON 'A MOONLESS LAND' WOULD HAVE BEEN ADDED BY A VERY SPECIAL GENT.
E.C
BIN
HE'S A FINISHER — THE CRÈME DE LA CRÈME.
NOW, SOME OF THESE MACHINES I DON'T MIND...
BUT THERE'S NO SUBSTITUTE FOR THE DELICATE HAND. KEEP IT TO THE SHOULDER OVER THERE!
AND THERE'S NO HAND AS DELICATE AS THIS ONE: OLD CECIL COX.
YOU'VE STILL GOT IT, CECIL.

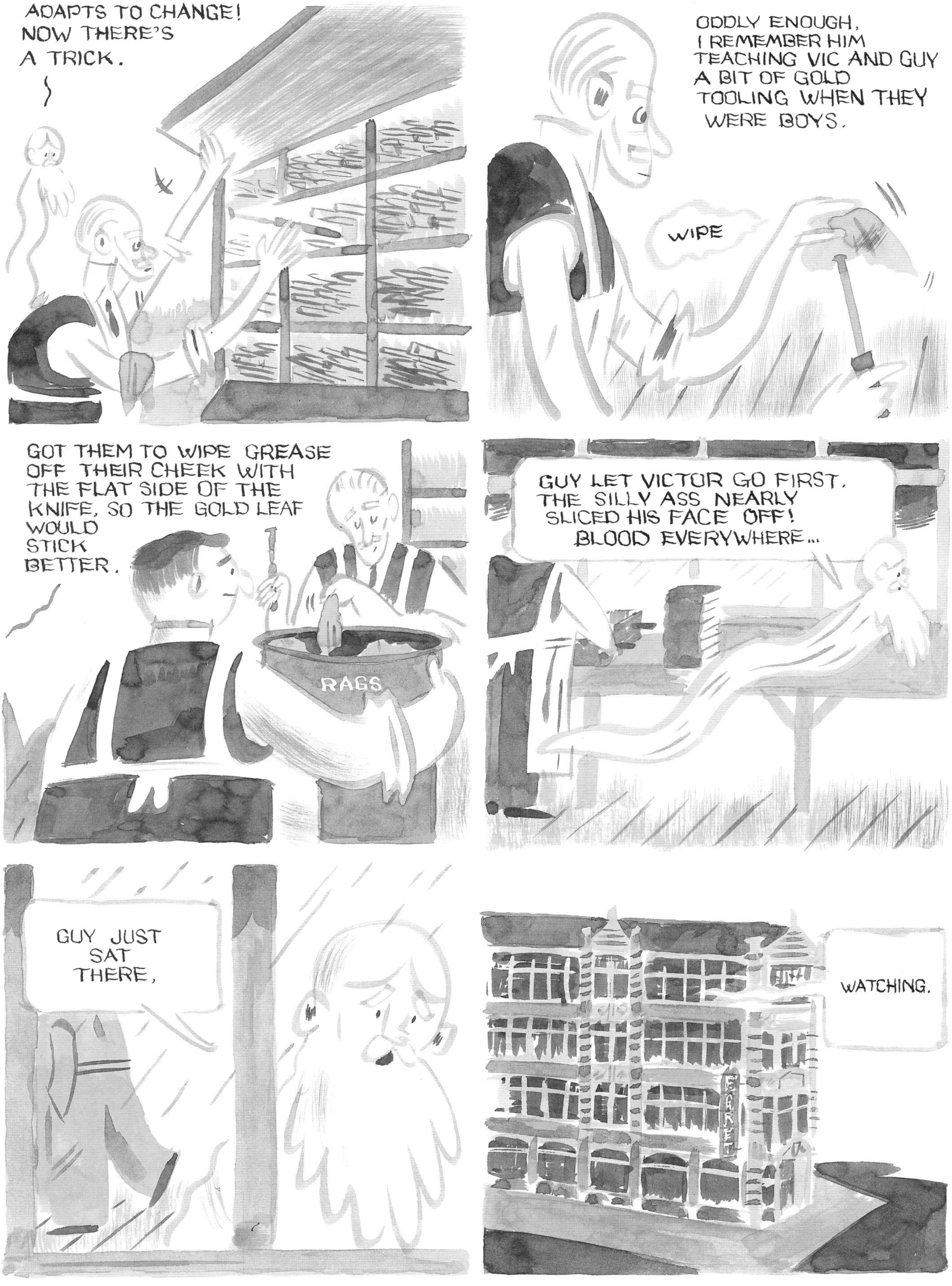
ADAPTS TO CHANGE! NOW THERE'S A TRICK.
ODDLY ENOUGH, I REMEMBER HIM TEACHING VIC AND GUY A BIT OF GOLD TOOLING WHEN THEY WERE BOYS.
WIPE
GOT THEM TO WIPE GREASE OFF THEIR CHEEK WITH THE FLAT SIDE OF THE KNIFE, SO THE GOLD LEAF WOULD STICK BETTER.
RAGS
GUY LET VICTOR GO FIRST. THE SILLY ASS NEARLY SLICED HIS FACE OFF! BLOOD EVERYWHERE...
GUY JUST SAT THERE,
WATCHING.

PART TWO:

A

Moonless

Land

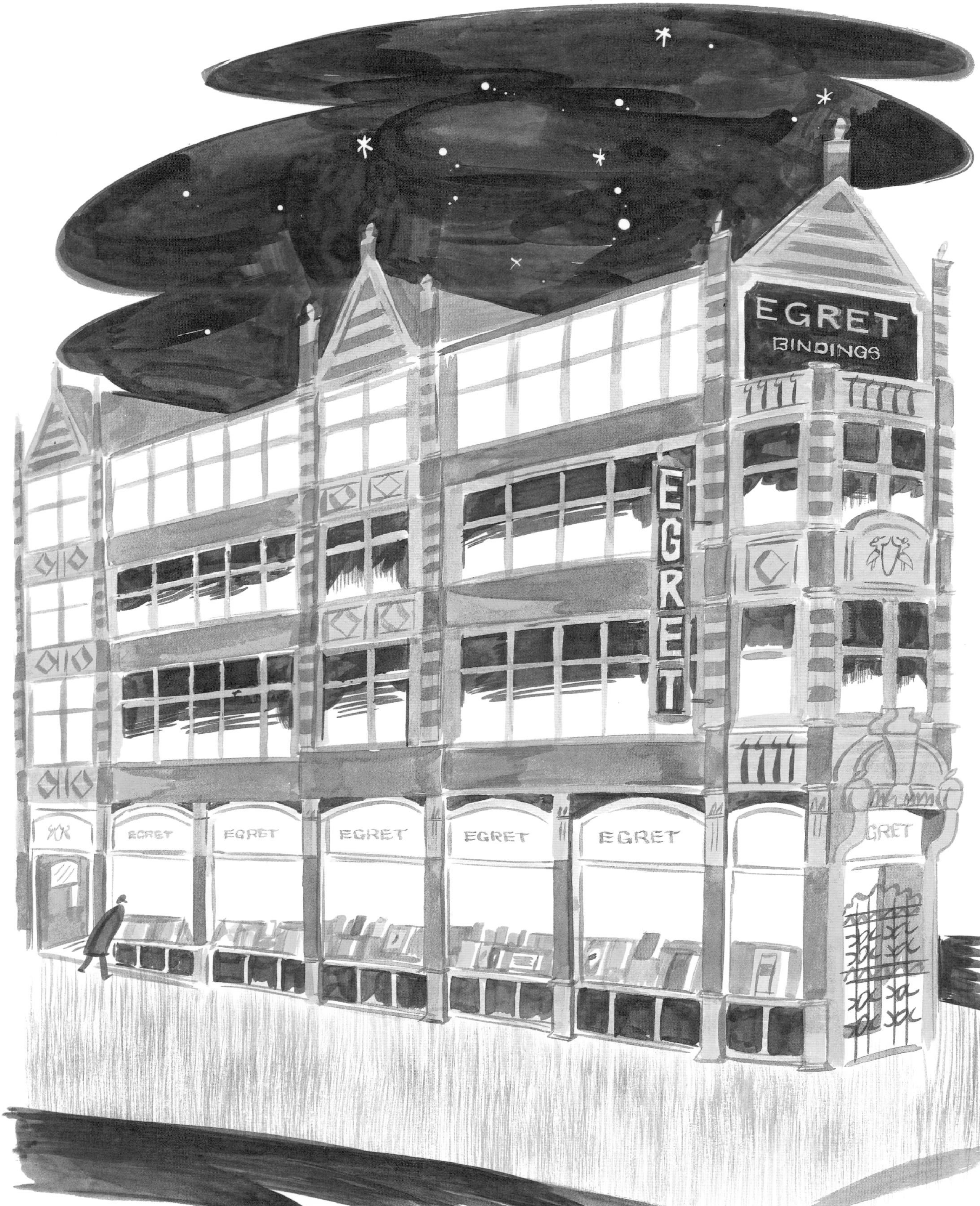
EGRET
BINDINGS
EGRET
EGRET
EGRET
EGRET
EGRET
EGRET
GRET

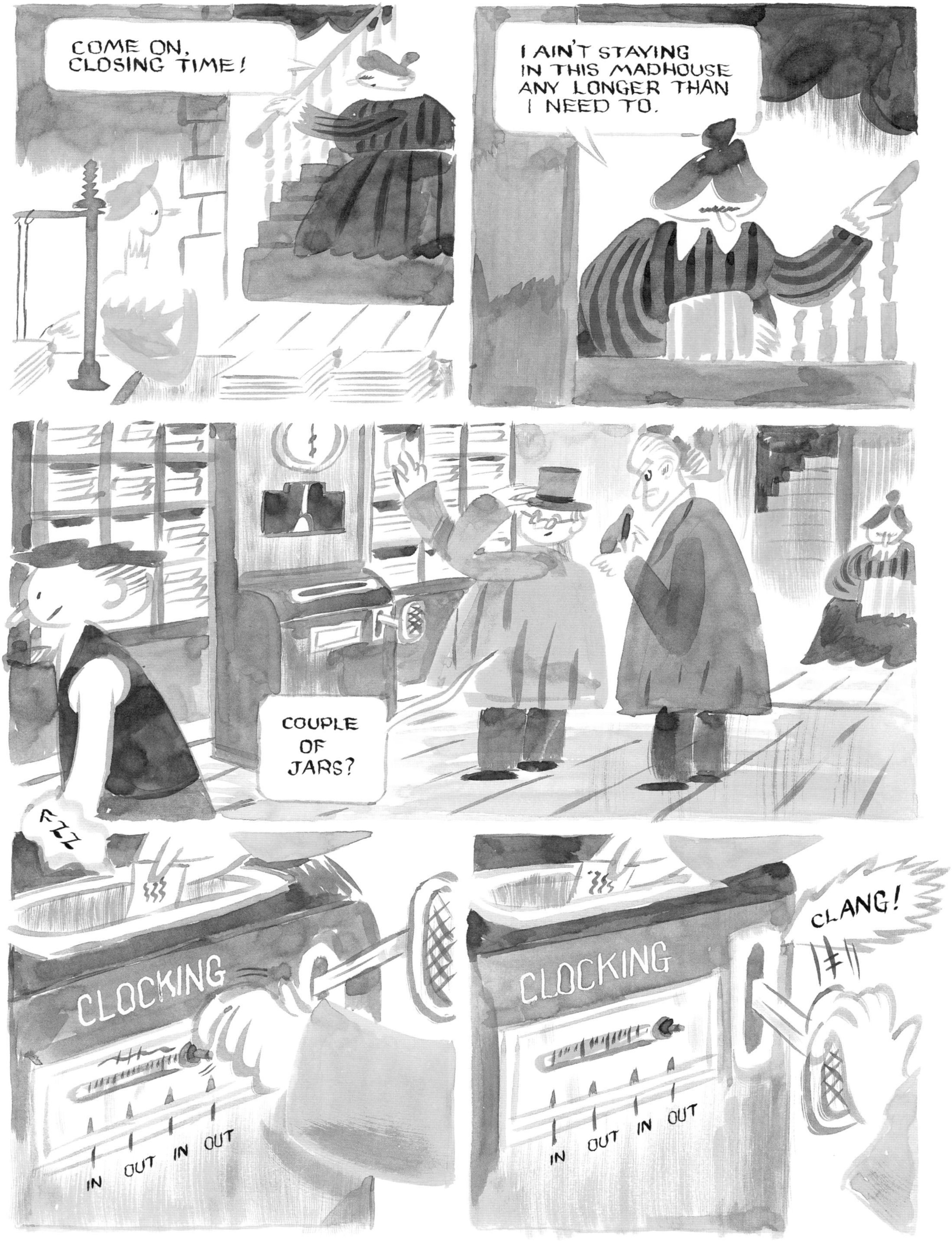
COME ON, CLOSING TIME!
I AIN'T STAYING IN THIS MADHOUSE ANY LONGER THAN I NEED TO.
COUPLE OF JARS?
ZZZ
CLOCKING
IN OUT IN OUT
CLANG!
CLOCKING
IN OUT IN OUT

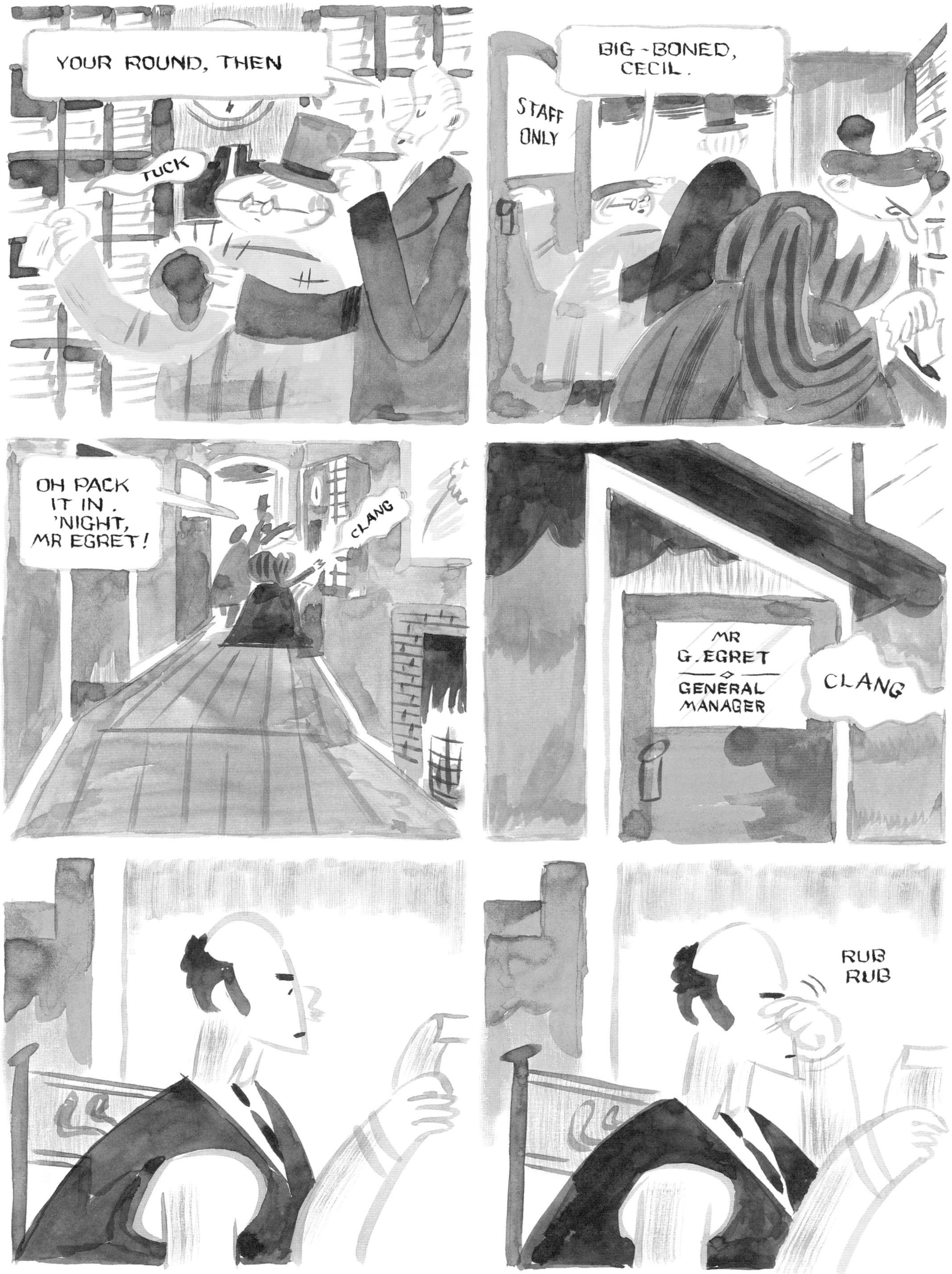
YOUR ROUND, THEN
TUCK
BIG-BONED, CECIL.
STAFF ONLY
OH PACK IT IN. 'NIGHT, MR EGRET!
CLANG
MR G. EGRET
GENERAL MANAGER
CLANG
RUB RUB

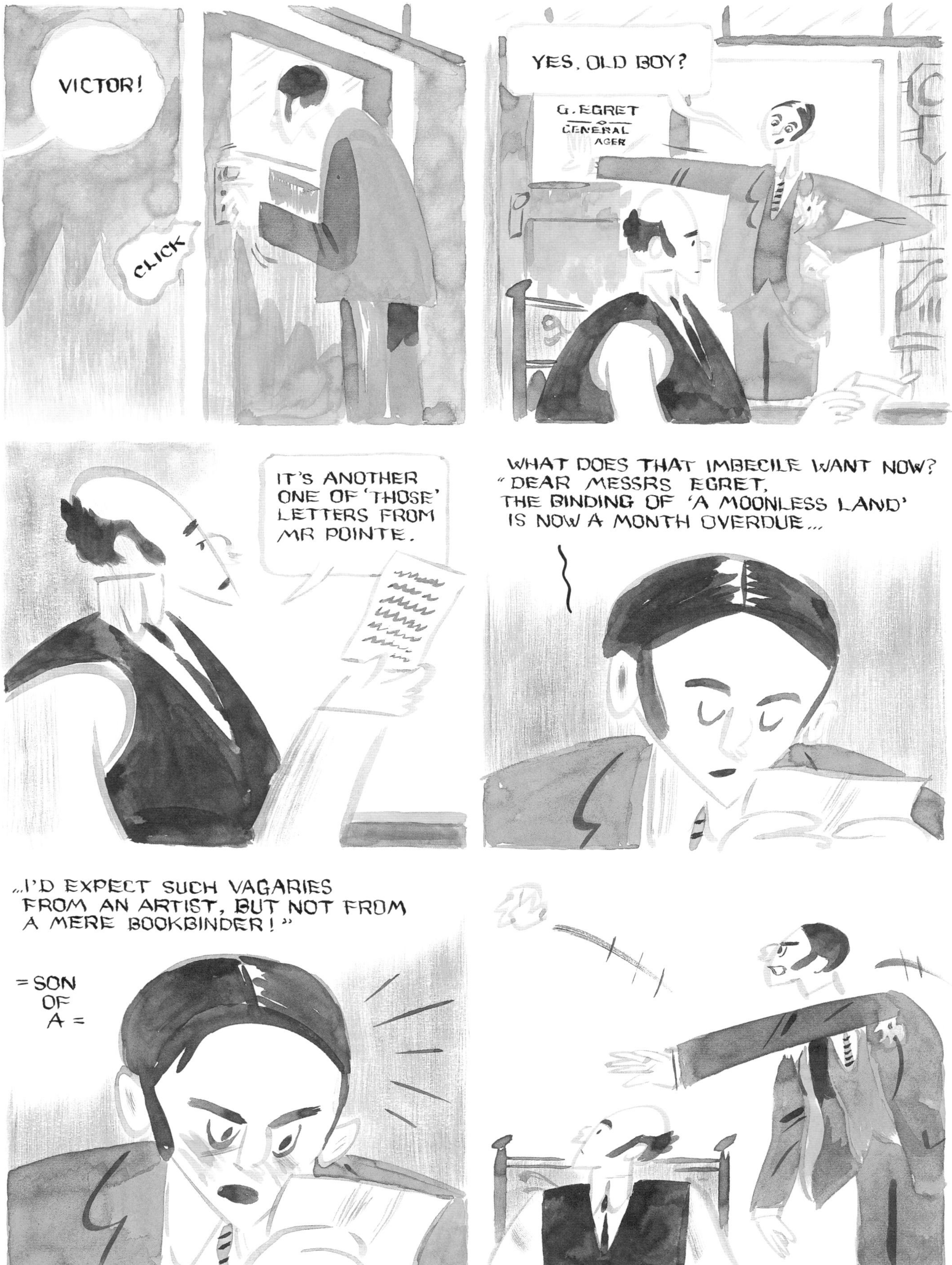

VICTOR!
CLICK
YES, OLD BOY?
G. EGRET GENERAL AGER
IT'S ANOTHER ONE OF 'THOSE' LETTERS FROM MR POINTE.
WHAT DOES THAT IMBECILE WANT NOW?
"DEAR MESSRS EGRET, THE BINDING OF 'A MOONLESS LAND' IS NOW A MONTH OVERDUE...
...I'D EXPECT SUCH VAGARIES FROM AN ARTIST, BUT NOT FROM A MERE BOOKBINDER!"
=SON OF A=

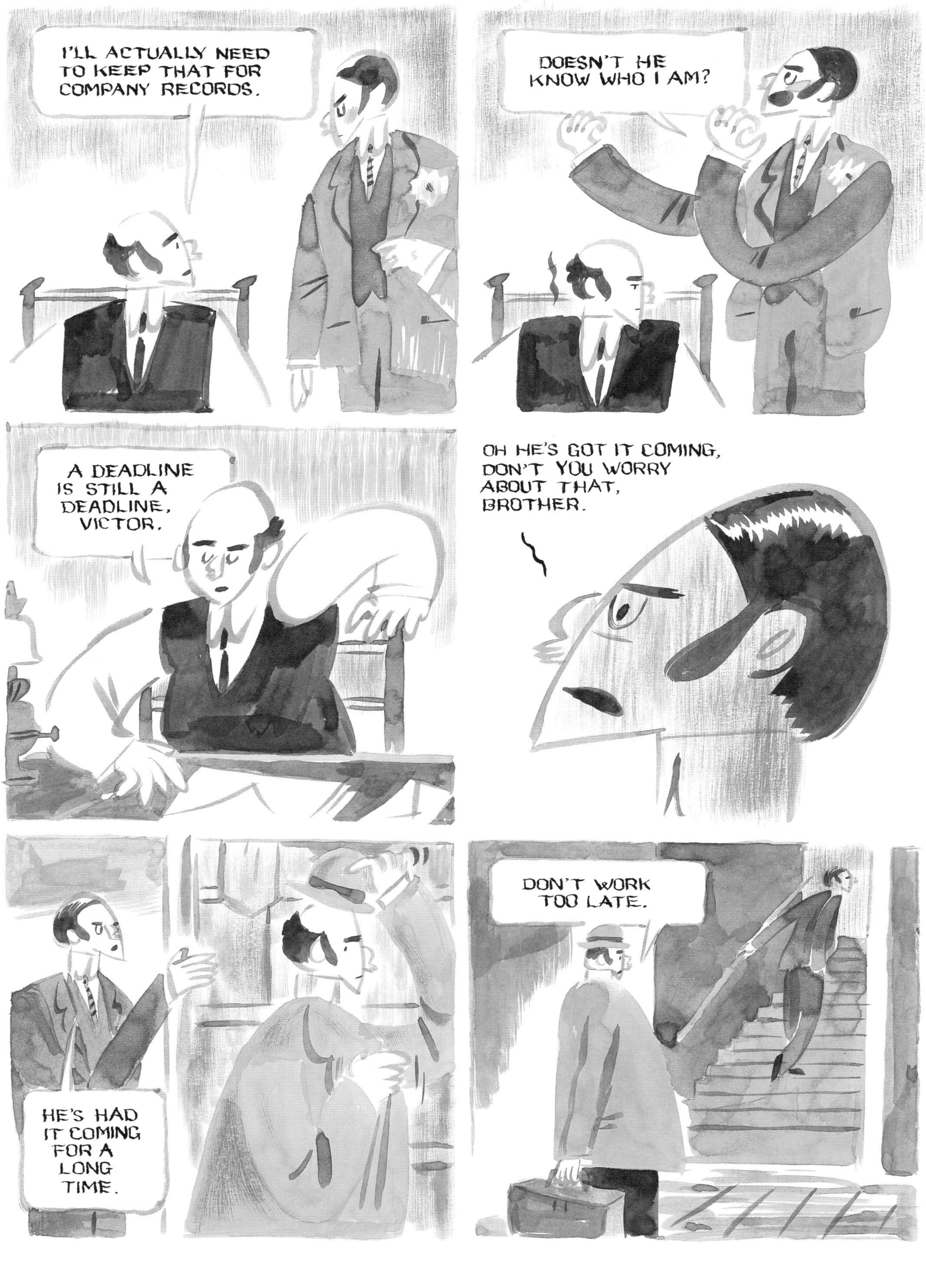
I'LL ACTUALLY NEED TO KEEP THAT FOR COMPANY RECORDS.
DOESN'T HE KNOW WHO I AM?
A DEADLINE IS STILL A DEADLINE, VICTOR.
OH HE'S GOT IT COMING, DON'T YOU WORRY ABOUT THAT, BROTHER.
HE'S HAD IT COMING FOR A LONG TIME.
DON'T WORK TOO LATE.

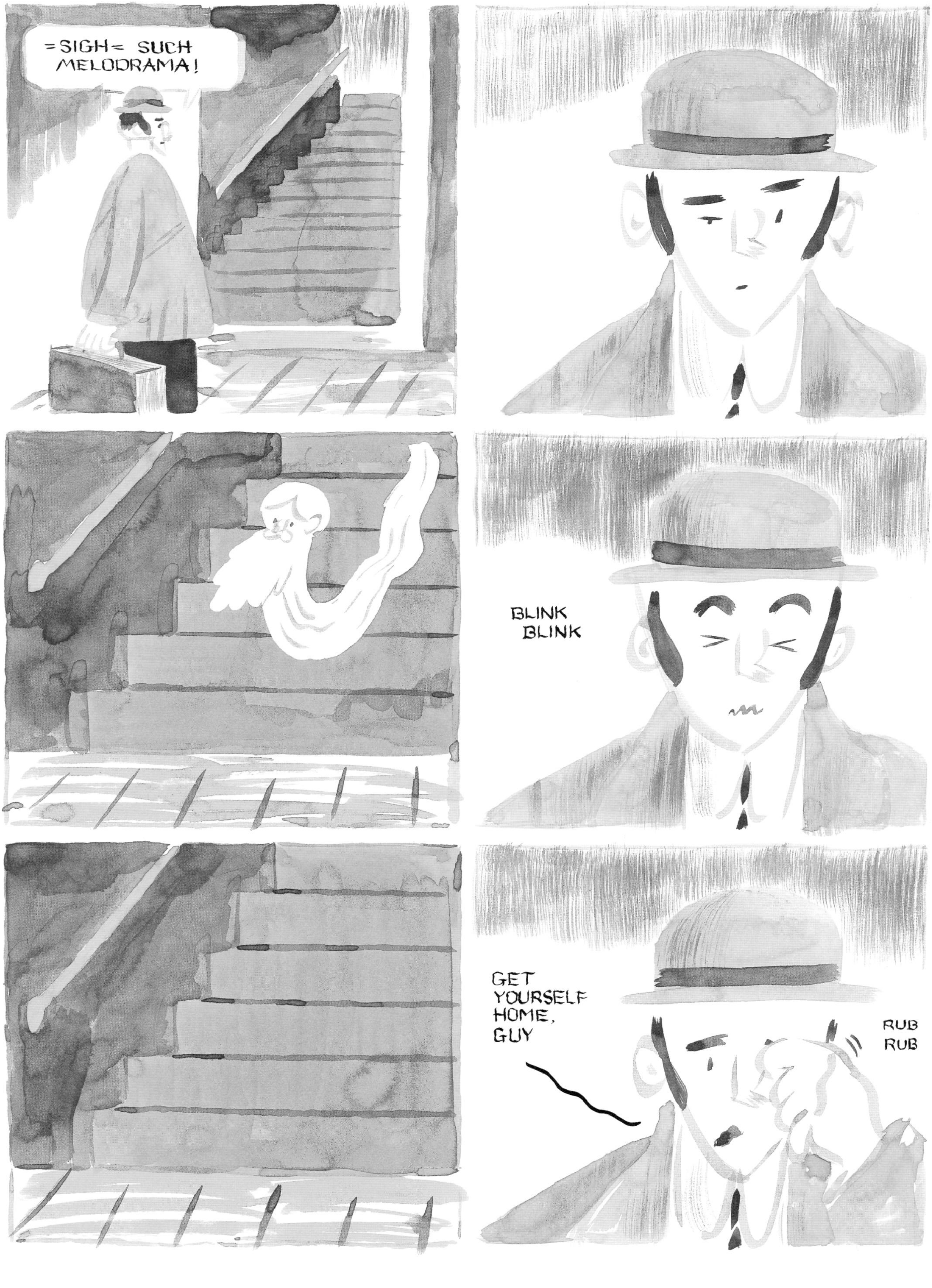
=SIGH= SUCH MELODRAMA!
BLINK BLINK
GET YOURSELF HOME, GUY
RUB RUB

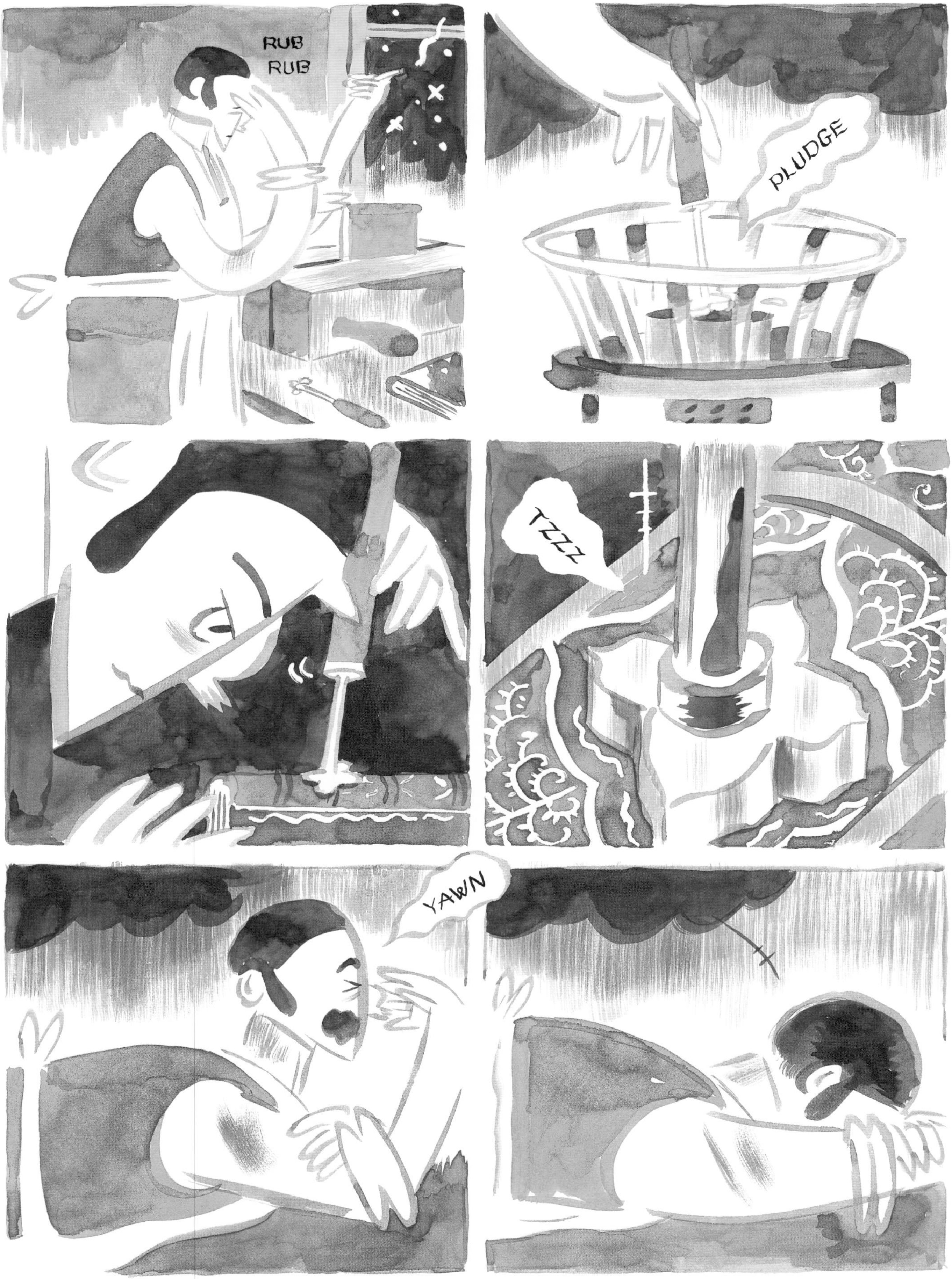
RUB
RUB
PLUDGE
TZZZ
YAWN

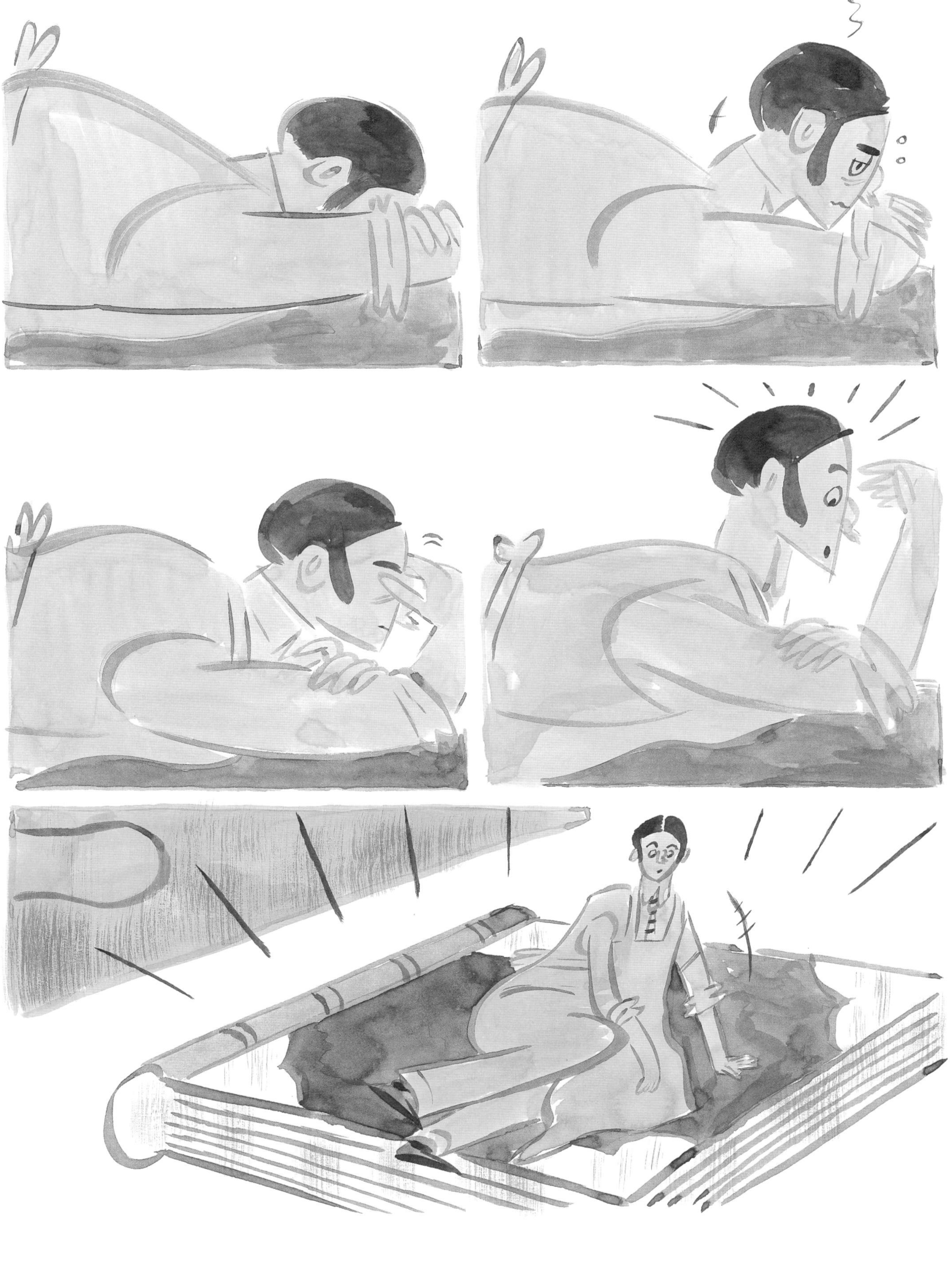

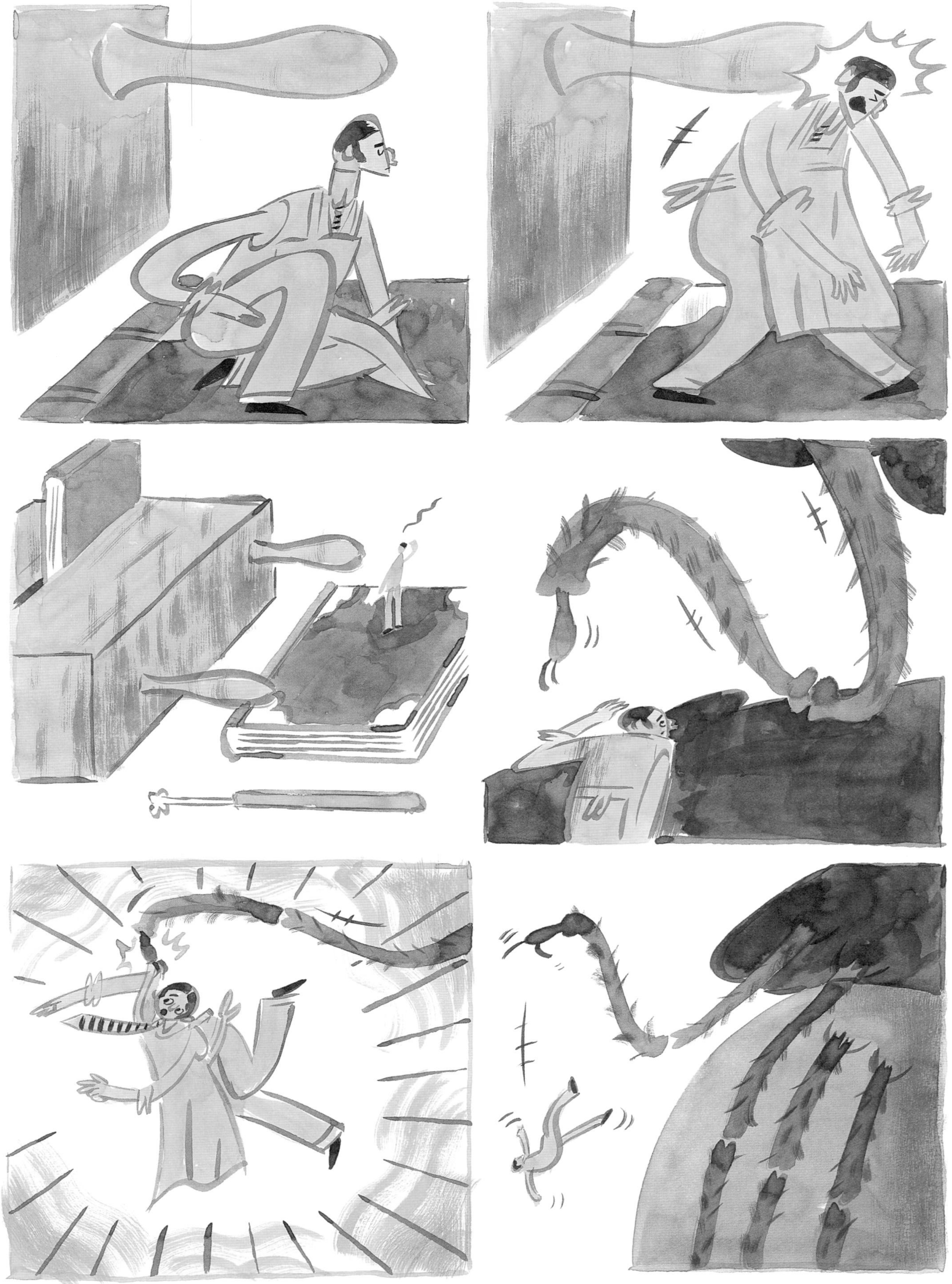

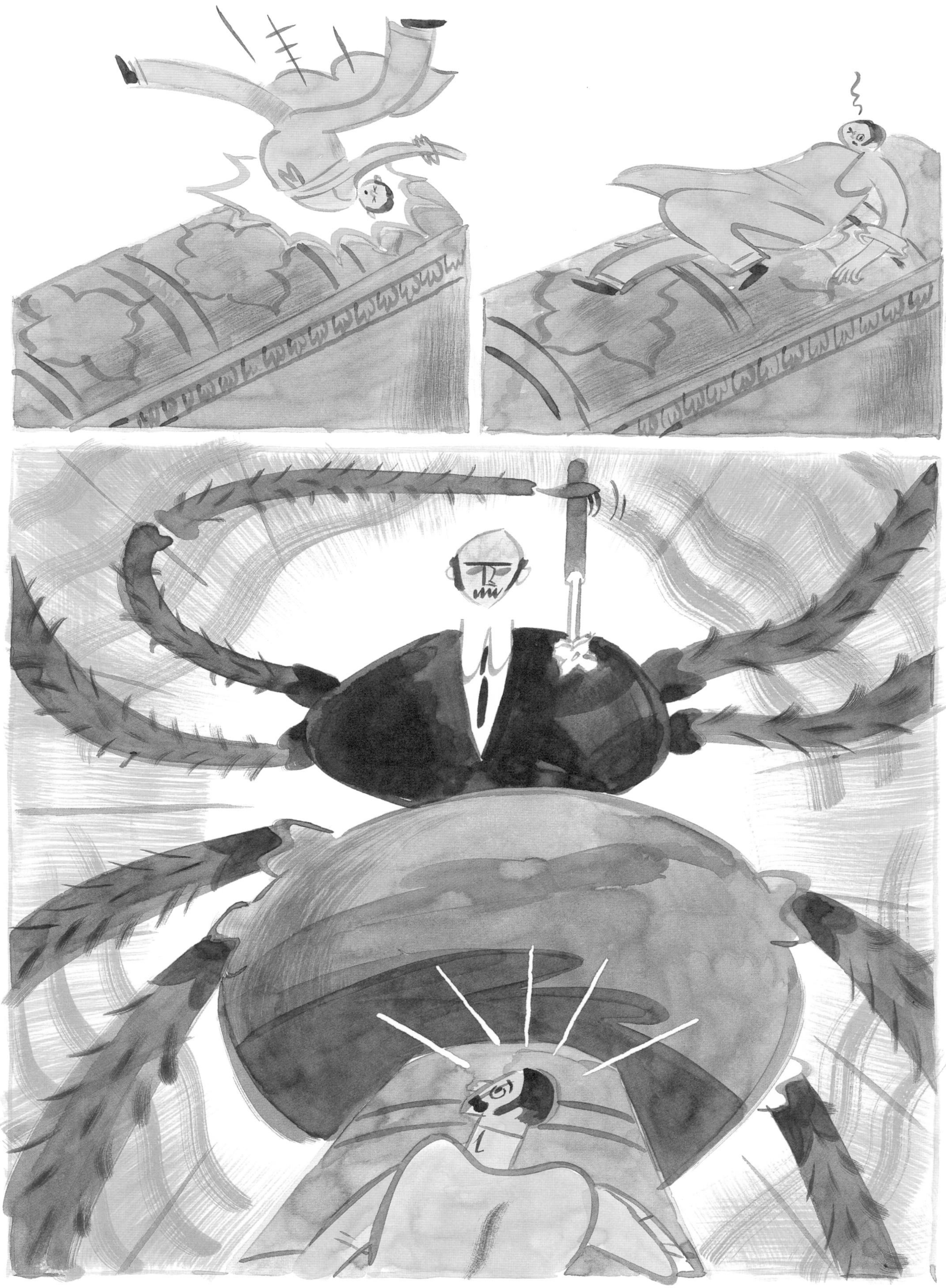

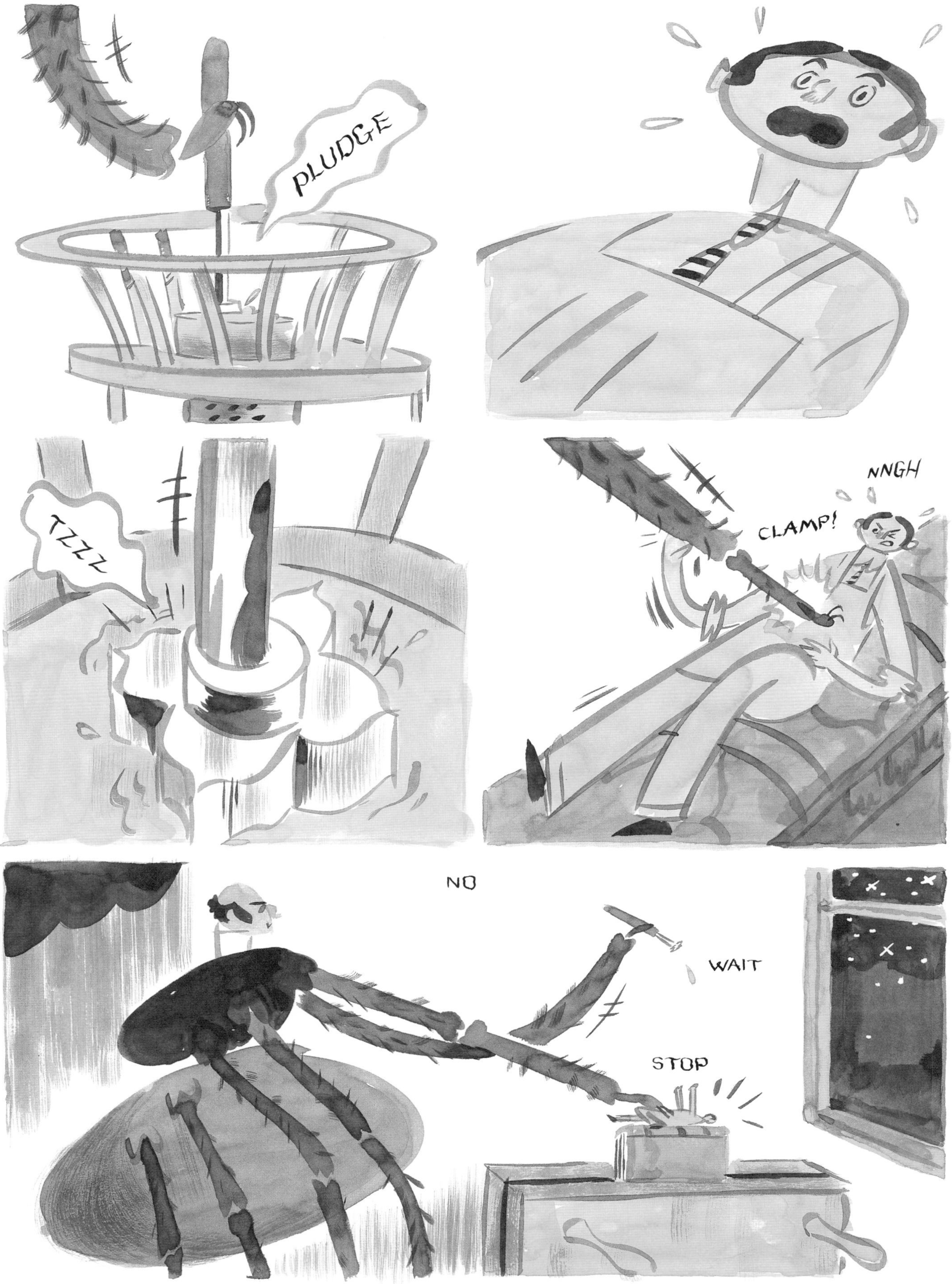
PLUDGE
TZZZ
NNGH
CLAMP!
NO
WAIT
STOP

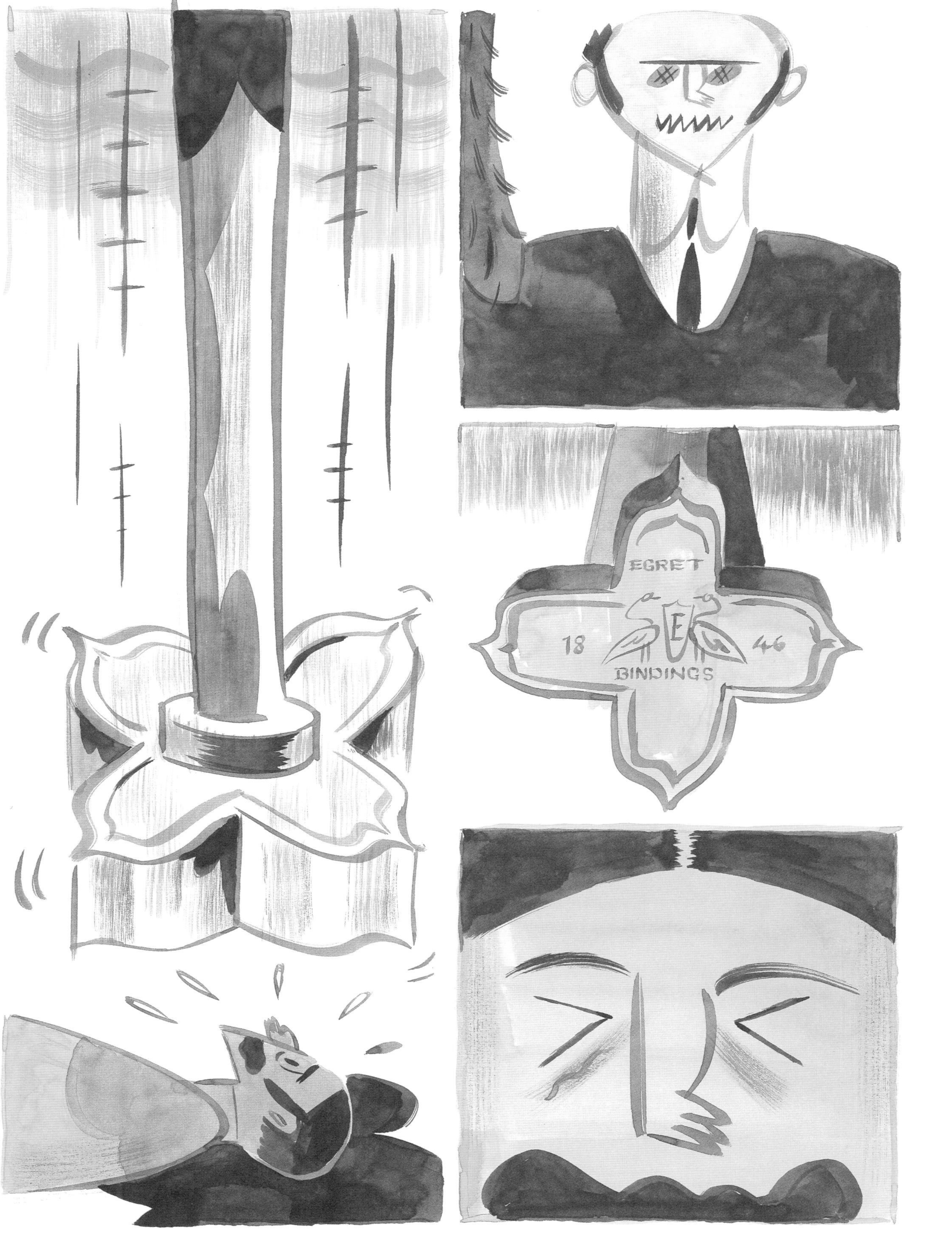
EGRET
E
18
46
BINDINGS

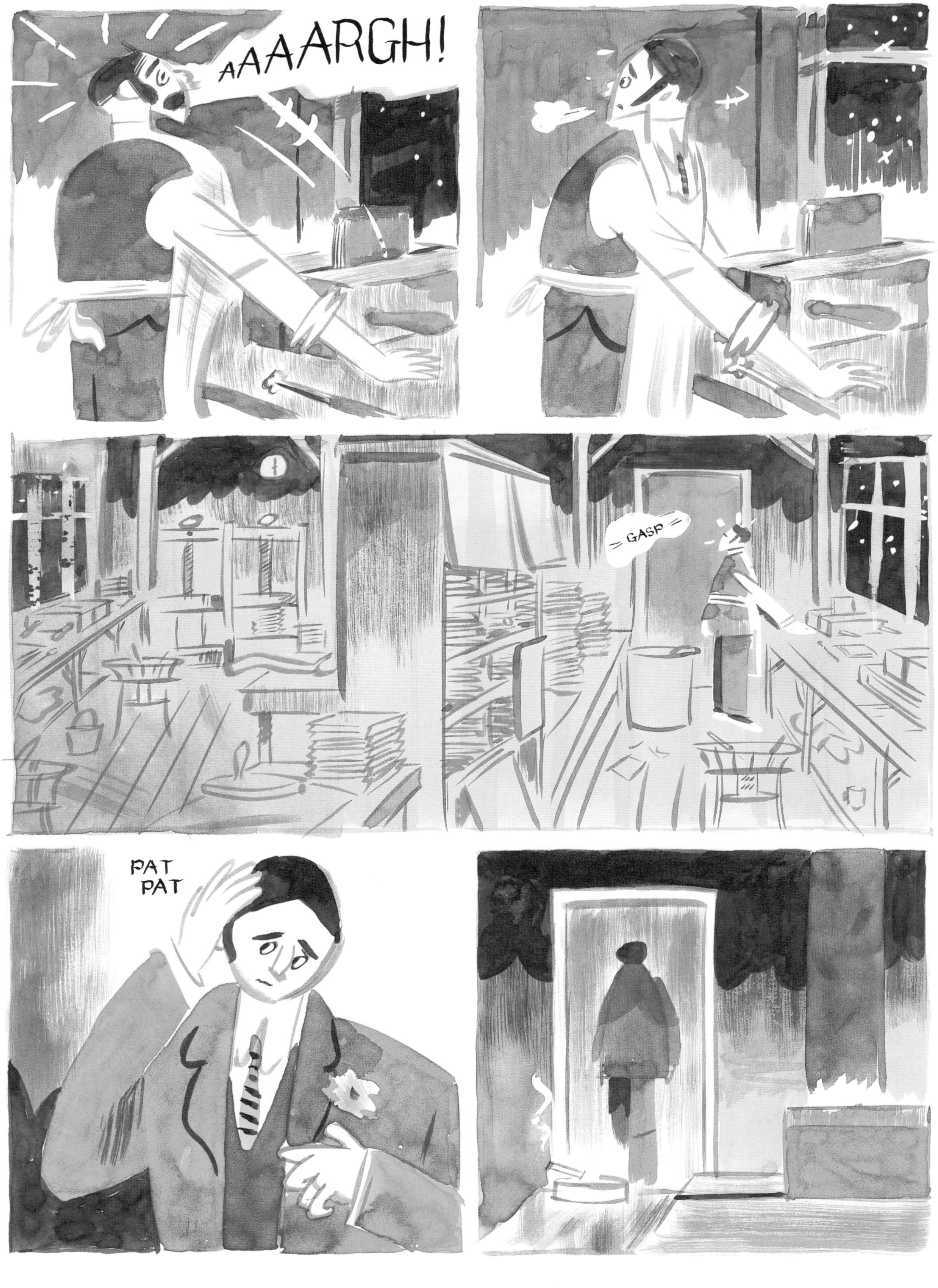
AAAARGH!
GASP
PAT PAT

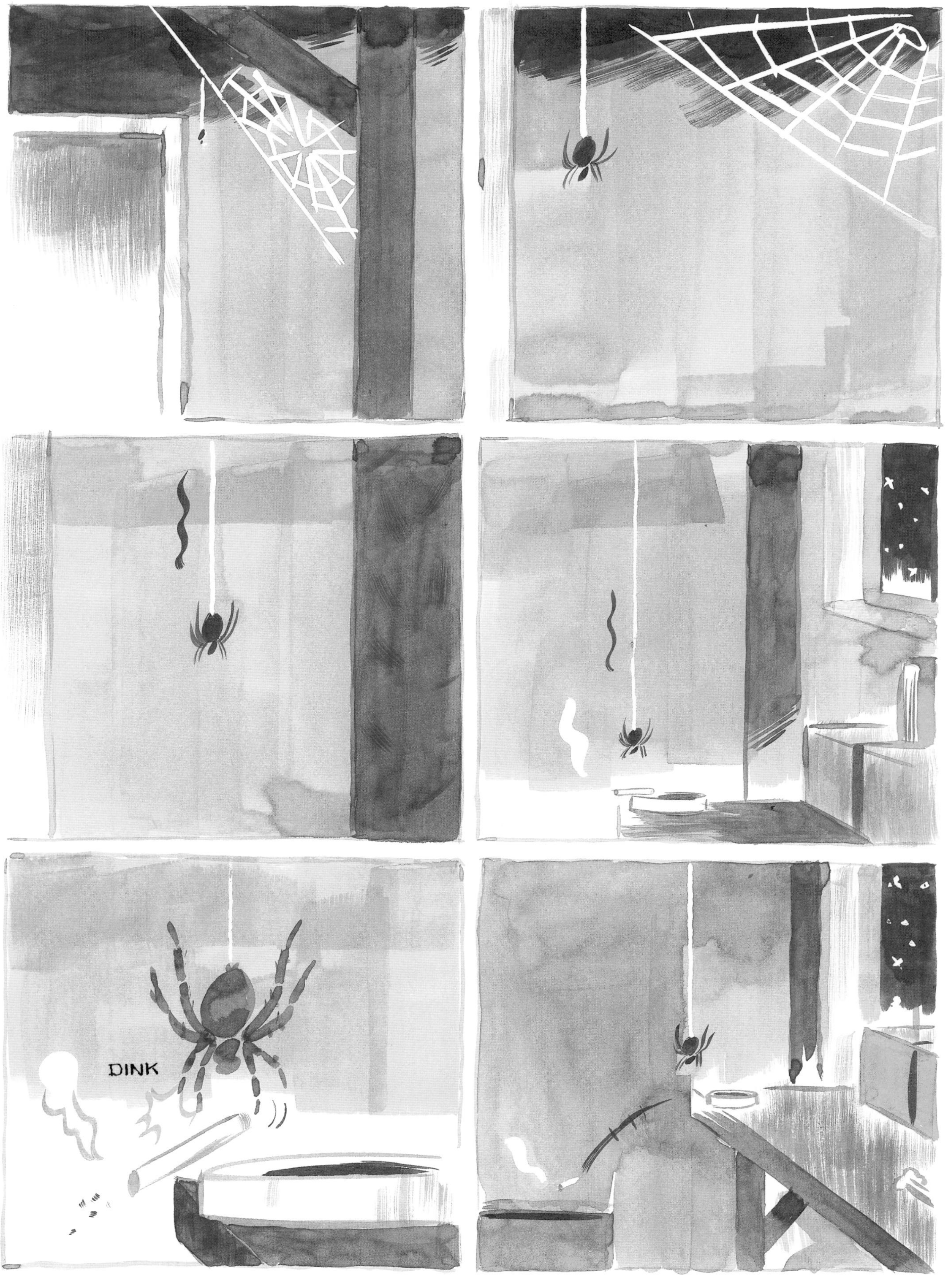
DINK

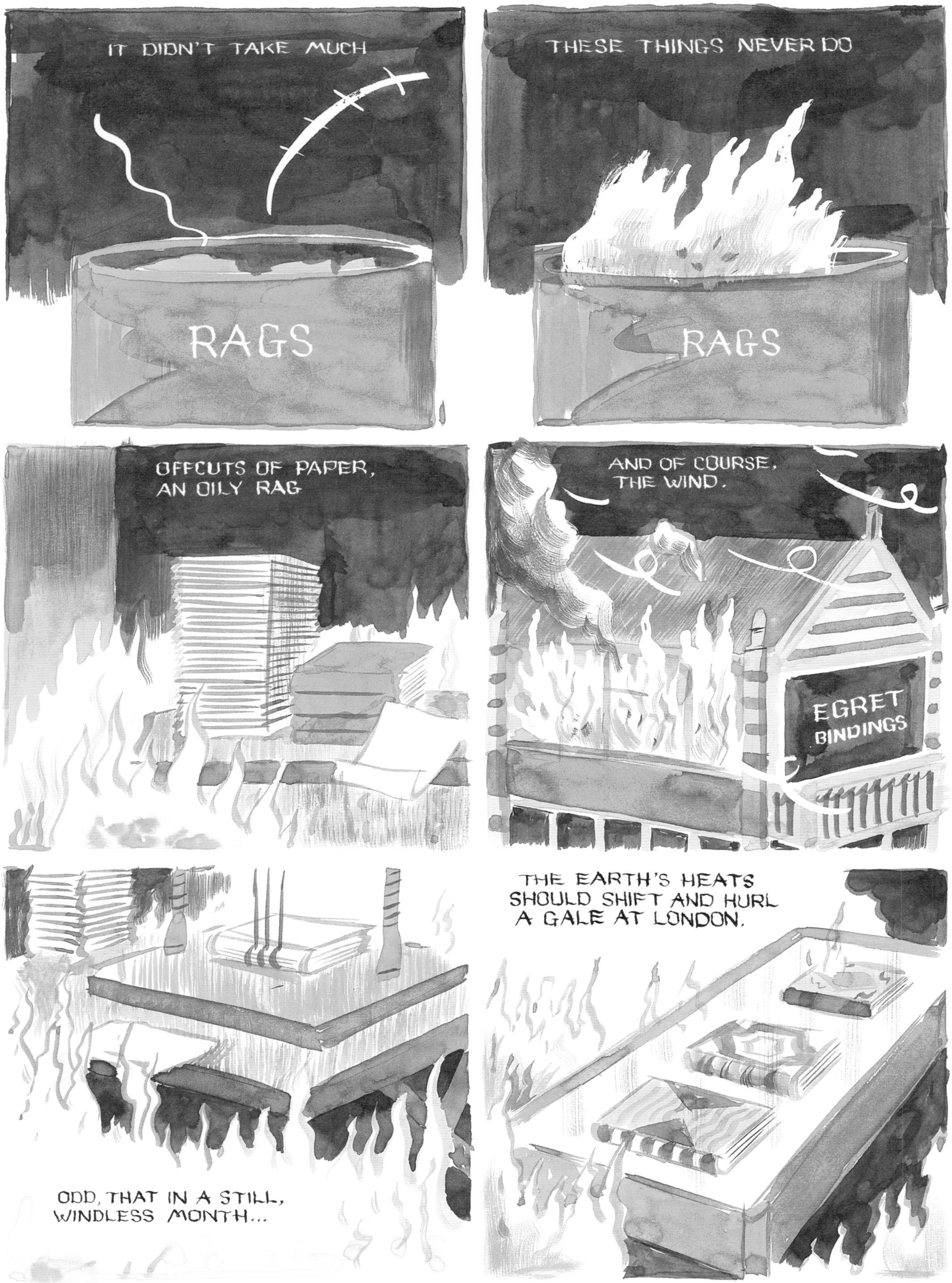
IT DIDN'T TAKE MUCH
RAGS
THESE THINGS NEVER DO
RAGS
OFFCUTS OF PAPER, AN OILY RAG
AND OF COURSE, THE WIND.
EGRET BINDINGS
ODD, THAT IN A STILL, WINDLESS MONTH...
THE EARTH'S HEATS SHOULD SHIFT AND HURL A GALE AT LONDON.

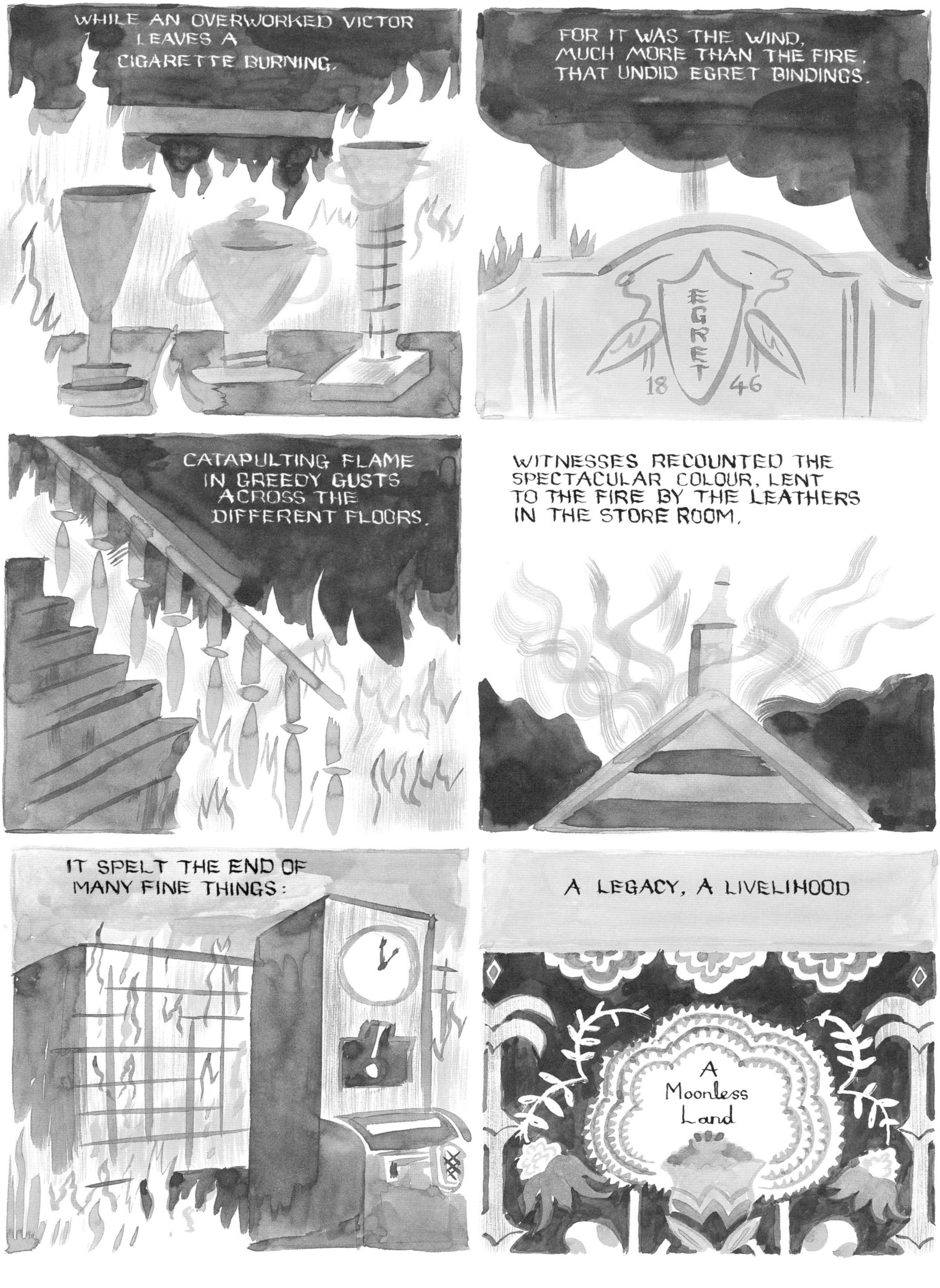
WHILE AN OVERWORKED VICTOR LEAVES A CIGARETTE BURNING,
FOR IT WAS THE WIND, MUCH MORE THAN THE FIRE, THAT UNDID EGRET BINDINGS.
EGRET
18 46
CATAPULTING FLAME IN GREEDY GUSTS ACROSS THE DIFFERENT FLOORS.
WITNESSES RECOUNTED THE SPECTACULAR COLOUR, LENT TO THE FIRE BY THE LEATHERS IN THE STORE ROOM,
IT SPELT THE END OF MANY FINE THINGS:
A LEGACY, A LIVELIHOOD
A Moonless Land

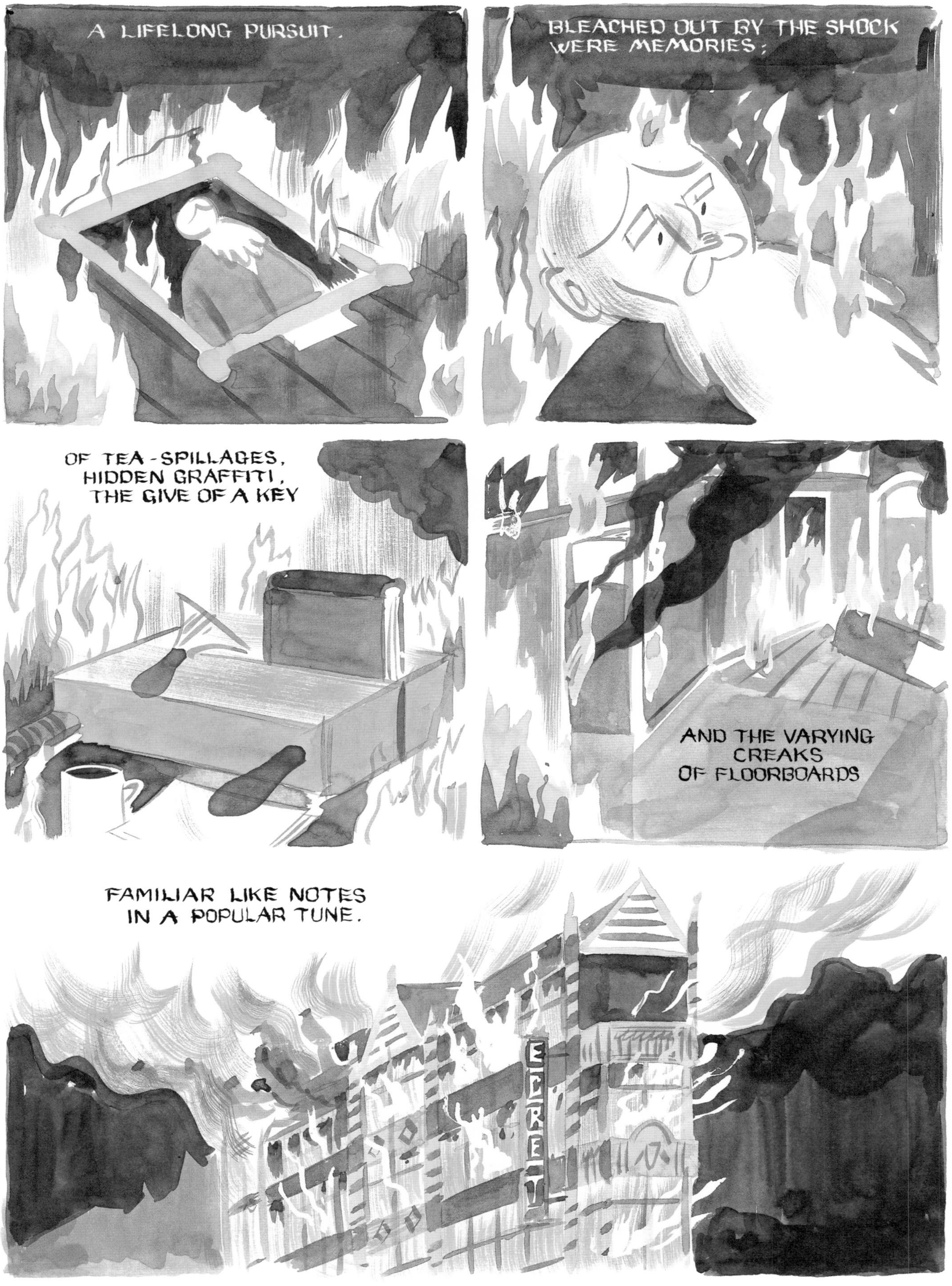
A LIFELONG PURSUIT.
BLEACHED OUT BY THE SHOCK WERE MEMORIES;
OF TEA-SPILLAGES, HIDDEN GRAFFITI, THE GIVE OF A KEY
AND THE VARYING CREAKS OF FLOORBOARDS
FAMILIAR LIKE NOTES IN A POPULAR TUNE.

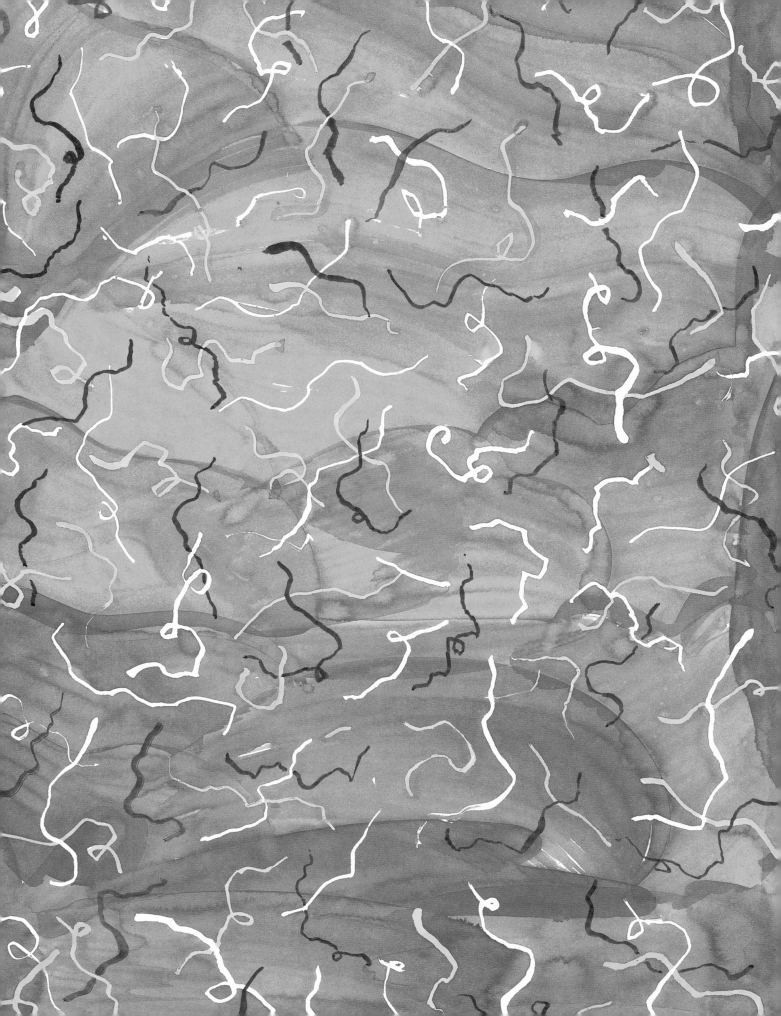

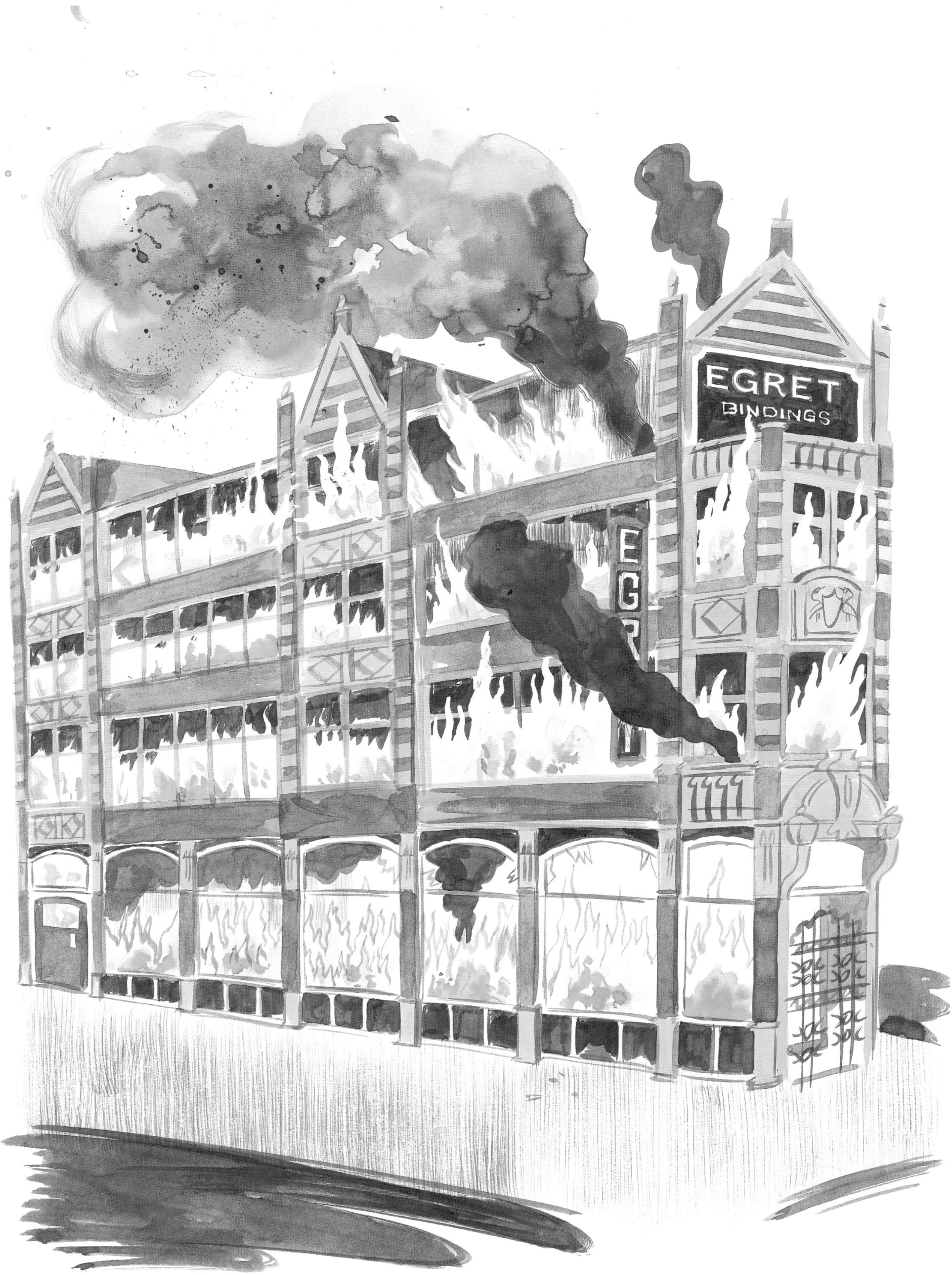
EGRET
BINDINGS
EGR

PART THREE:

Pleasure In Ruin

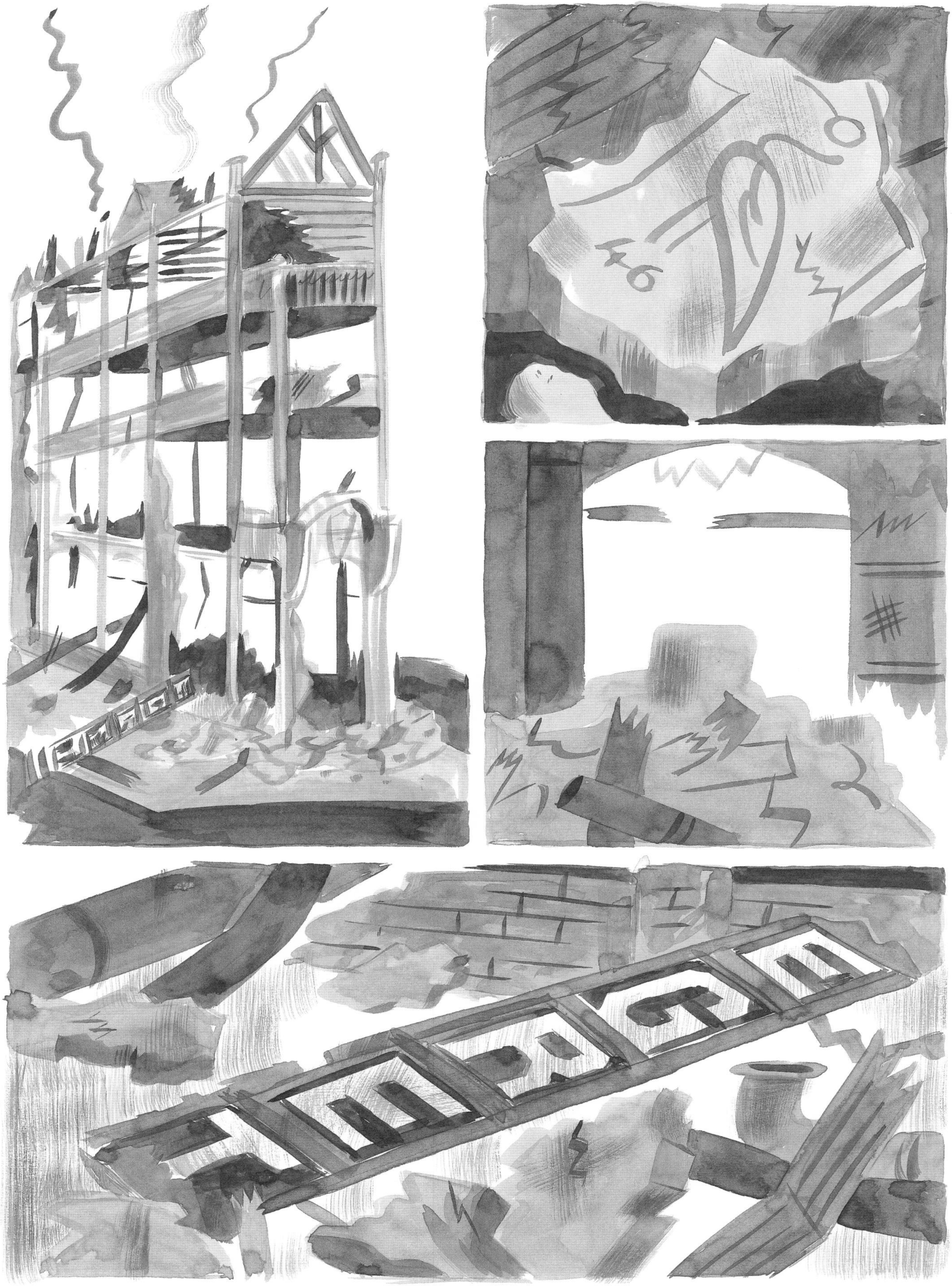

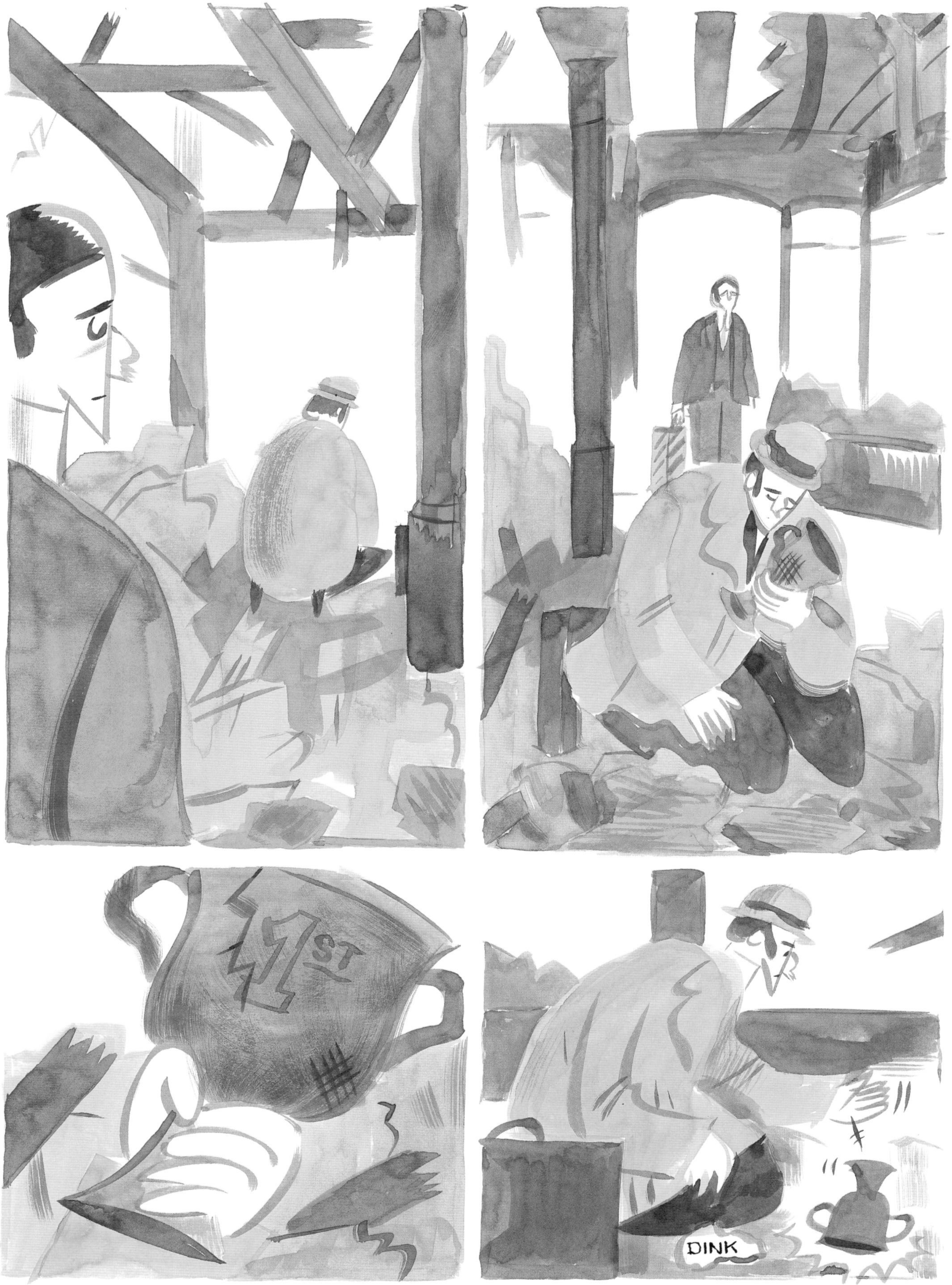
1ST
DINK

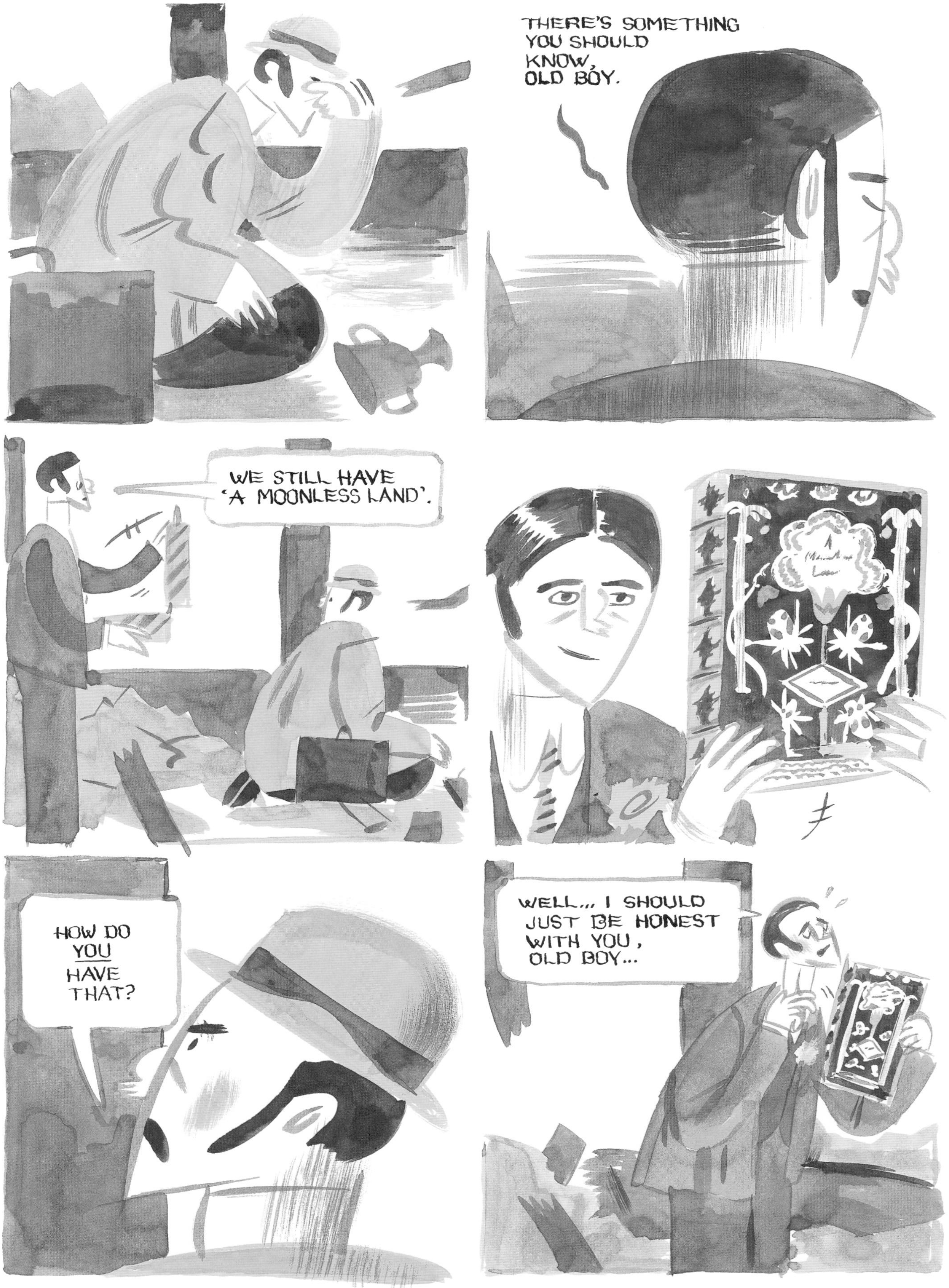
THERE'S SOMETHING YOU SHOULD KNOW, OLD BOY.
WE STILL HAVE 'A MOONLESS LAND'.
HOW DO YOU HAVE THAT?
WELL... I SHOULD JUST BE HONEST WITH YOU, OLD BOY...

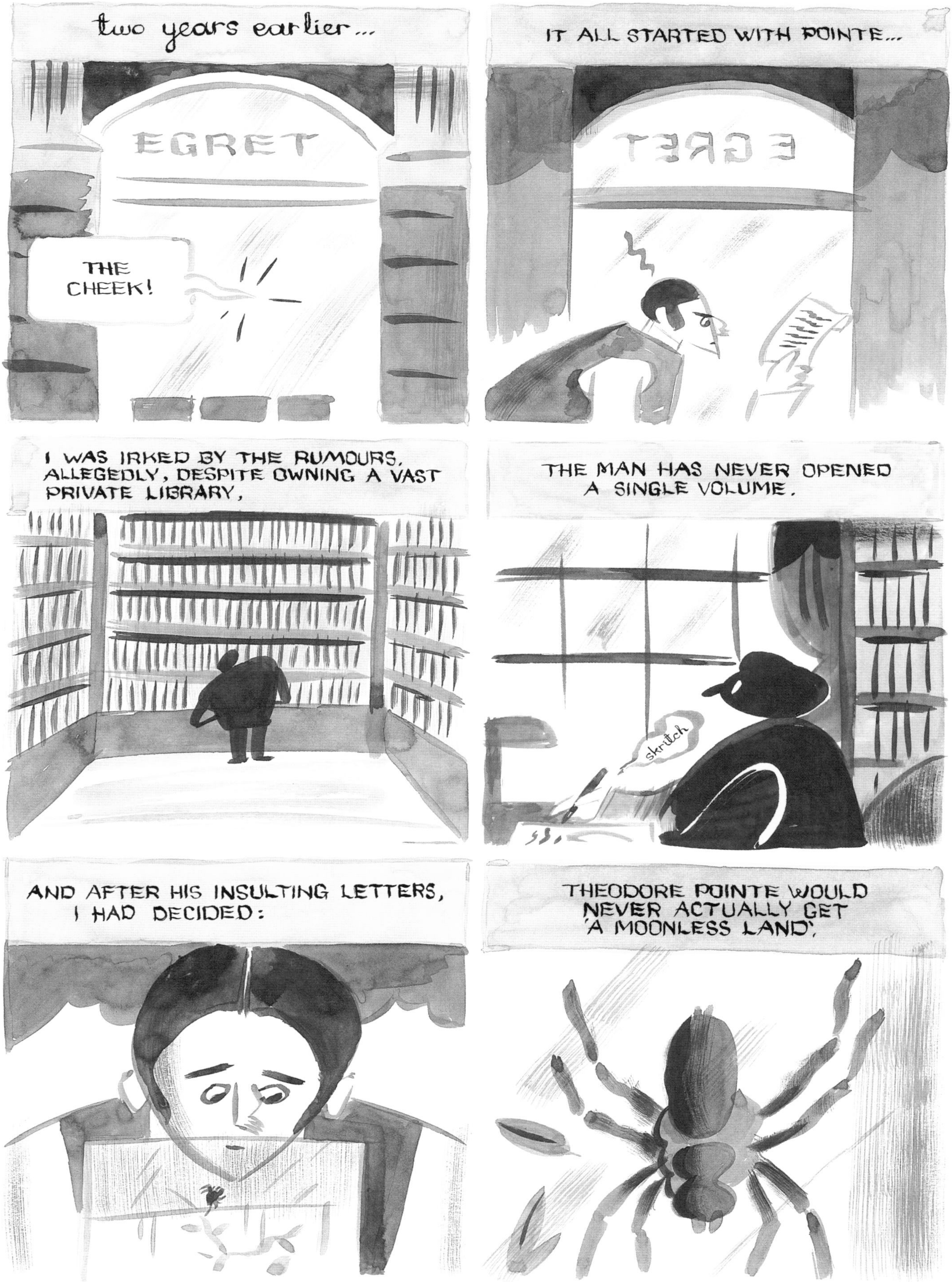
two years earlier...
EGRET
THE CHEEK!
IT ALL STARTED WITH POINTE...
I WAS IRKED BY THE RUMOURS, ALLEGEDLY, DESPITE OWNING A VAST PRIVATE LIBRARY,
THE MAN HAS NEVER OPENED A SINGLE VOLUME.
skritch
AND AFTER HIS INSULTING LETTERS, I HAD DECIDED:
THEODORE POINTE WOULD NEVER ACTUALLY GET 'A MOONLESS LAND'.

MY IDEA WAS TO MAKE A SECOND, COUNTERFEIT BOOK FOR POINTE. IT SHOULD BE PASSABLE AS THE ORIGINAL, YET WORTHLESS IN COMPARISON.
skritch
A Moonless Land
THE UNCUT PAGES WOULD CONTAIN NOTHING BUT FILTH,
skritch
AND THE JEWELS ~ ALL 1,500 OF THEM ~ WOULD BE DUDS.
GARNET
AMETHYST
EMERALD
RUBIES
IF THERE WAS ANY DIFFERENCE IN THE SLEIGHT OF HAND ON EITHER BOOK, YOU'D SUSPECT SOMETHING. SO I HOUNDED THE SAME BUNCH THAT WORKED ON THE ORIGINAL: STANZA, RON AND CECIL.

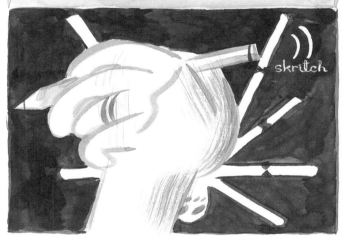

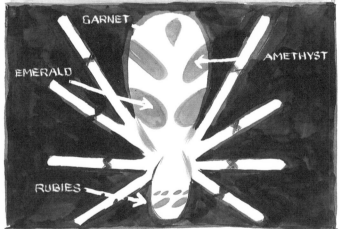

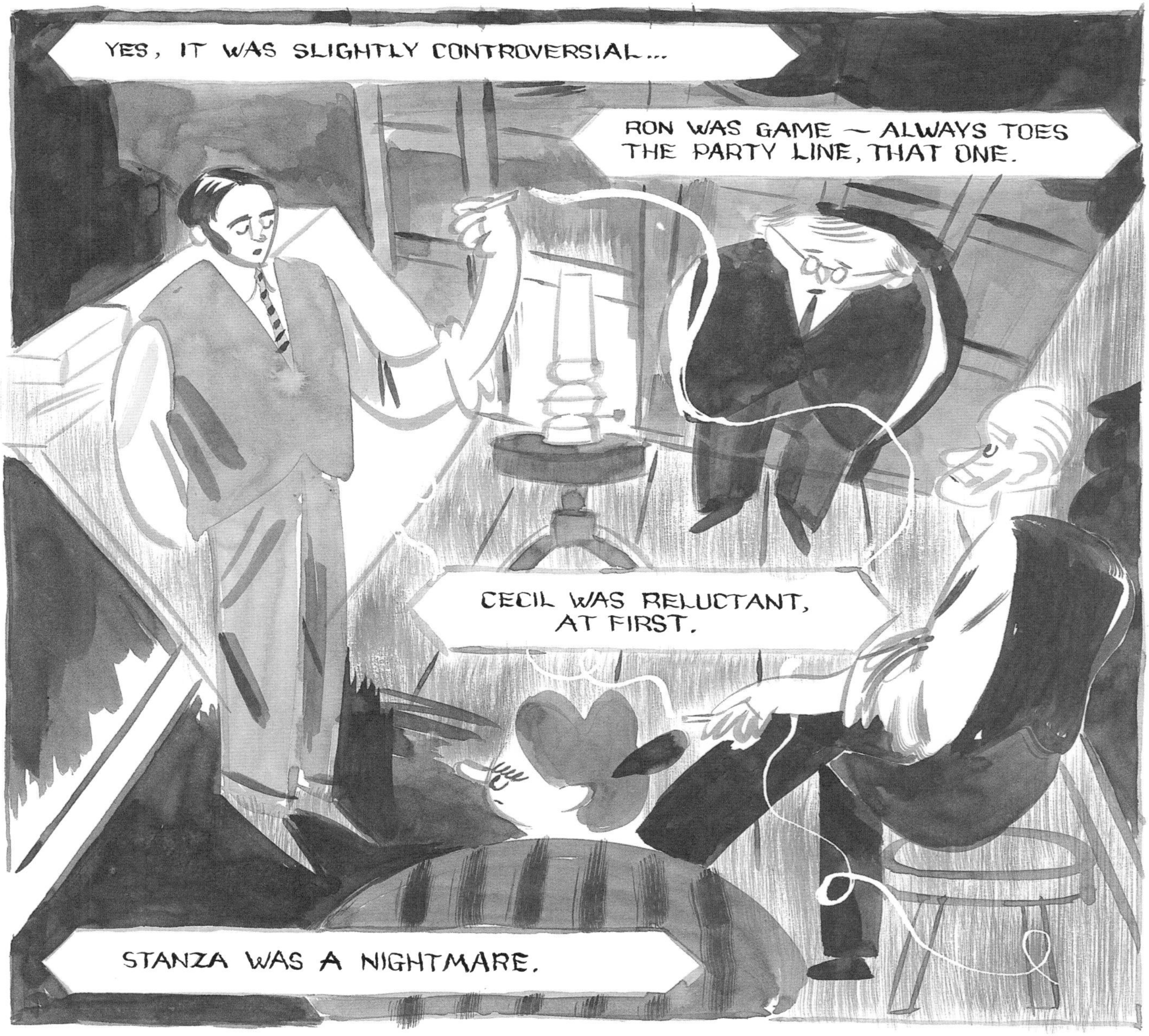
YES, IT WAS SLIGHTLY CONTROVERSIAL...
RON WAS GAME ~ ALWAYS TOES THE PARTY LINE, THAT ONE.
CECIL WAS RELUCTANT, AT FIRST.
STANZA WAS A NIGHTMARE.
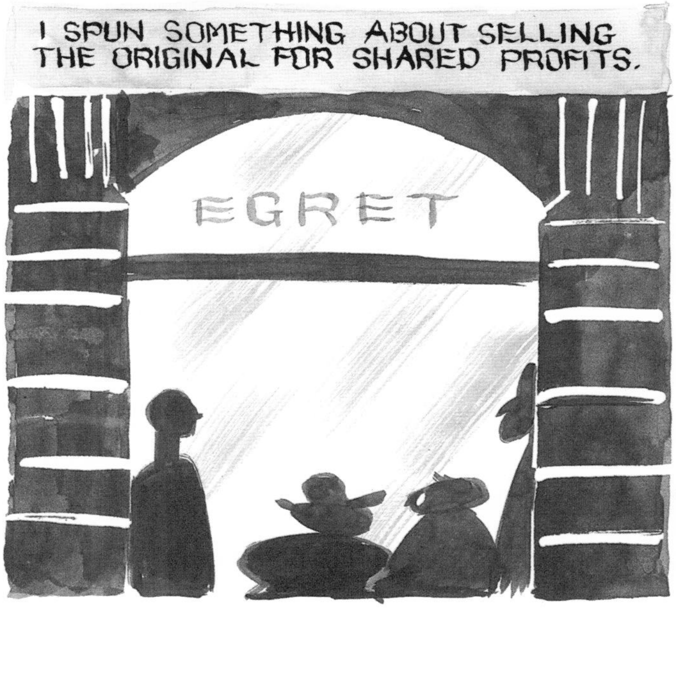
I SPUN SOMETHING ABOUT SELLING THE ORIGINAL FOR SHARED PROFITS.
EGRET
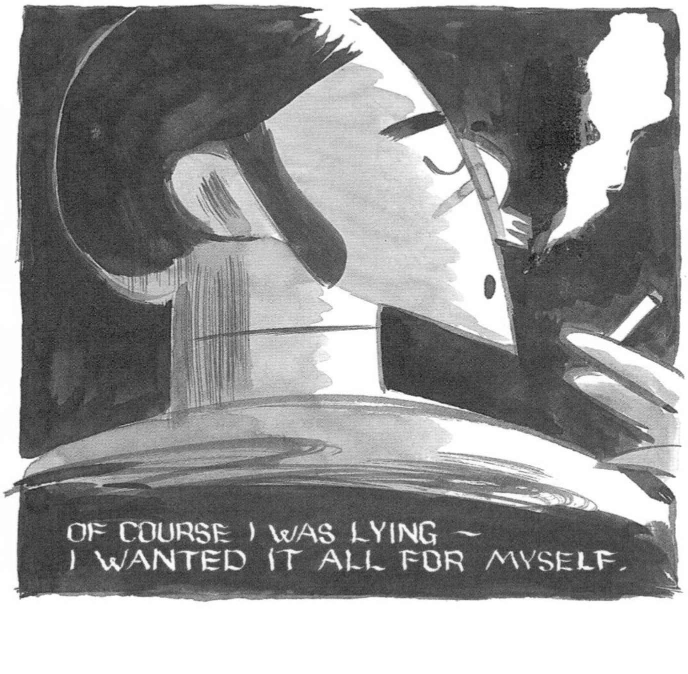
OF COURSE I WAS LYING ~ I WANTED IT ALL FOR MYSELF.

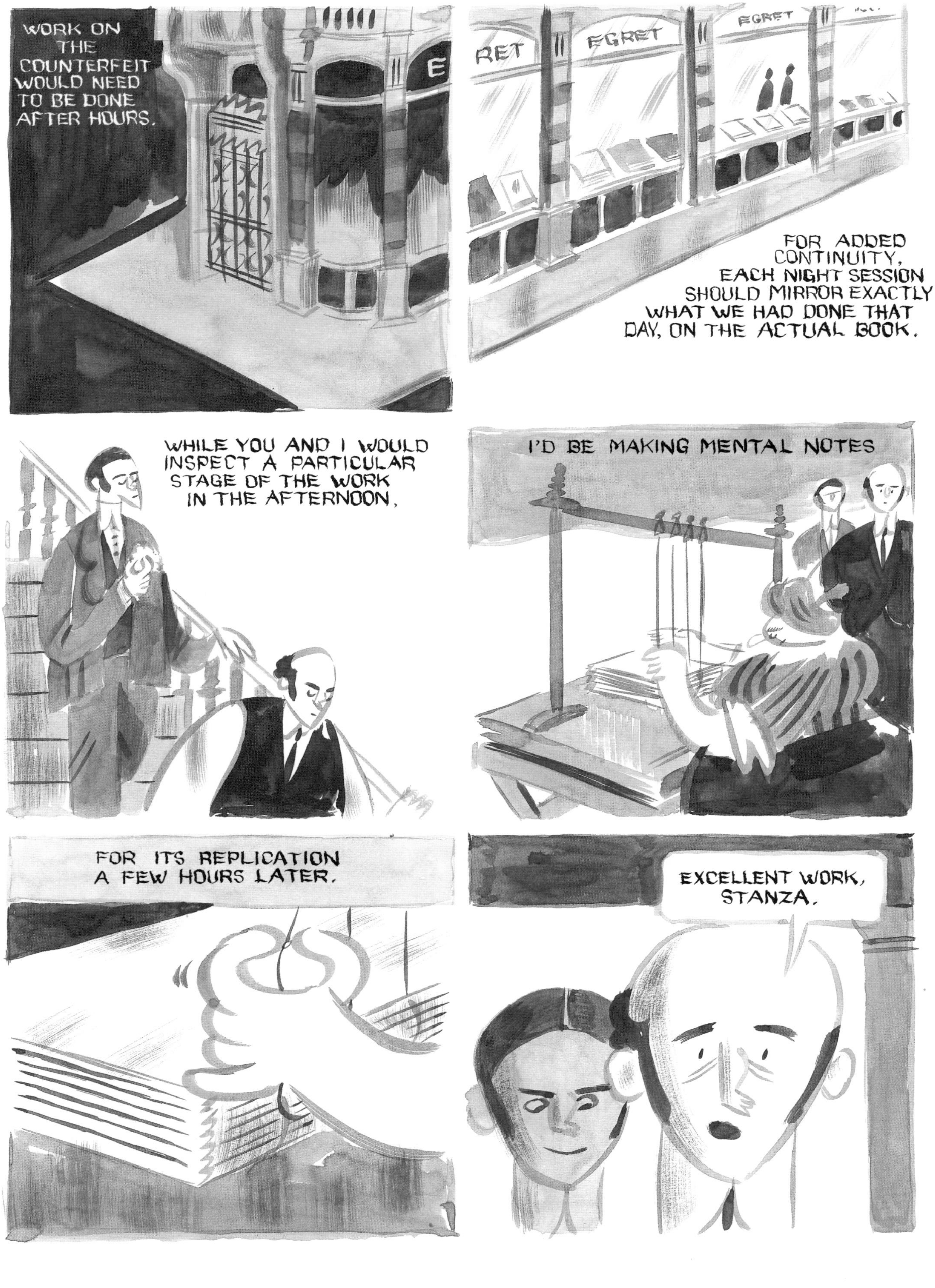
WORK ON THE COUNTERFEIT WOULD NEED TO BE DONE AFTER HOURS.
RET
EGRET
EGRET
FOR ADDED CONTINUITY, EACH NIGHT SESSION SHOULD MIRROR EXACTLY WHAT WE HAD DONE THAT DAY, ON THE ACTUAL BOOK.
WHILE YOU AND I WOULD INSPECT A PARTICULAR STAGE OF THE WORK IN THE AFTERNOON,
I'D BE MAKING MENTAL NOTES
FOR ITS REPLICATION A FEW HOURS LATER.
EXCELLENT WORK, STANZA.

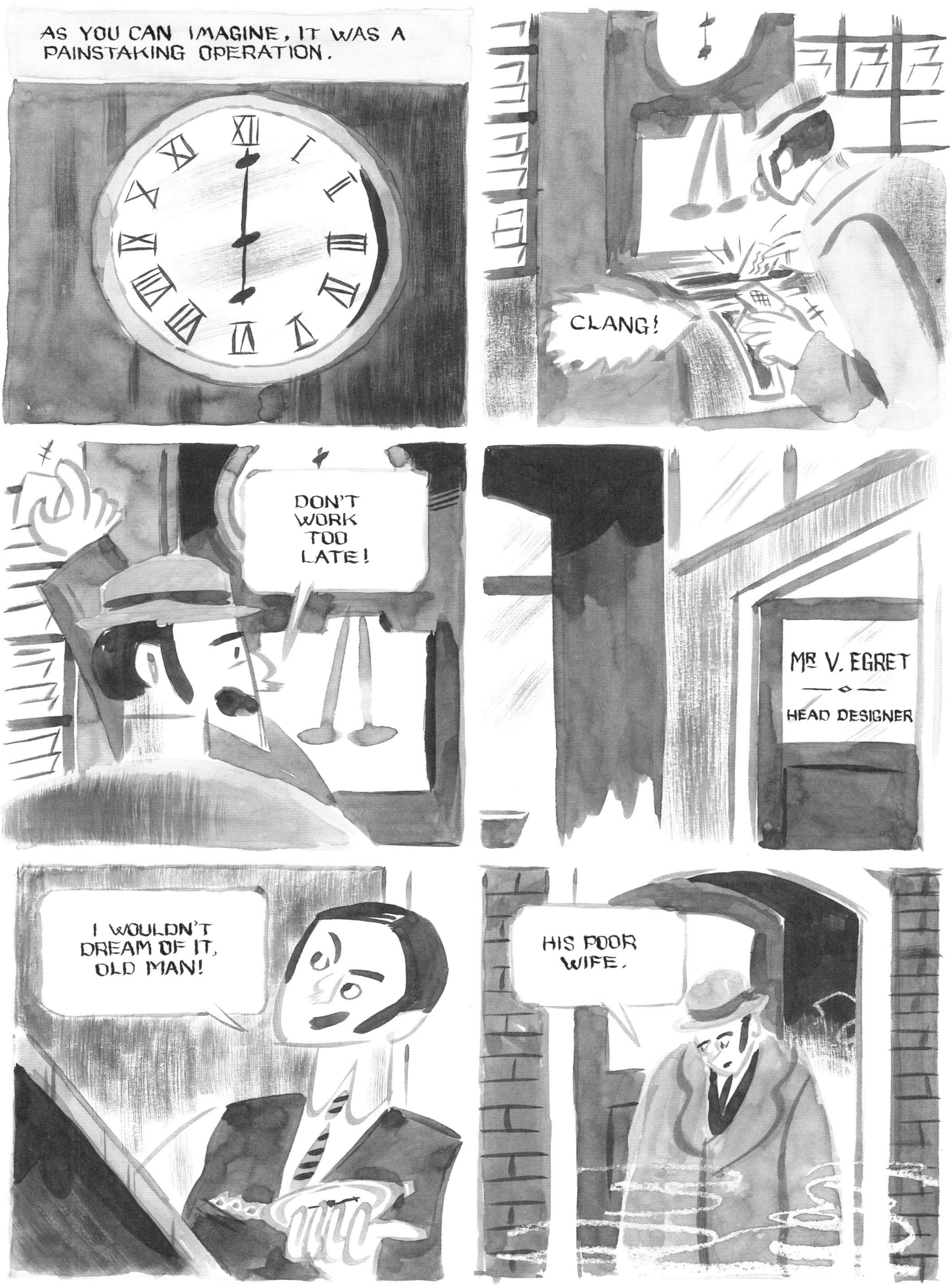
AS YOU CAN IMAGINE, IT WAS A PAINSTAKING OPERATION.
CLANG!
DON'T WORK TOO LATE!
MR V. EGRET
HEAD DESIGNER
I WOULDN'T DREAM OF IT, OLD MAN!
HIS POOR WIFE.

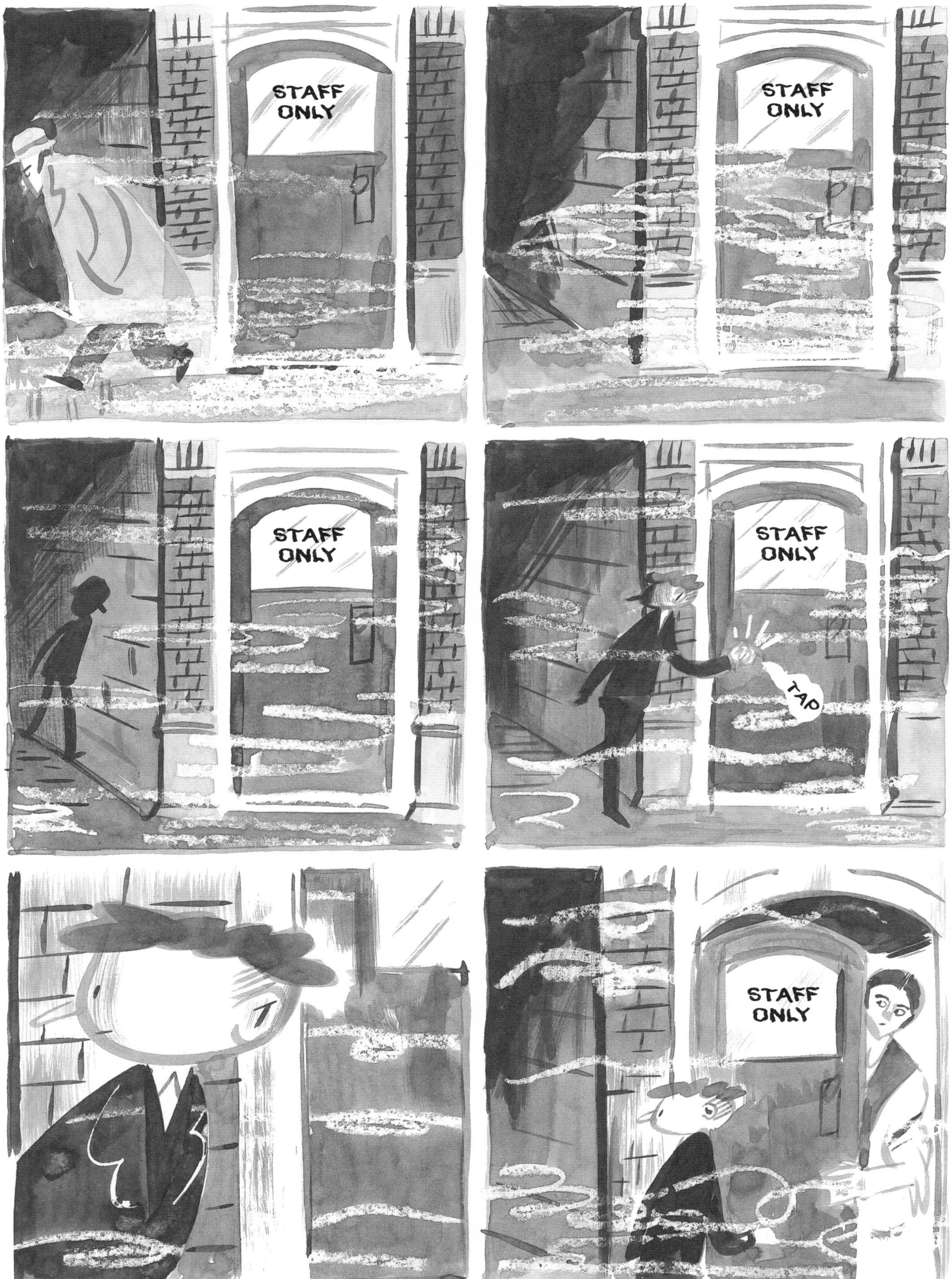
STAFF ONLY
STAFF ONLY
STAFF ONLY
STAFF ONLY
TAP
STAFF ONLY

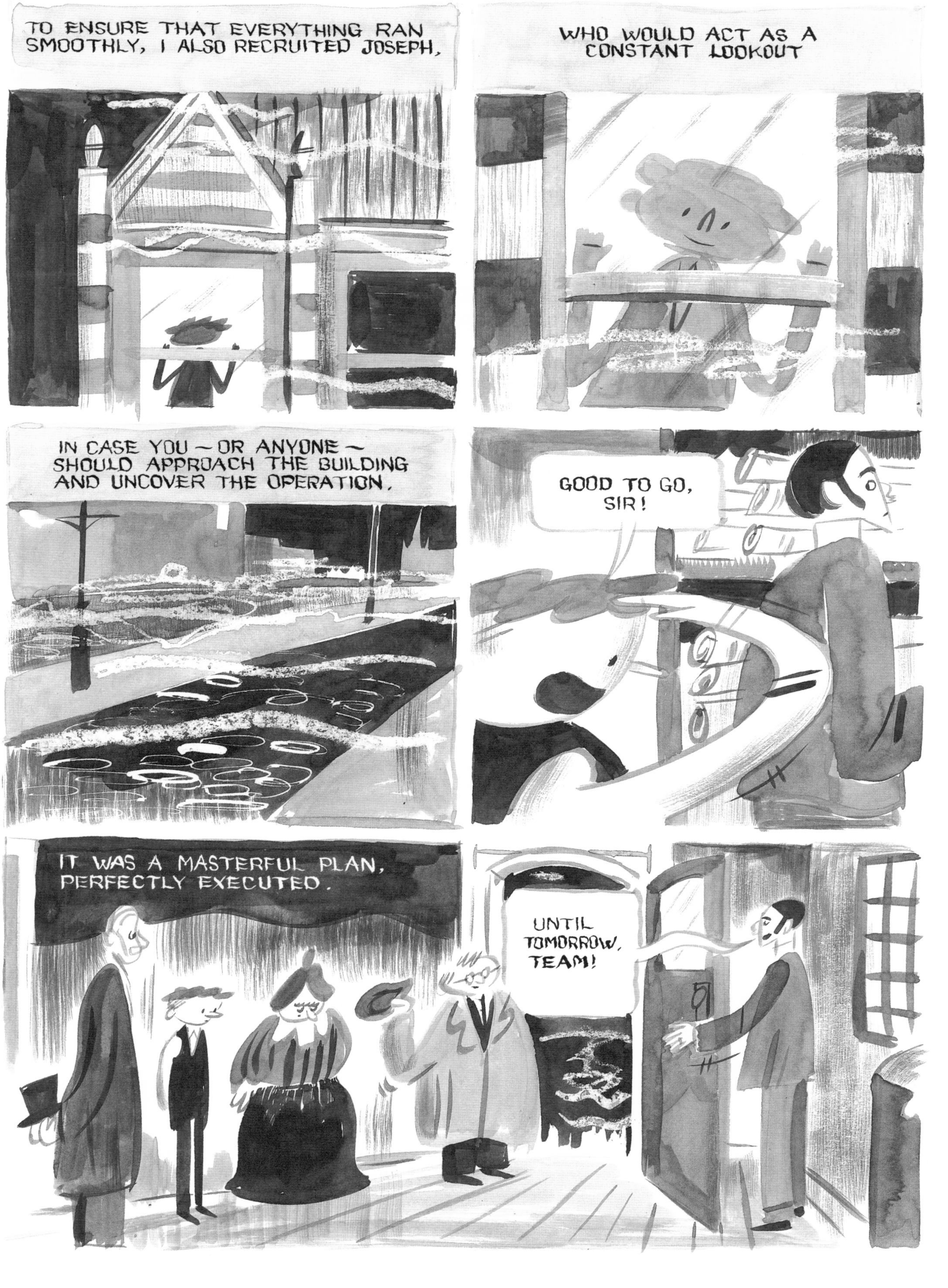
TO ENSURE THAT EVERYTHING RAN SMOOTHLY, I ALSO RECRUITED JOSEPH,
WHO WOULD ACT AS A CONSTANT LOOKOUT
IN CASE YOU — OR ANYONE — SHOULD APPROACH THE BUILDING AND UNCOVER THE OPERATION.
GOOD TO GO, SIR!
IT WAS A MASTERFUL PLAN, PERFECTLY EXECUTED.
UNTIL TOMORROW, TEAM!

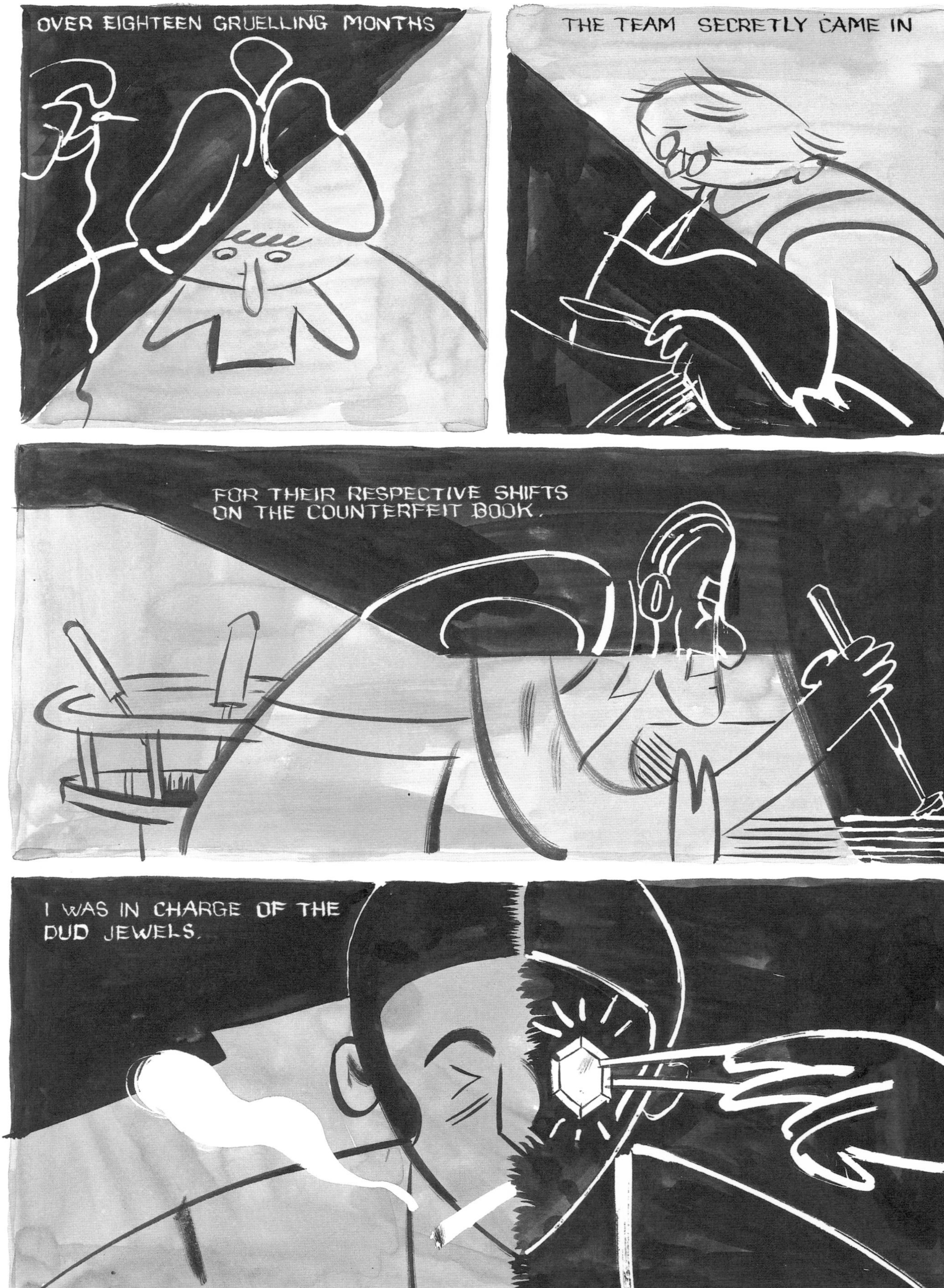
OVER EIGHTEEN GRUELLING MONTHS
THE TEAM SECRETLY CAME IN
FOR THEIR RESPECTIVE SHIFTS ON THE COUNTERFEIT BOOK.
I WAS IN CHARGE OF THE DUD JEWELS.

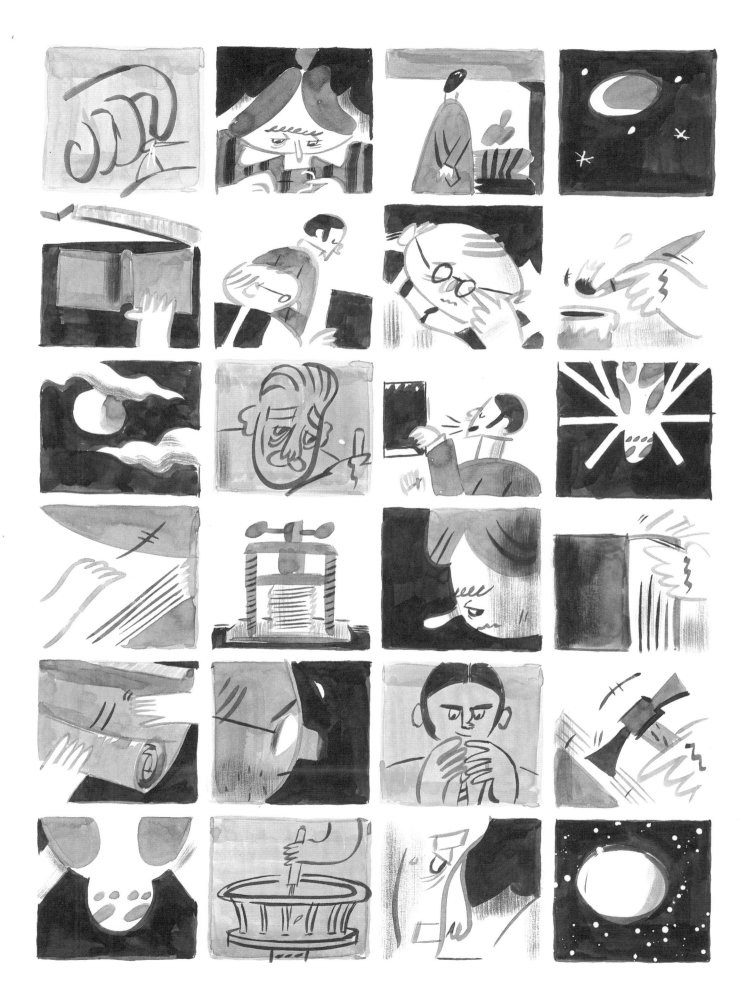

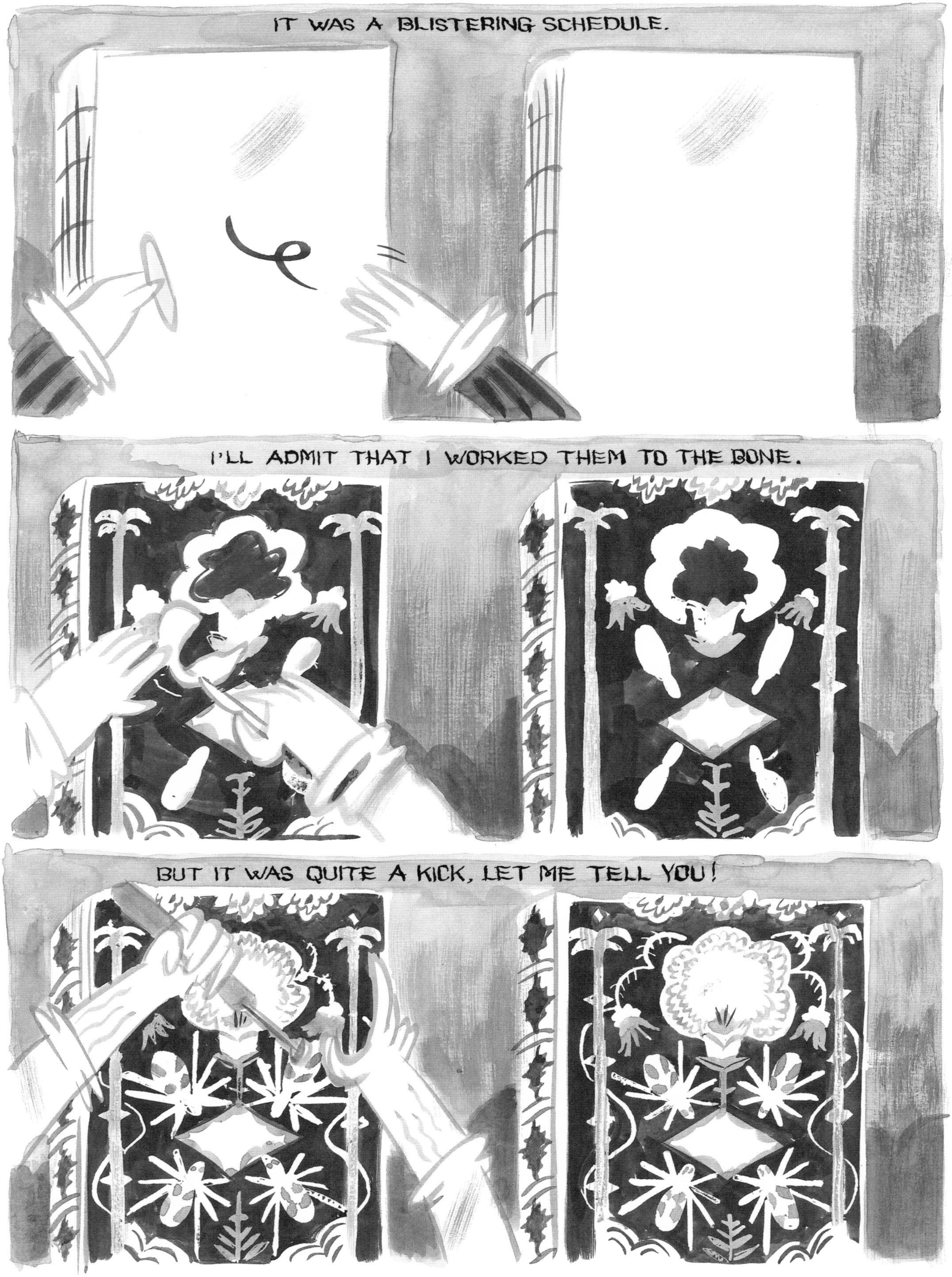
IT WAS A BLISTERING SCHEDULE.
I'LL ADMIT THAT I WORKED THEM TO THE BONE.
BUT IT WAS QUITE A KICK, LET ME TELL YOU!

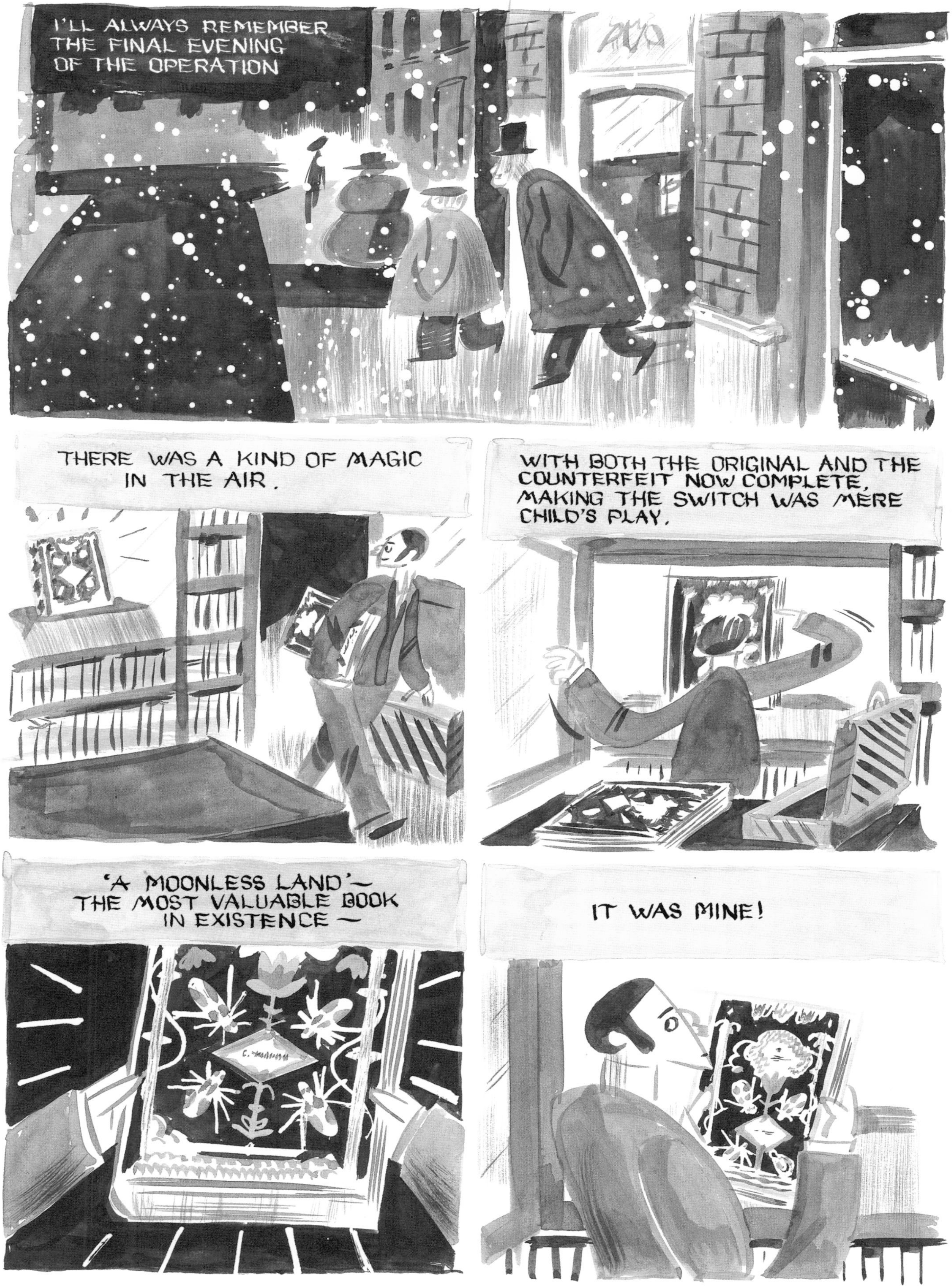
I'LL ALWAYS REMEMBER THE FINAL EVENING OF THE OPERATION
THERE WAS A KIND OF MAGIC IN THE AIR.
WITH BOTH THE ORIGINAL AND THE COUNTERFEIT NOW COMPLETE, MAKING THE SWITCH WAS MÉRE CHILD'S PLAY.
'A MOONLESS LAND'— THE MOST VALUABLE BOOK IN EXISTENCE—
IT WAS MINE!

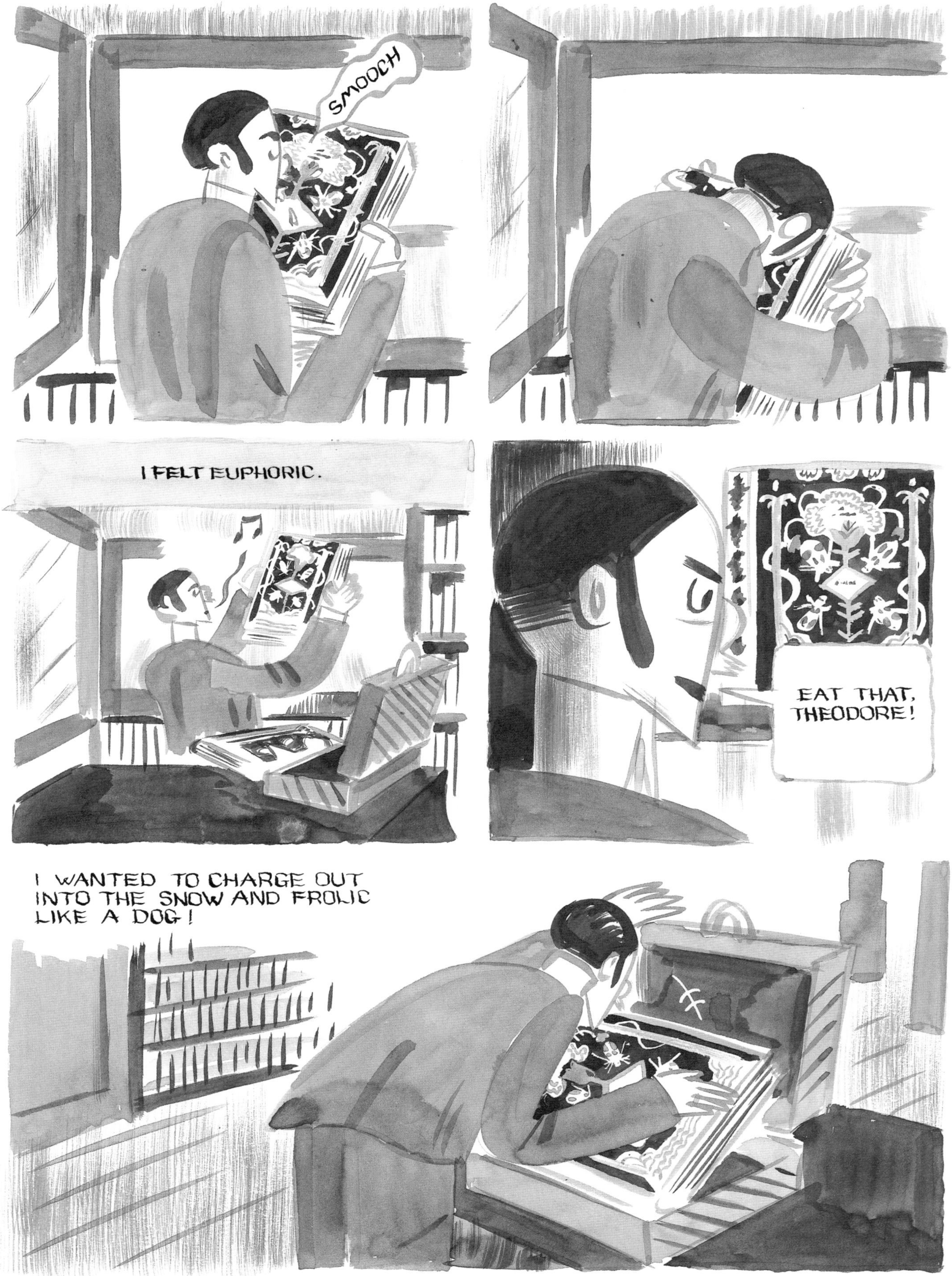
SMOOCH
I FELT EUPHORIC.
EAT THAT, THEODORE!
I WANTED TO CHARGE OUT INTO THE SNOW AND FROLIC LIKE A DOG!

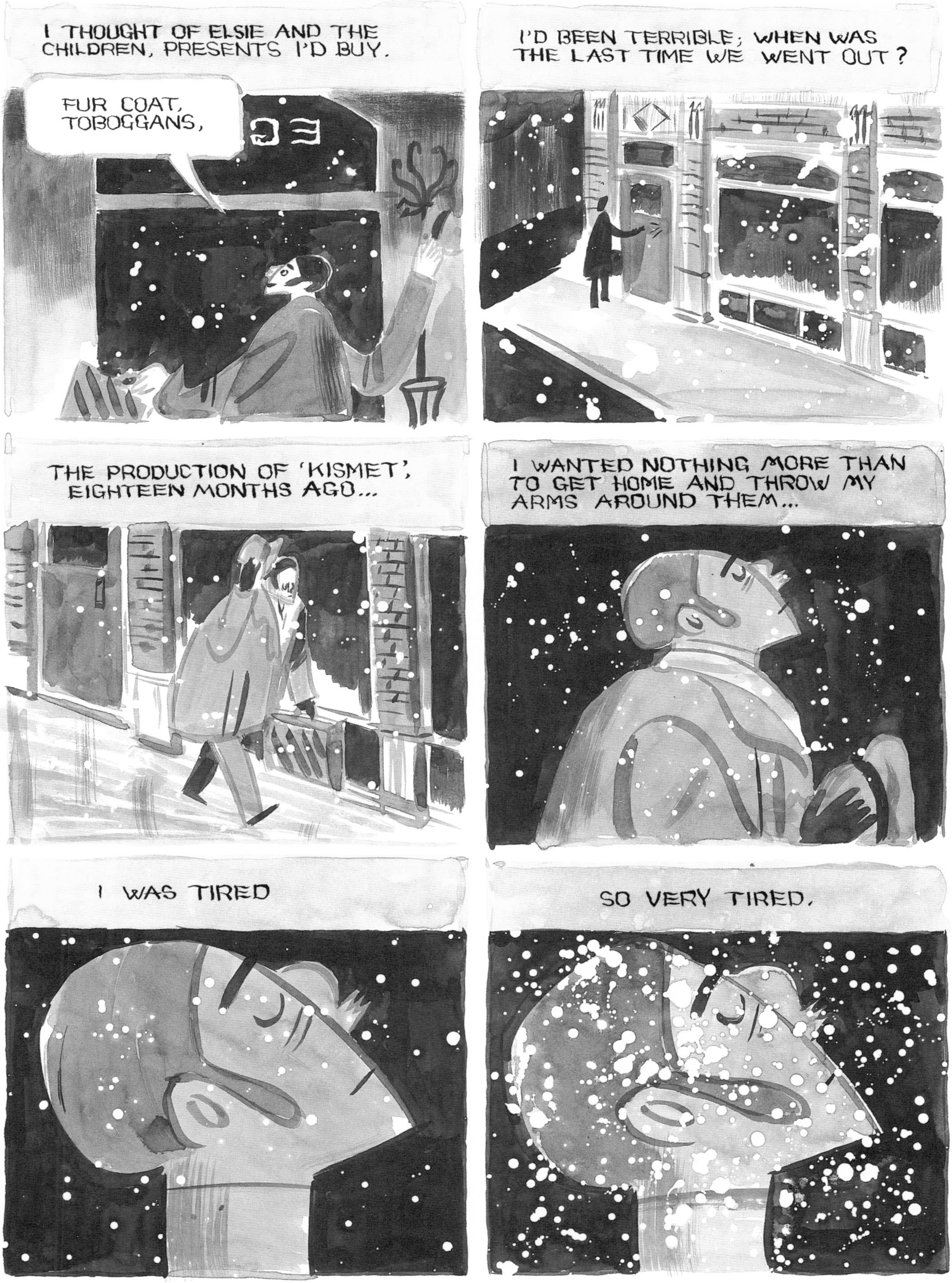
I THOUGHT OF ELSIE AND THE CHILDREN, PRESENTS I'D BUY.
FUR COAT, TOBOGGANS,
I'D BEEN TERRIBLE; WHEN WAS THE LAST TIME WE WENT OUT ?
THE PRODUCTION OF 'KISMET', EIGHTEEN MONTHS AGO...
I WANTED NOTHING MORE THAN TO GET HOME AND THROW MY ARMS AROUND THEM...
I WAS TIRED
SO VERY TIRED.

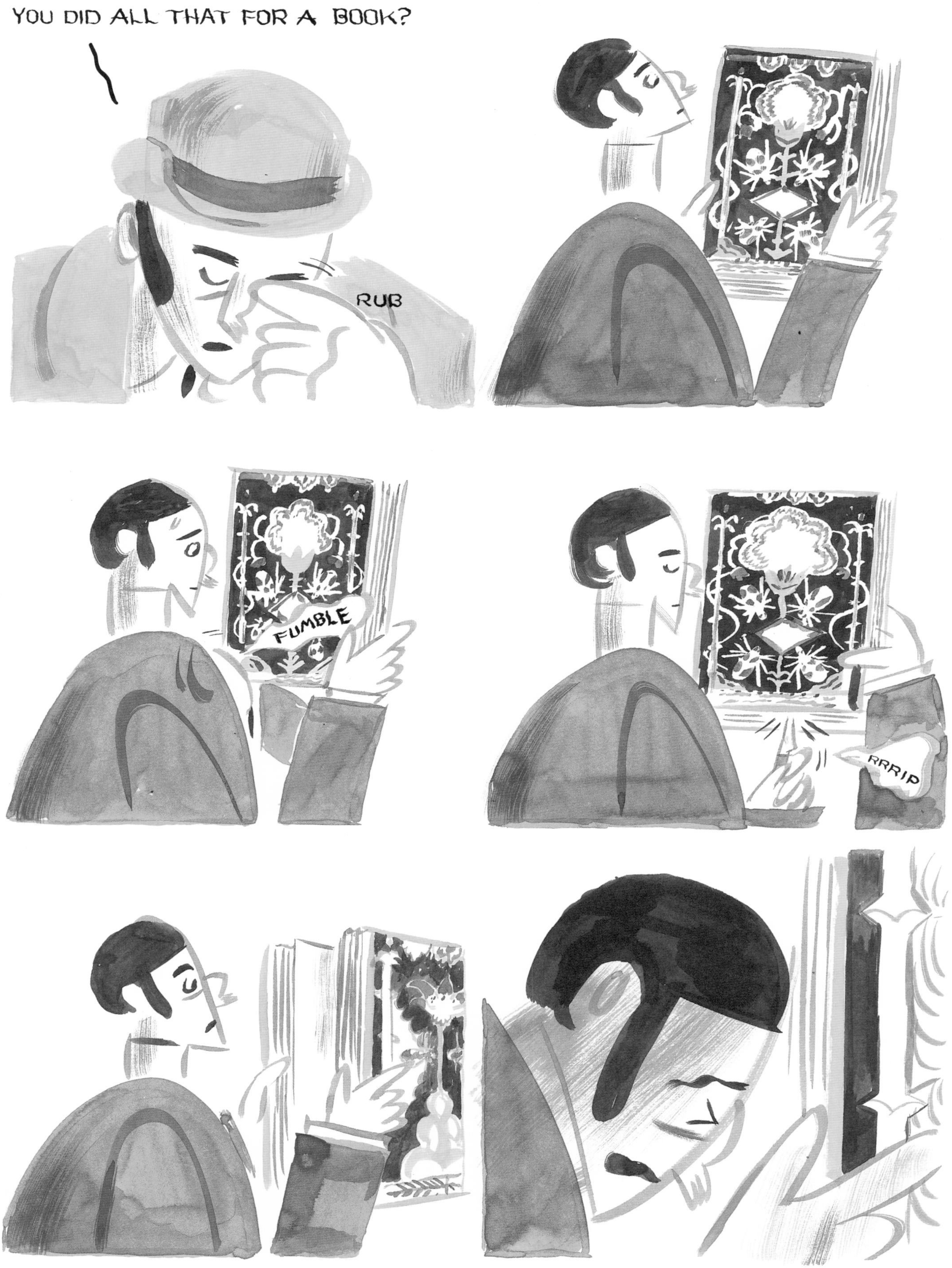
YOU DID ALL THAT FOR A BOOK?
RUB
FUMBLE
RRRIP

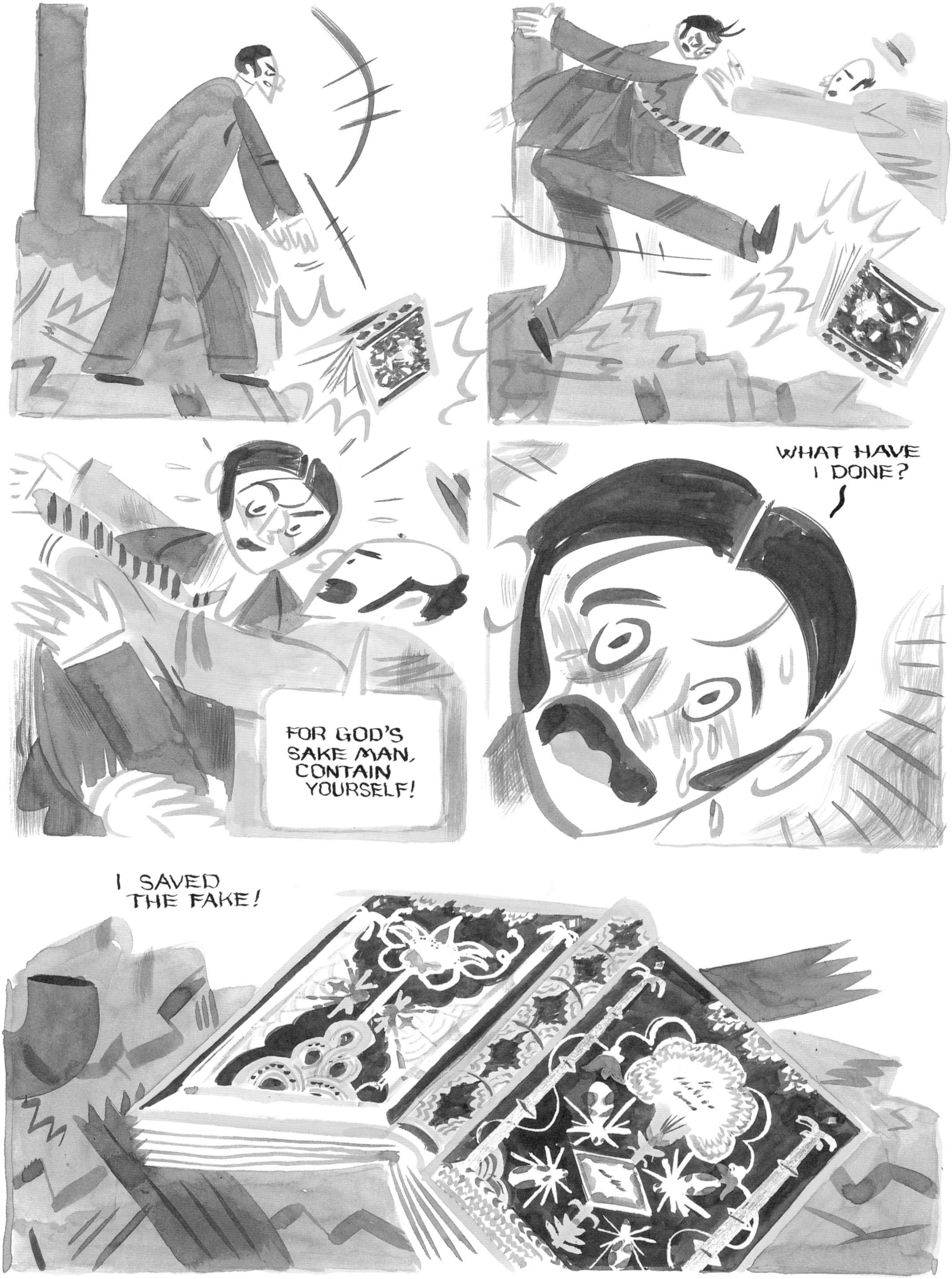
FOR GOD'S SAKE MAN, CONTAIN YOURSELF!
WHAT HAVE I DONE?
I SAVED THE FAKE!

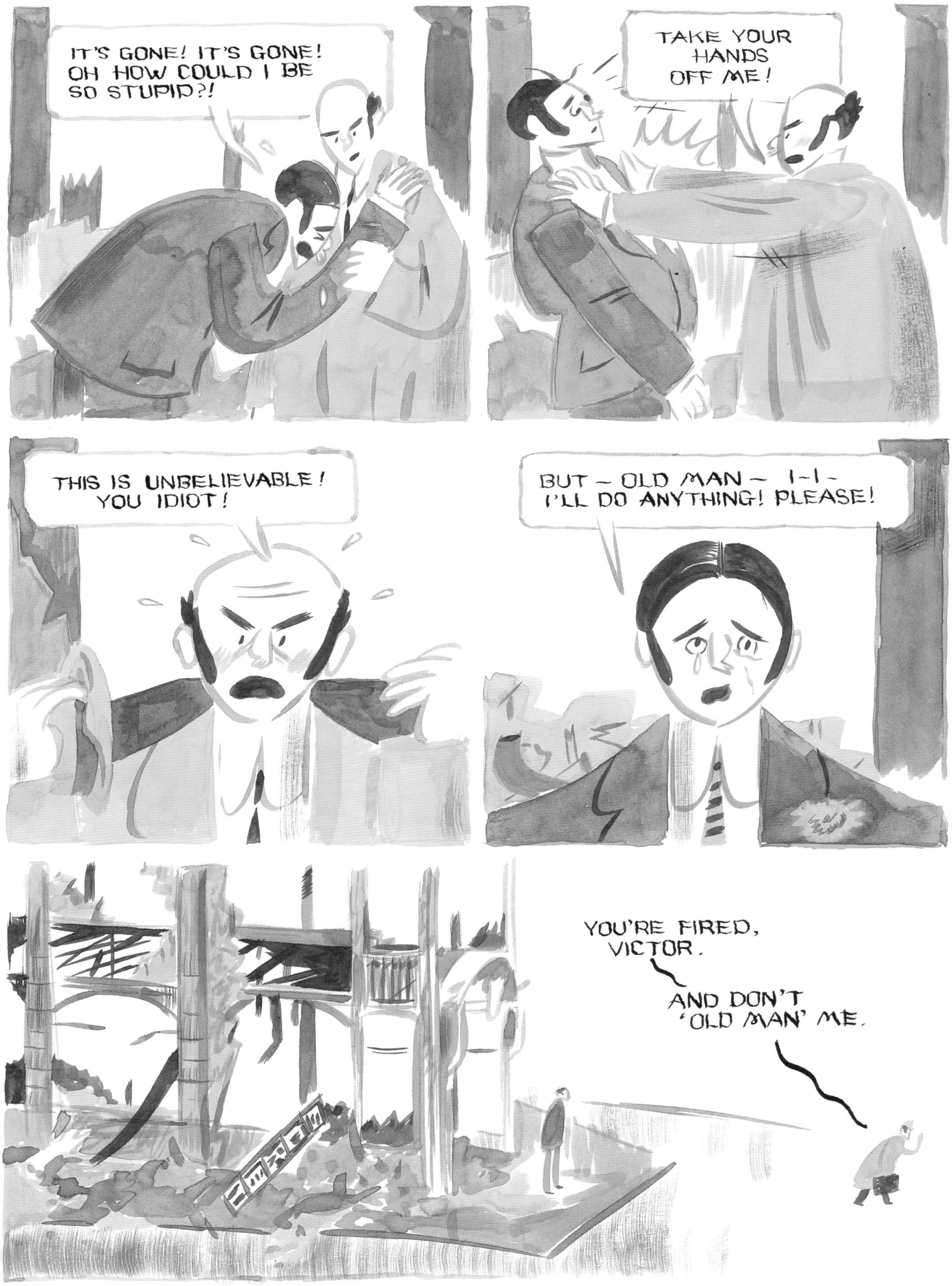
IT'S GONE! IT'S GONE! OH HOW COULD I BE SO STUPID?!
TAKE YOUR HANDS OFF ME!
THIS IS UNBELIEVABLE! YOU IDIOT!
BUT – OLD MAN – I-I- I'LL DO ANYTHING! PLEASE!
YOU'RE FIRED, VICTOR.
AND DON'T 'OLD MAN' ME.

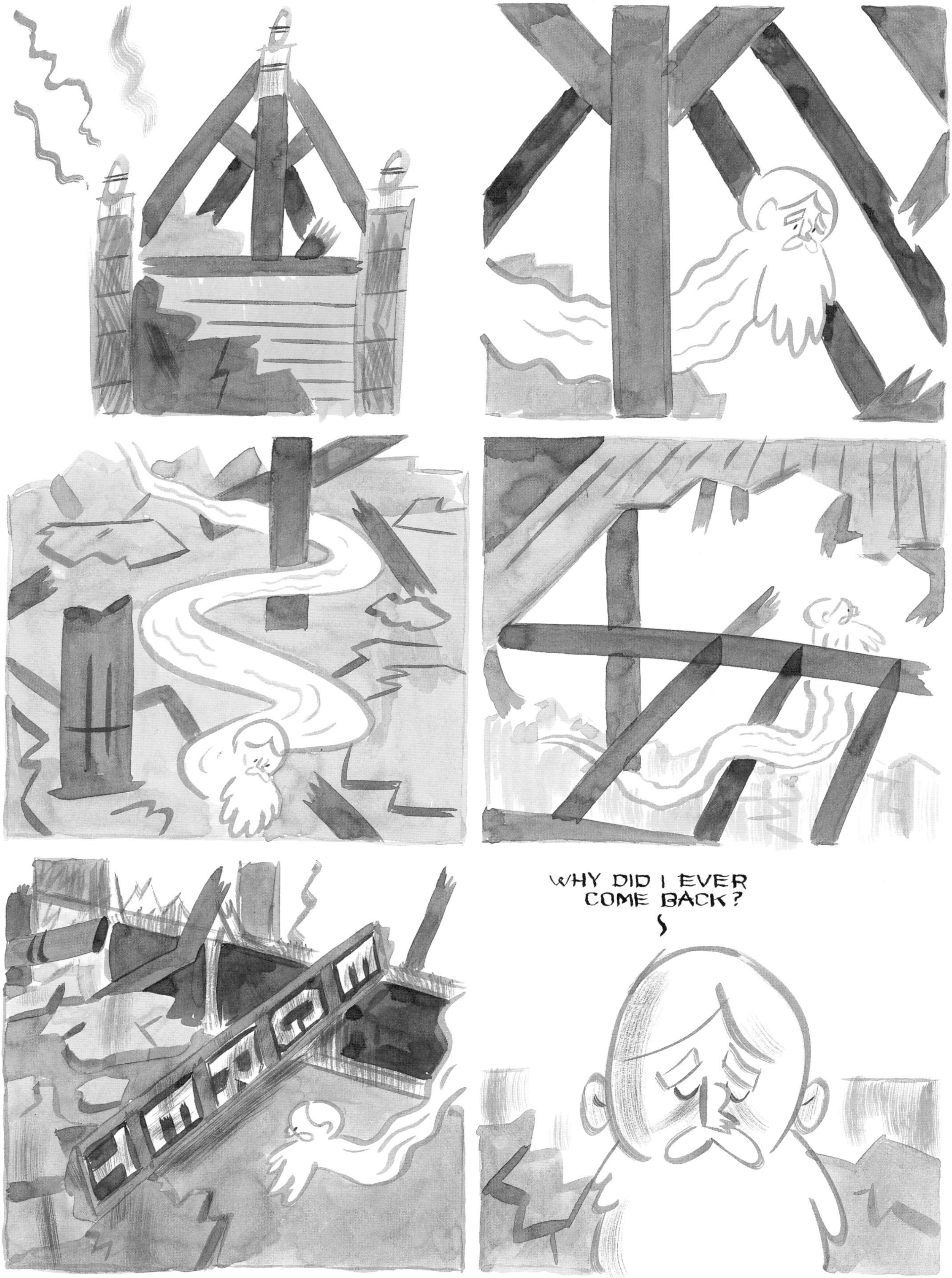
WHY DID I EVER COME BACK?

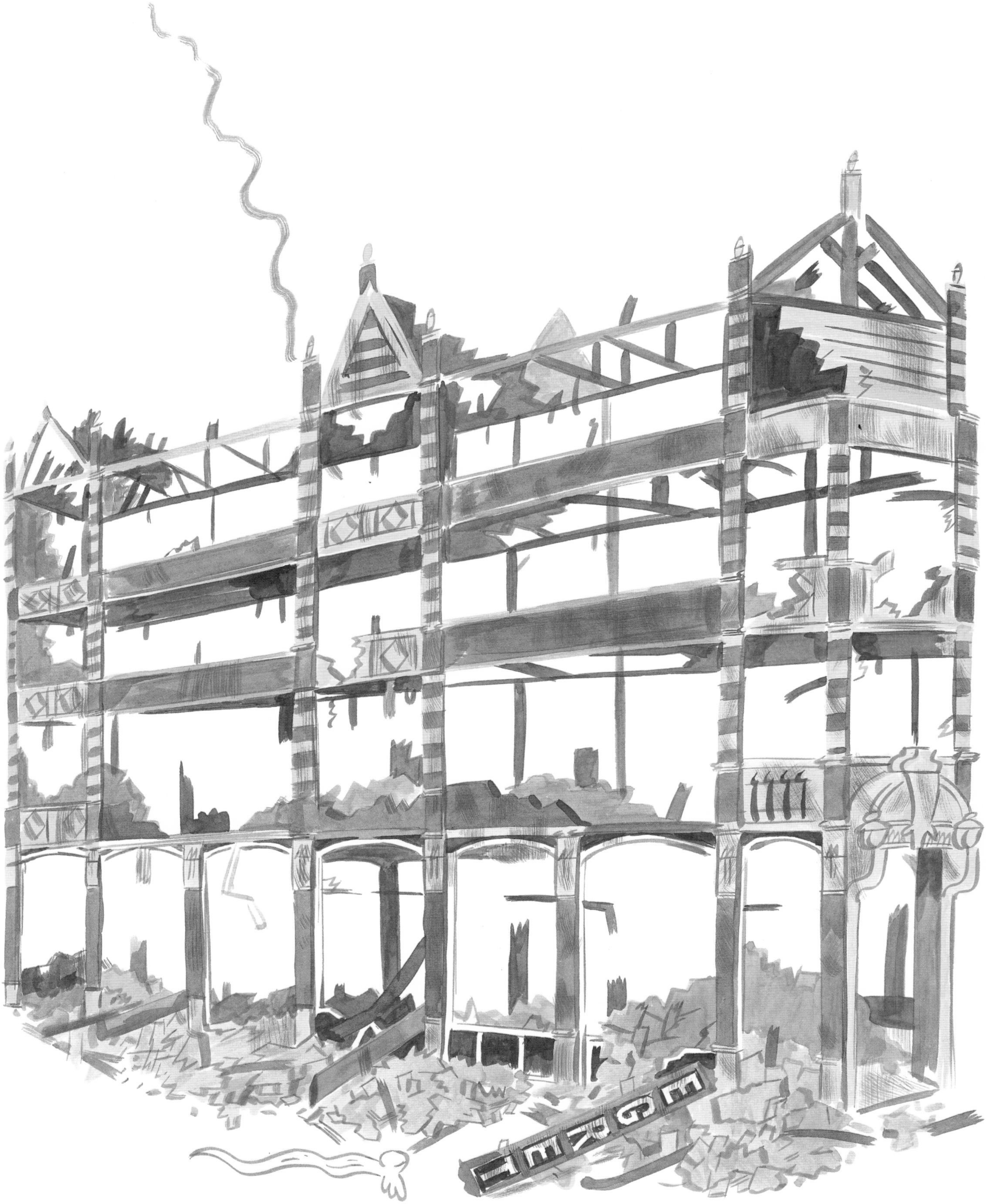

PART
FOUR:

The
Whole
Circus

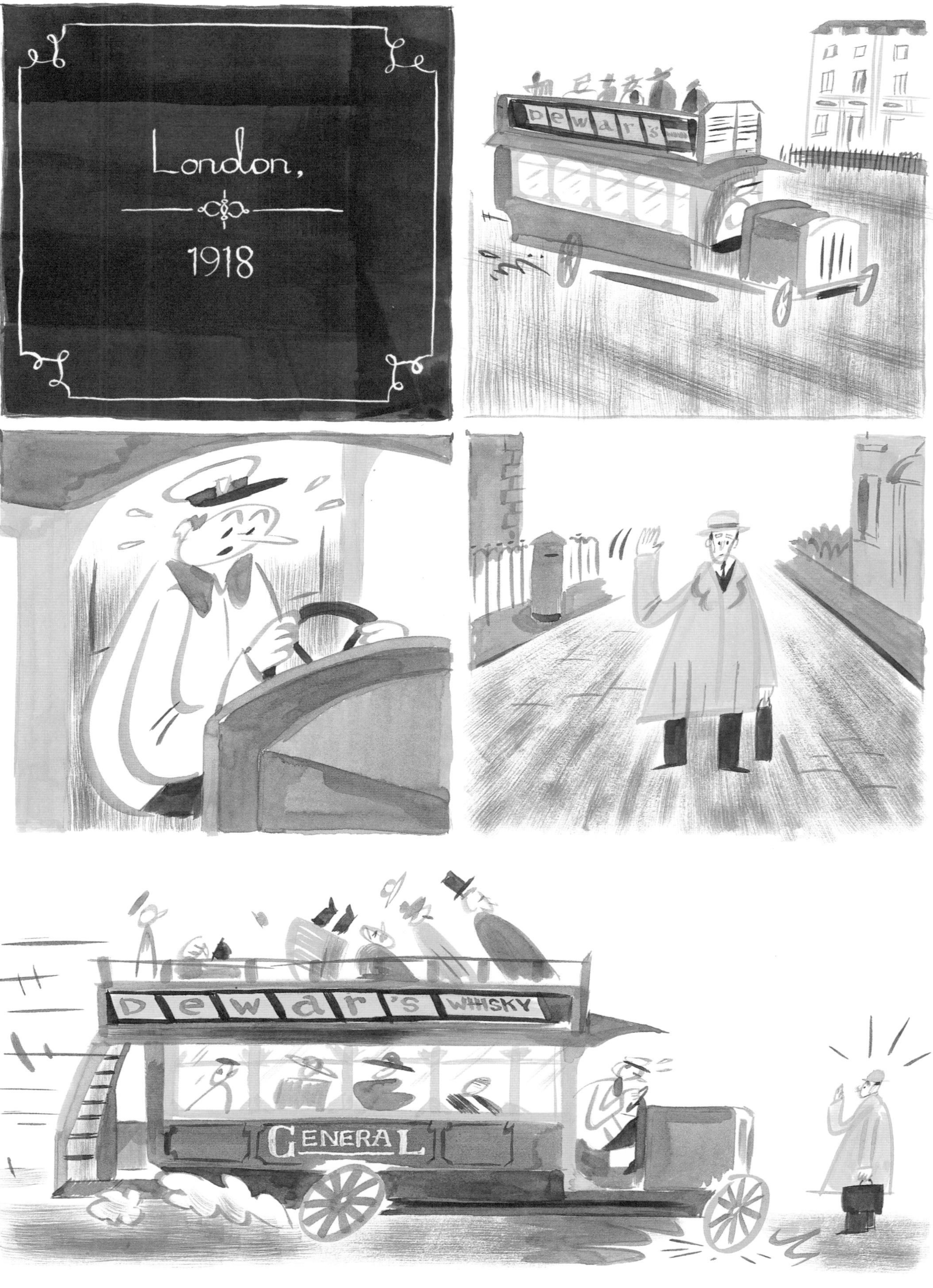
London,
1918
Dewar's
Dewar's WHISKY
GENERAL

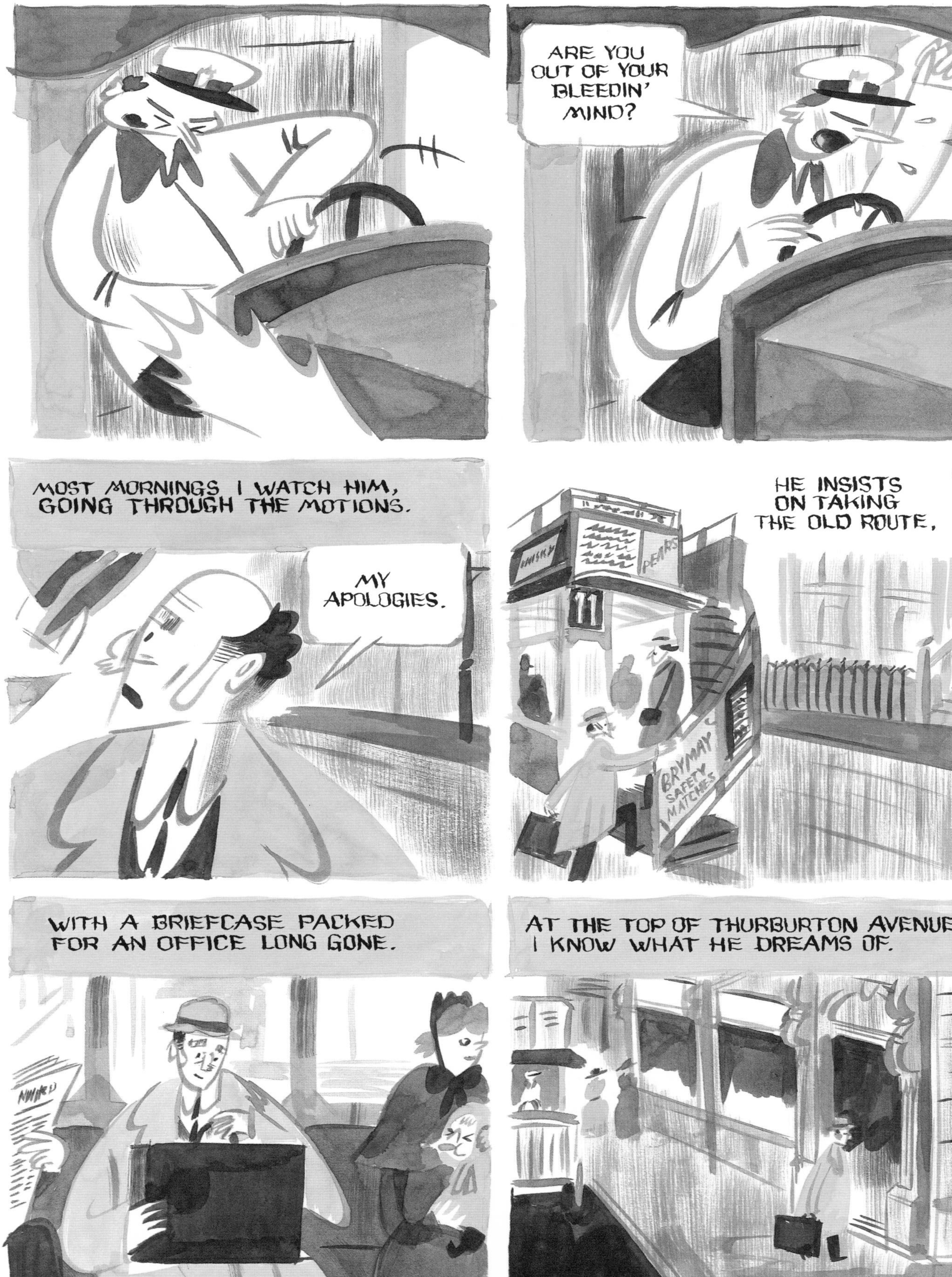
ARE YOU OUT OF YOUR BLEEDIN' MIND?
MOST MORNINGS I WATCH HIM, GOING THROUGH THE MOTIONS.
MY APOLOGIES.
HE INSISTS ON TAKING THE OLD ROUTE,
PEARS
11
BRYMAY SAFETY MATCHES
WITH A BRIEFCASE PACKED FOR AN OFFICE LONG GONE.
AT THE TOP OF THURBURTON AVENUE, I KNOW WHAT HE DREAMS OF.

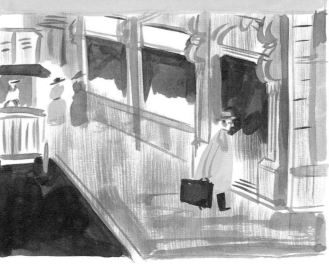

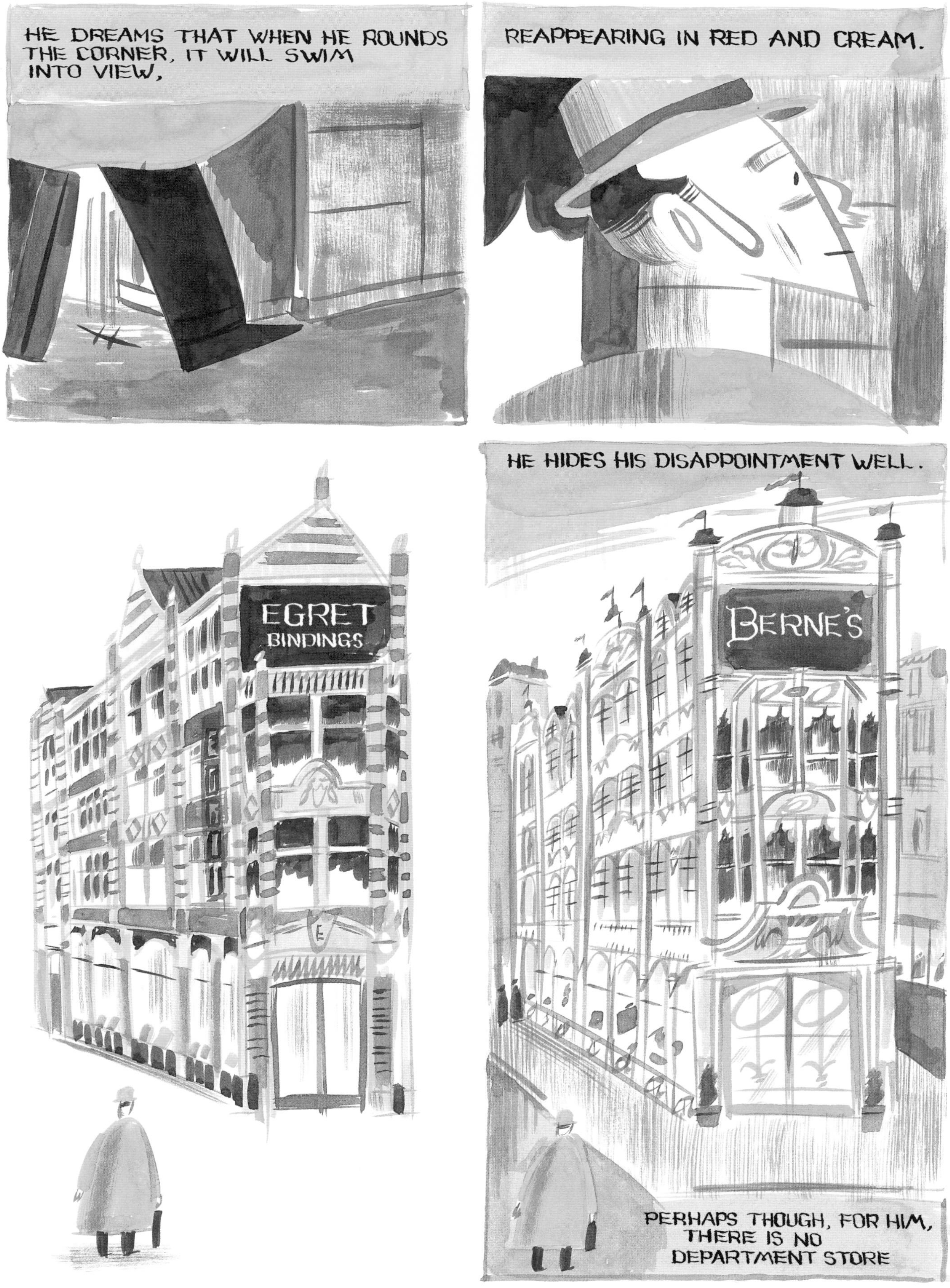
HE DREAMS THAT WHEN HE ROUNDS THE CORNER, IT WILL SWIM INTO VIEW,
REAPPEARING IN RED AND CREAM.
EGRET BINDINGS
HE HIDES HIS DISAPPOINTMENT WELL.
BERNE'S
PERHAPS THOUGH, FOR HIM, THERE IS NO DEPARTMENT STORE

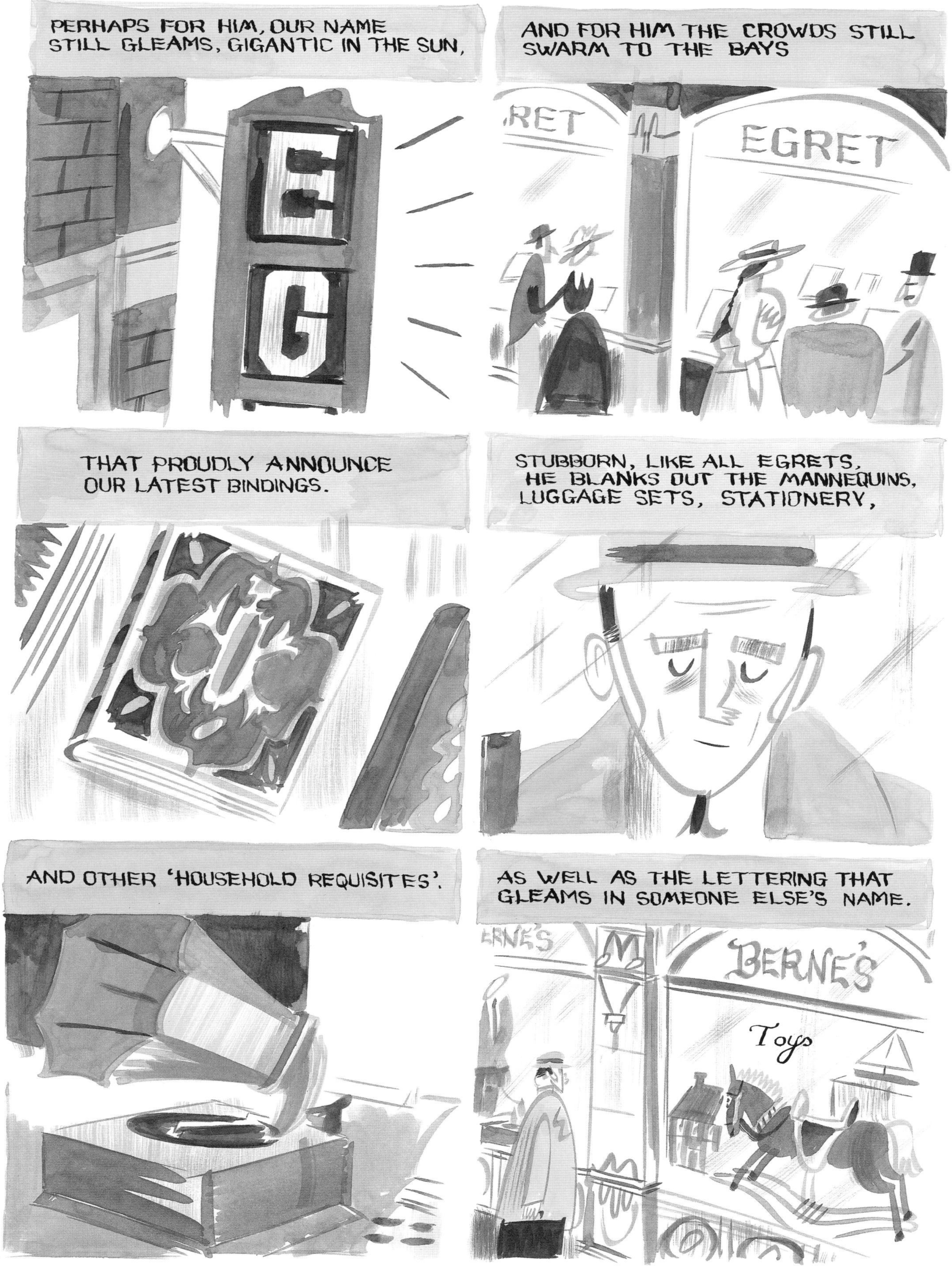
PERHAPS FOR HIM, OUR NAME STILL GLEAMS, GIGANTIC IN THE SUN,
AND FOR HIM THE CROWDS STILL SWARM TO THE BAYS
RET
EGRET
THAT PROUDLY ANNOUNCE OUR LATEST BINDINGS.
STUBBORN, LIKE ALL EGRETS, HE BLANKS OUT THE MANNEQUINS, LUGGAGE SETS, STATIONERY,
AND OTHER 'HOUSEHOLD REQUISITES'.
AS WELL AS THE LETTERING THAT GLEAMS IN SOMEONE ELSE'S NAME.
ERNE'S
BERNE'S
Toys

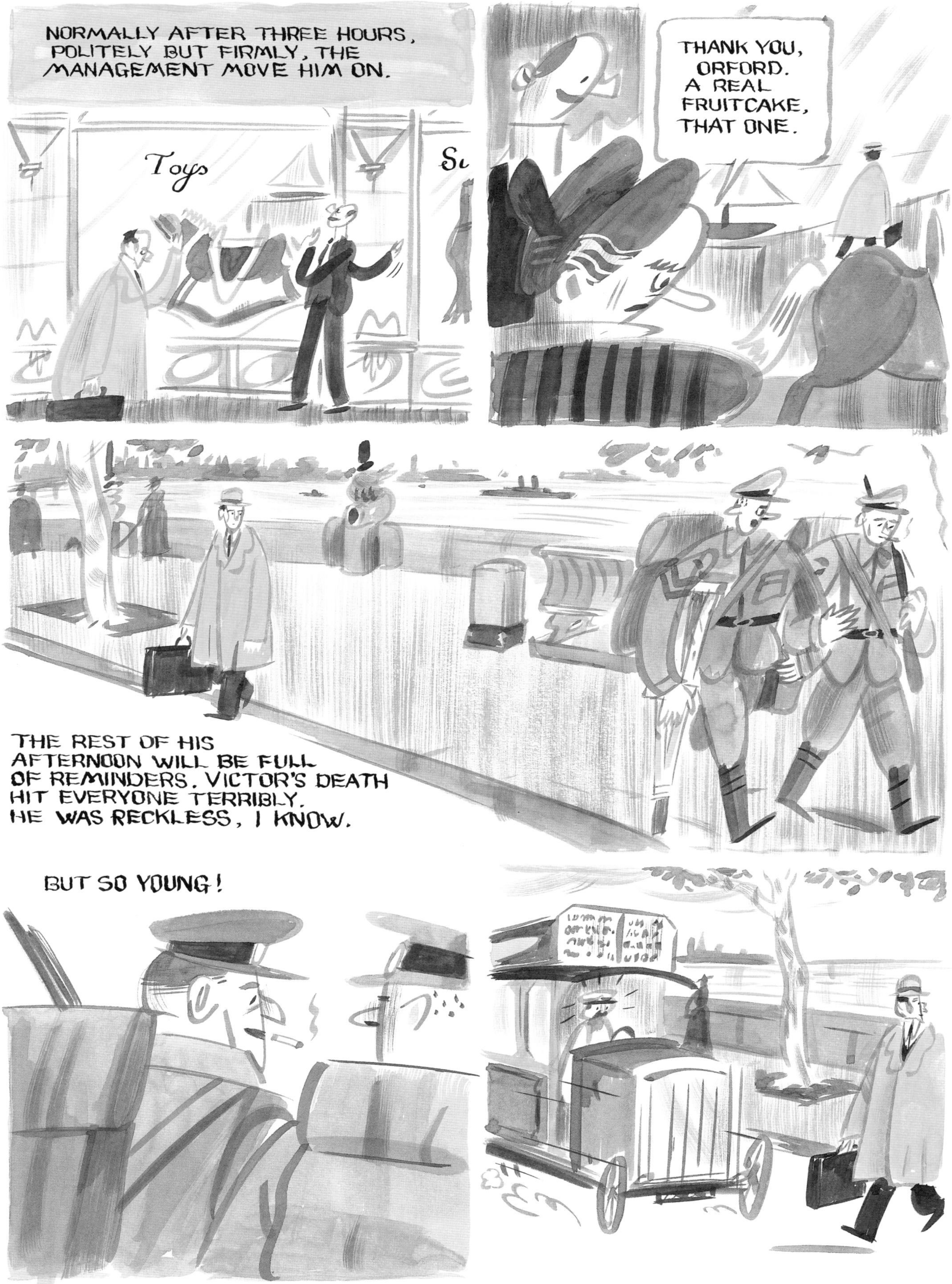
NORMALLY AFTER THREE HOURS, POLITELY BUT FIRMLY, THE MANAGEMENT MOVE HIM ON.
Toys
THANK YOU, ORFORD. A REAL FRUITCAKE, THAT ONE.
THE REST OF HIS AFTERNOON WILL BE FULL OF REMINDERS. VICTOR'S DEATH HIT EVERYONE TERRIBLY. HE WAS RECKLESS, I KNOW.
BUT SO YOUNG!

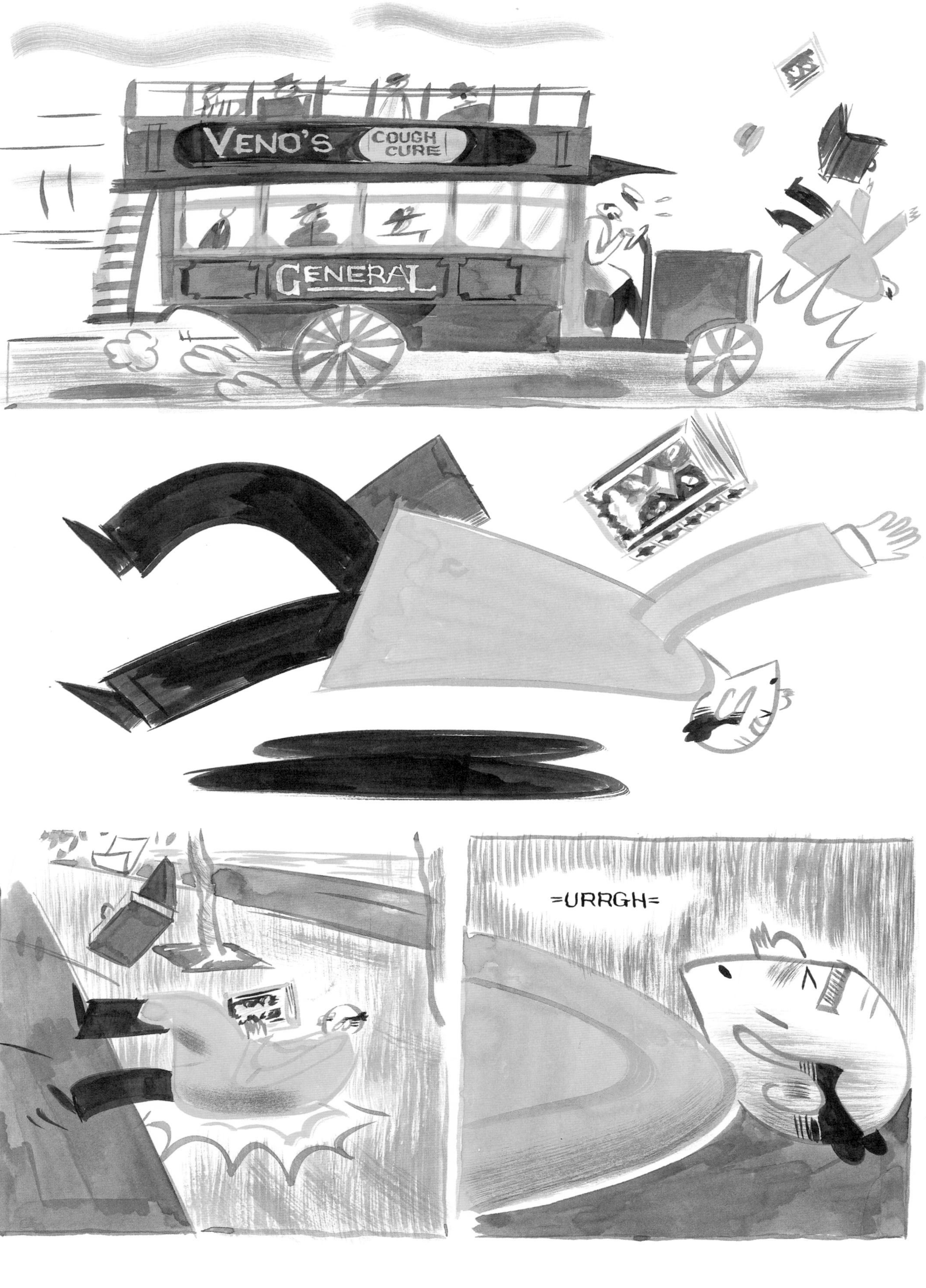
VENO'S
COUGH CURE
GENERAL
=URRGH=

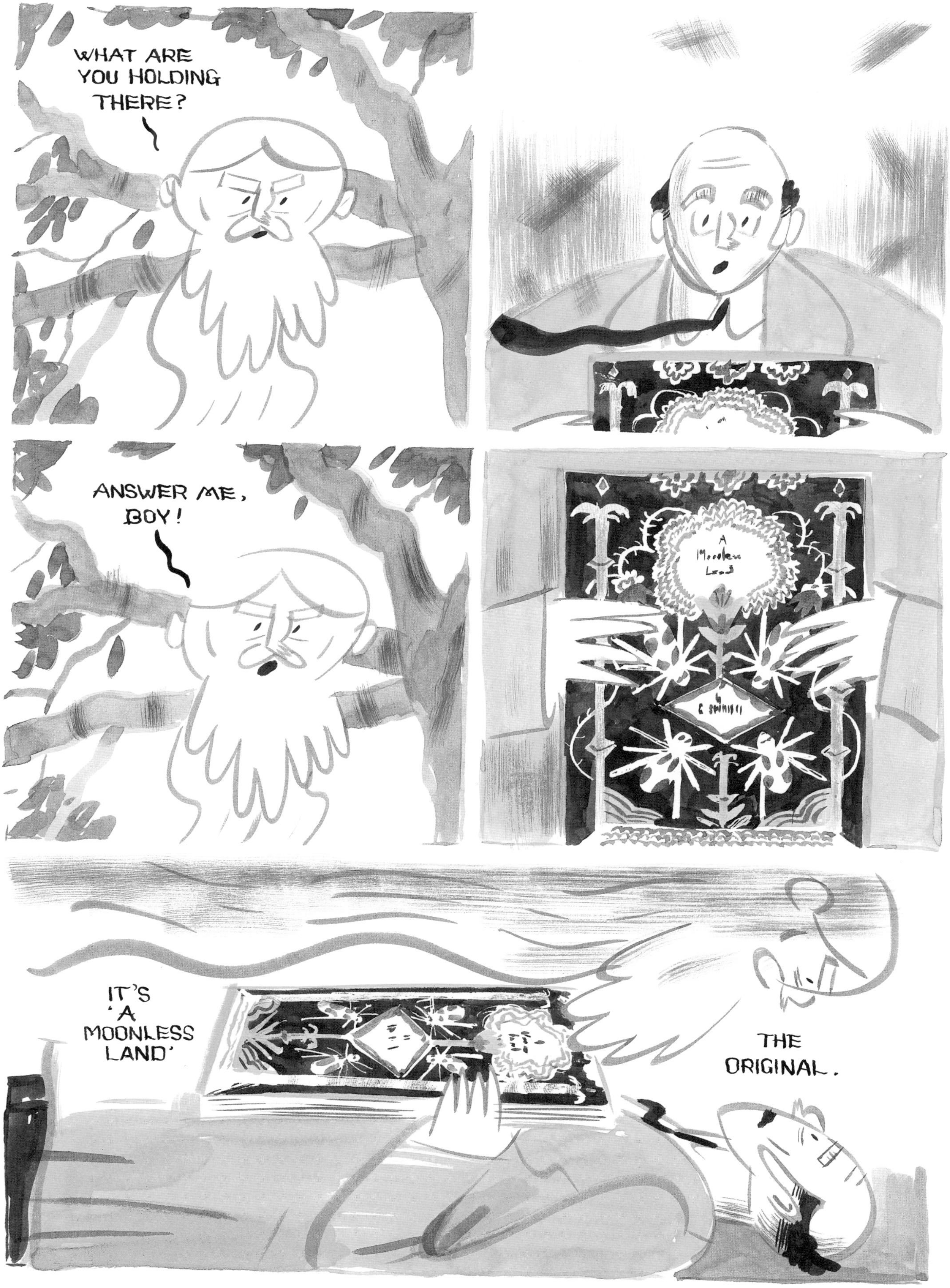
WHAT ARE YOU HOLDING THERE?
ANSWER ME, BOY!
IT'S 'A MOONLESS LAND'
THE ORIGINAL.

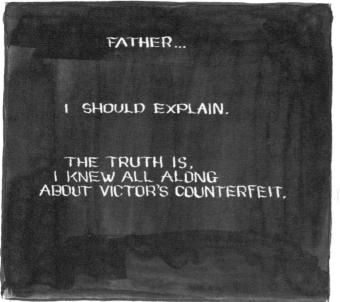
FATHER...

I SHOULD EXPLAIN.

THE TRUTH IS,
I KNEW ALL ALONG
ABOUT VICTOR'S COUNTERFEIT.

HE CALLED IT 'MASTERFUL',
BUT VICTOR'S GRAND PLAN
UNRAVELLED ON DAY ONE.

I REMEMBER THAT I RETURNED
FOR A FORGOTTEN UMBRELLA.
VICTOR'S 'SENTRIES' HAD LET
HIM DOWN.

JOSEPH WAS DITHERING,
EMPTYING PAPER SHAVINGS
OUT THE BACK.

CECIL COX WAS DOZING —
THOSE WERE PUNISHING
HOURS FOR A VETERAN.

ALL THIS ON THE ONE NIGHT
VICTOR TOOK OFF — TO SEE
'KISMET' AT THE GARRICK.

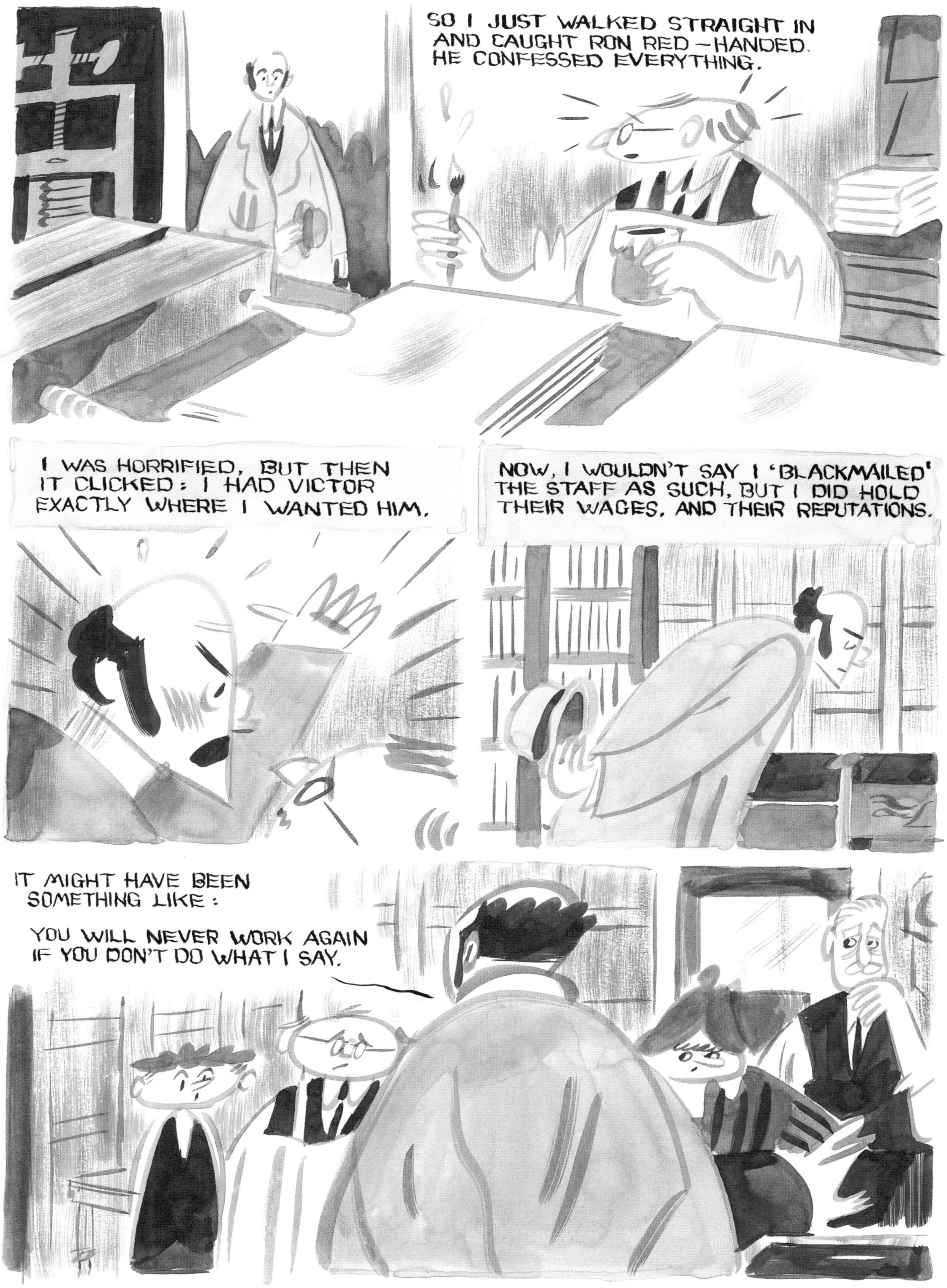
SO I JUST WALKED STRAIGHT IN AND CAUGHT RON RED-HANDED. HE CONFESSED EVERYTHING.
I WAS HORRIFIED, BUT THEN IT CLICKED: I HAD VICTOR EXACTLY WHERE I WANTED HIM.
NOW, I WOULDN'T SAY I 'BLACKMAILED' THE STAFF AS SUCH, BUT I DID HOLD THEIR WAGES, AND THEIR REPUTATIONS.
IT MIGHT HAVE BEEN SOMETHING LIKE:
YOU WILL NEVER WORK AGAIN IF YOU DON'T DO WHAT I SAY.

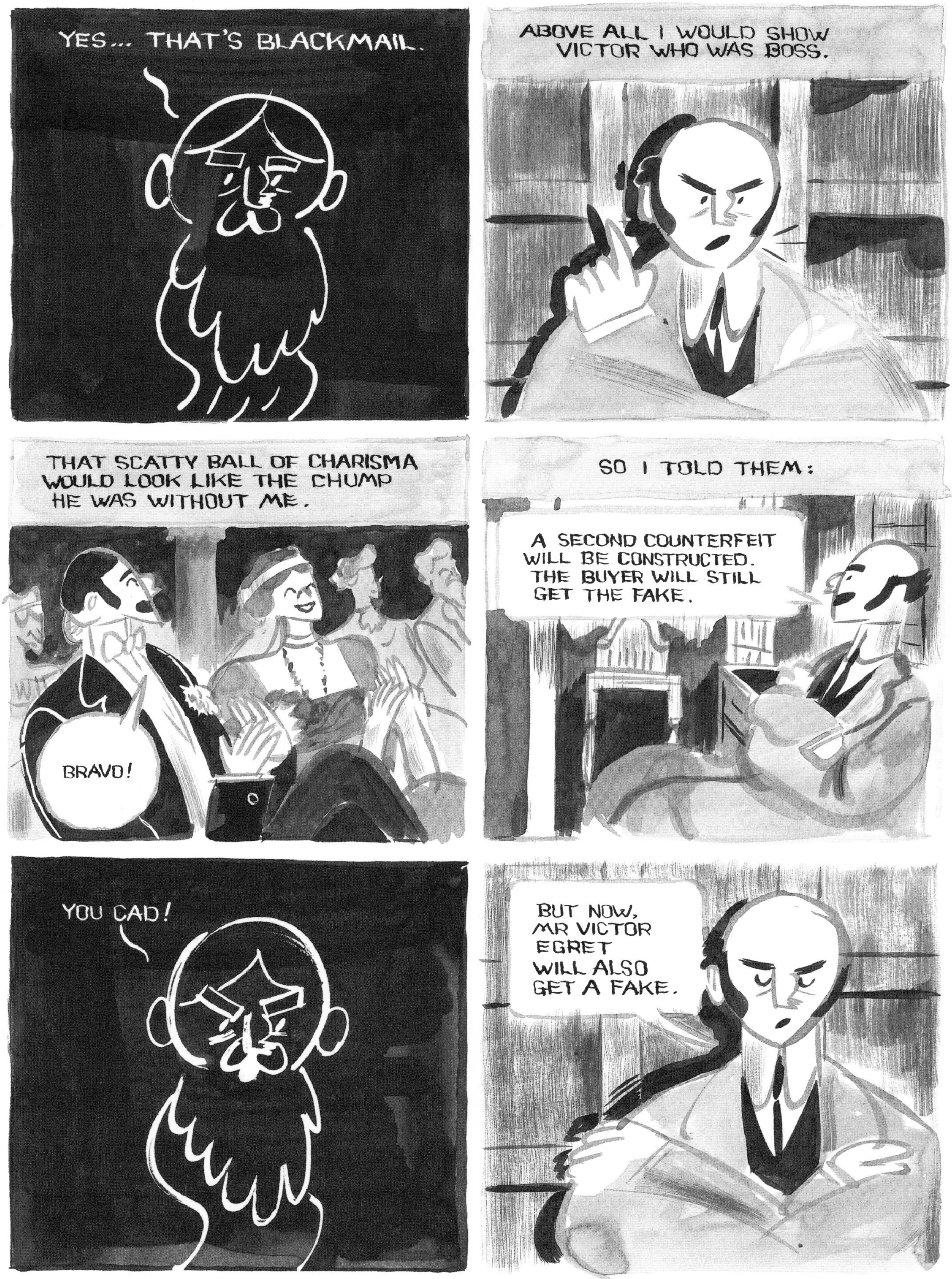
YES... THAT'S BLACKMAIL.
ABOVE ALL I WOULD SHOW VICTOR WHO WAS BOSS.
THAT SCATTY BALL OF CHARISMA WOULD LOOK LIKE THE CHUMP HE WAS WITHOUT ME.
BRAVO!
SO I TOLD THEM:
A SECOND COUNTERFEIT WILL BE CONSTRUCTED. THE BUYER WILL STILL GET THE FAKE.
YOU CAD!
BUT NOW, MR VICTOR EGRET WILL ALSO GET A FAKE.

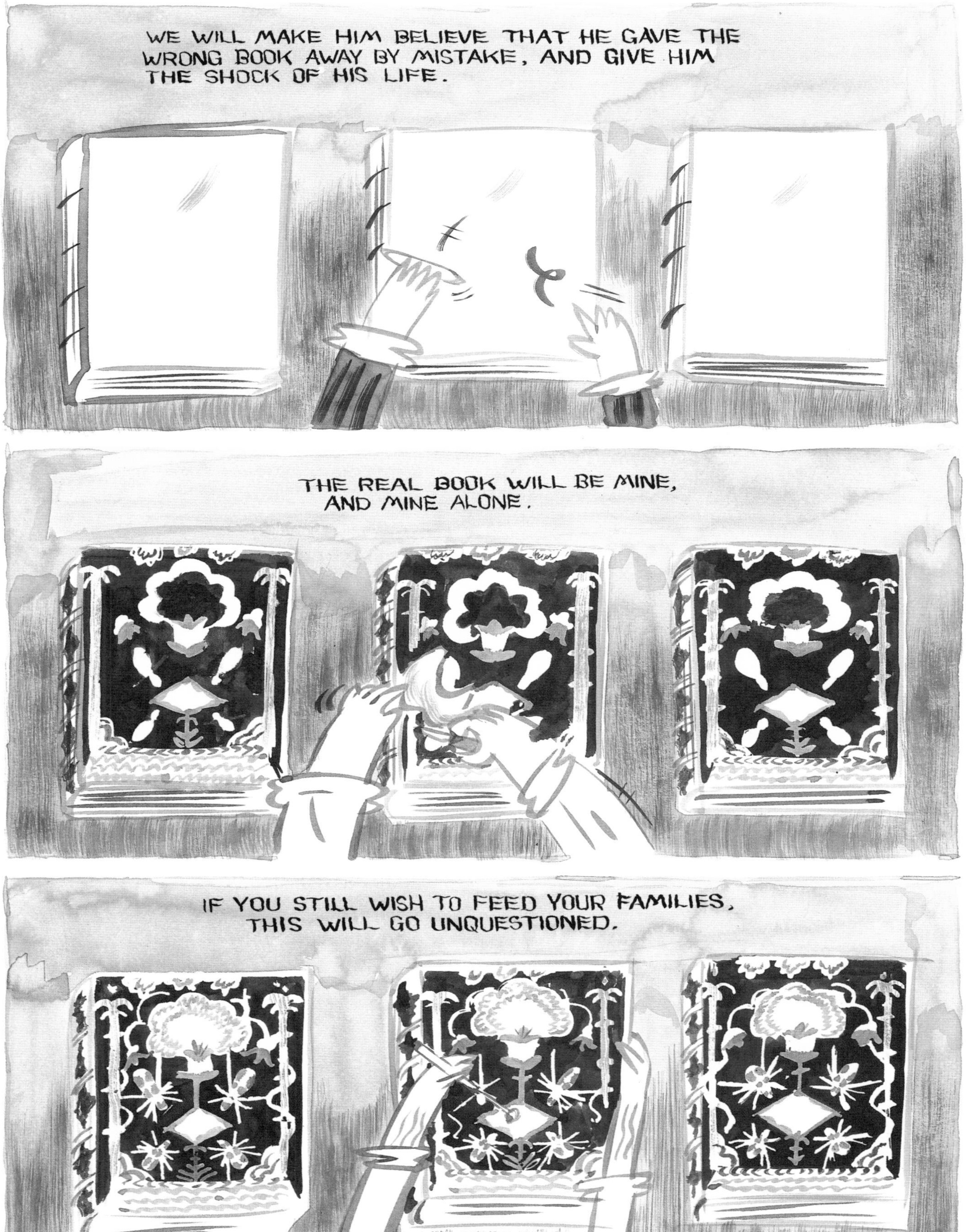
WE WILL MAKE HIM BELIEVE THAT HE GAVE THE WRONG BOOK AWAY BY MISTAKE, AND GIVE HIM THE SHOCK OF HIS LIFE.
THE REAL BOOK WILL BE MINE, AND MINE ALONE.
IF YOU STILL WISH TO FEED YOUR FAMILIES, THIS WILL GO UNQUESTIONED.

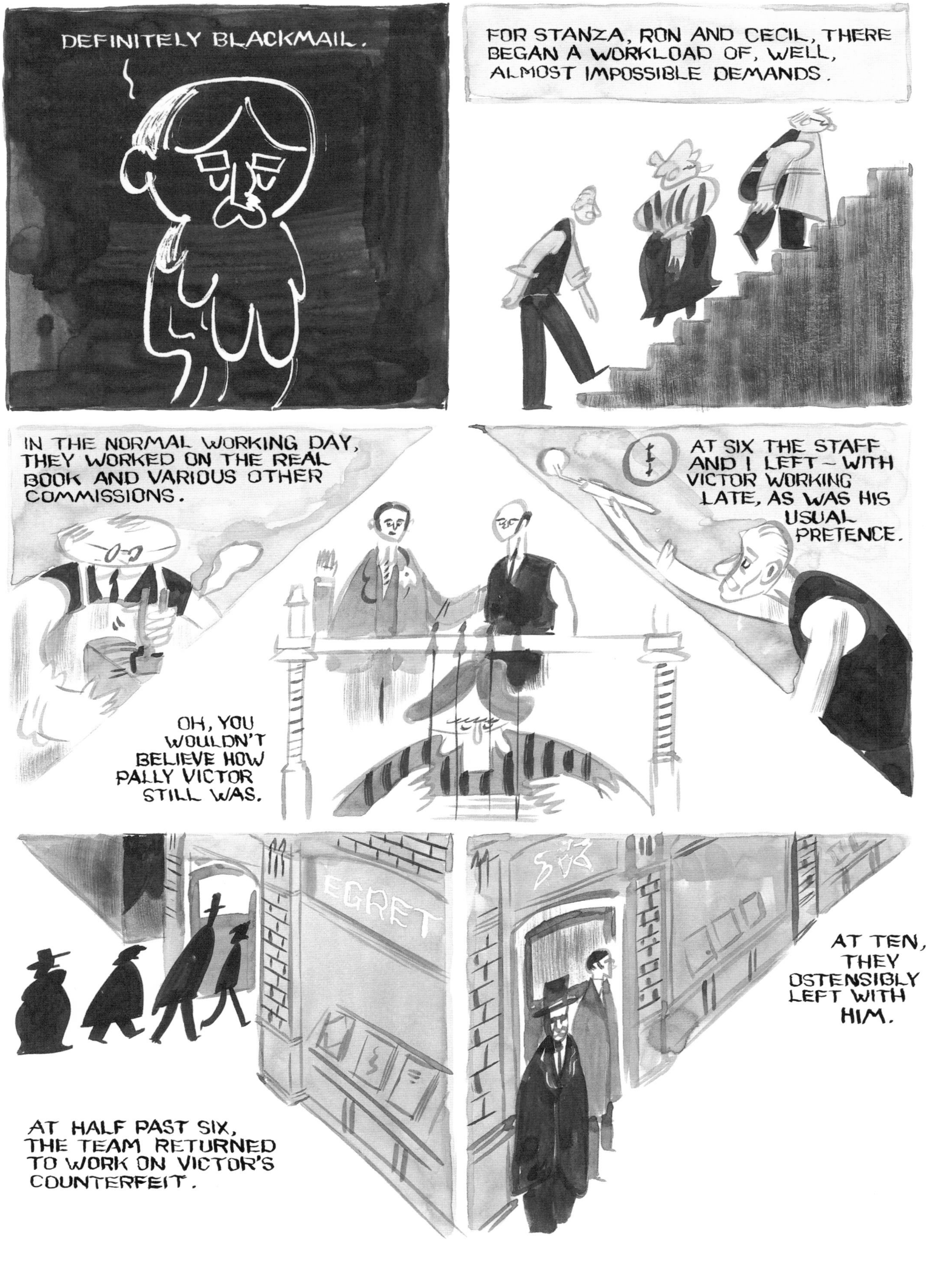
DEFINITELY BLACKMAIL.
FOR STANZA, RON AND CECIL, THERE BEGAN A WORKLOAD OF, WELL, ALMOST IMPOSSIBLE DEMANDS.
IN THE NORMAL WORKING DAY, THEY WORKED ON THE REAL BOOK AND VARIOUS OTHER COMMISSIONS.
OH, YOU WOULDN'T BELIEVE HOW PALLY VICTOR STILL WAS.
AT SIX THE STAFF AND I LEFT – WITH VICTOR WORKING LATE, AS WAS HIS USUAL PRETENCE.
EGRET
AT HALF PAST SIX, THE TEAM RETURNED TO WORK ON VICTOR'S COUNTERFEIT.
AT TEN, THEY OSTENSIBLY LEFT WITH HIM.

ONLY TO RETURN WITH ME IN THE DEAD OF NIGHT TO WORK ON THE SECOND COUNTERFEIT.

THE TEAM HAD TO STUDY VICTOR'S COUNTERFEIT INTENSELY, SO AS TO PRODUCE AN EXACT COUNTERFEIT OF THE COUNTERFEIT.

THIS INCLUDED SOURCING THE DUD JEWELS FROM THE SAME SUPPLIER.

I INLAID THEM MYSELF. IT WAS THE ONE PART OF THE PROCESS THAT PUT ME ON EDGE, TRYING TO IMITATE VICTOR'S HAND.

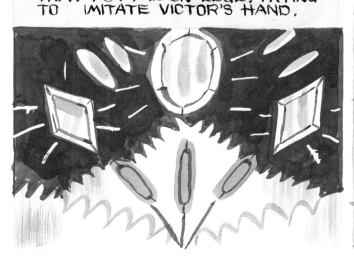

WE WERE EXHAUSTED — OPERATING IN A KIND OF SOMNAMBULIST TRANCE.

THE TEAM UPDATED ME ON EACH STAGE OF VICTOR'S OPERATION, SO WE WERE MIRRORING IT EXACTLY.

ON THE WEEK BEFORE THE DREADFUL FIRE, THE SCHEDULE WAS TO HAVE THE ORIGINAL COMPLETE AND ON DISPLAY ON THE FRIDAY. VICTOR PLANNED TO SWITCH IT WITH HIS COUNTERFEIT ON THE FRIDAY EVENING.

I THEREFORE HAD TO CALCULATE A WAY TO REMOVE THE ORIGINAL BEFORE HE DID, PREFERABLY ON THE FRIDAY MORNING.

ON THE THURSDAY EVENING WE PULLED AN EXTRA LONG SHIFT.

EGRET BINDINGS

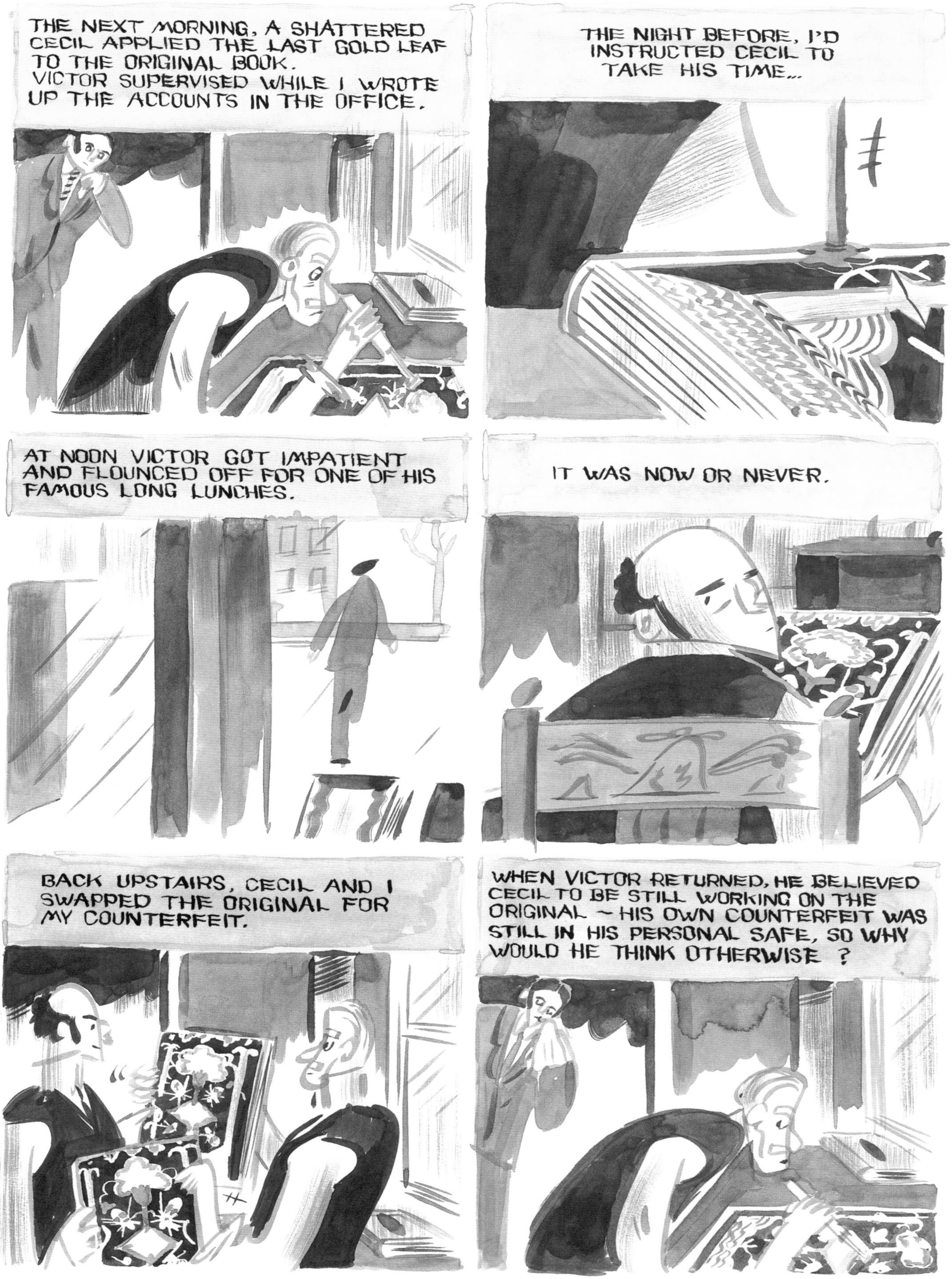
THE NEXT MORNING, A SHATTERED CECIL APPLIED THE LAST GOLD LEAF TO THE ORIGINAL BOOK.
VICTOR SUPERVISED WHILE I WROTE UP THE ACCOUNTS IN THE OFFICE.
THE NIGHT BEFORE, I'D INSTRUCTED CECIL TO TAKE HIS TIME...
AT NOON VICTOR GOT IMPATIENT AND FLOUNCED OFF FOR ONE OF HIS FAMOUS LONG LUNCHES.
IT WAS NOW OR NEVER.
BACK UPSTAIRS, CECIL AND I SWAPPED THE ORIGINAL FOR MY COUNTERFEIT.
WHEN VICTOR RETURNED, HE BELIEVED CECIL TO BE STILL WORKING ON THE ORIGINAL ~ HIS OWN COUNTERFEIT WAS STILL IN HIS PERSONAL SAFE, SO WHY WOULD HE THINK OTHERWISE ?

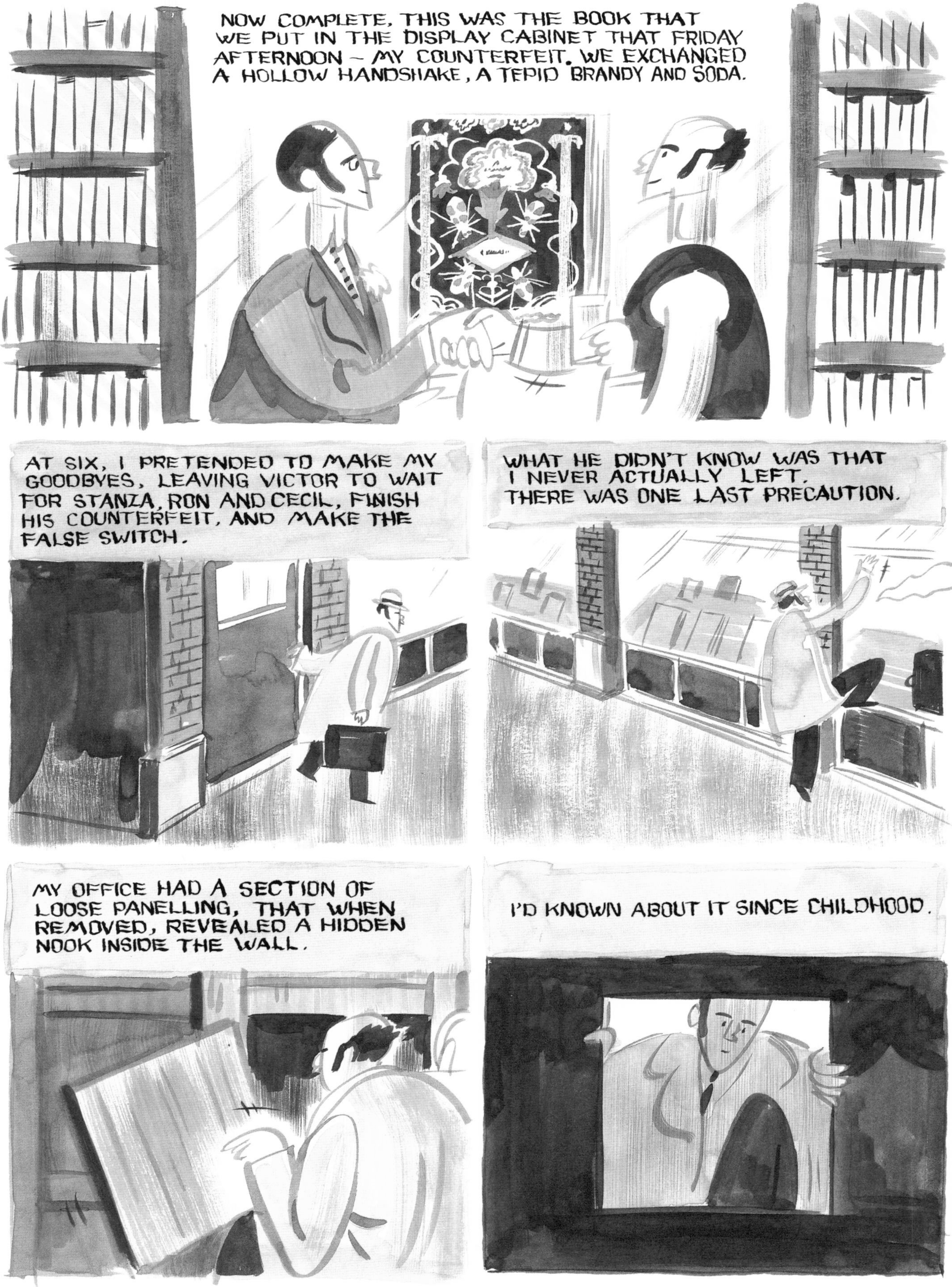
NOW COMPLETE, THIS WAS THE BOOK THAT WE PUT IN THE DISPLAY CABINET THAT FRIDAY AFTERNOON – MY COUNTERFEIT. WE EXCHANGED A HOLLOW HANDSHAKE, A TEPID BRANDY AND SODA.
AT SIX, I PRETENDED TO MAKE MY GOODBYES, LEAVING VICTOR TO WAIT FOR STANZA, RON AND CECIL, FINISH HIS COUNTERFEIT, AND MAKE THE FALSE SWITCH.
WHAT HE DIDN'T KNOW WAS THAT I NEVER ACTUALLY LEFT. THERE WAS ONE LAST PRECAUTION.
MY OFFICE HAD A SECTION OF LOOSE PANELLING, THAT WHEN REMOVED, REVEALED A HIDDEN NOOK INSIDE THE WALL.
I'D KNOWN ABOUT IT SINCE CHILDHOOD.

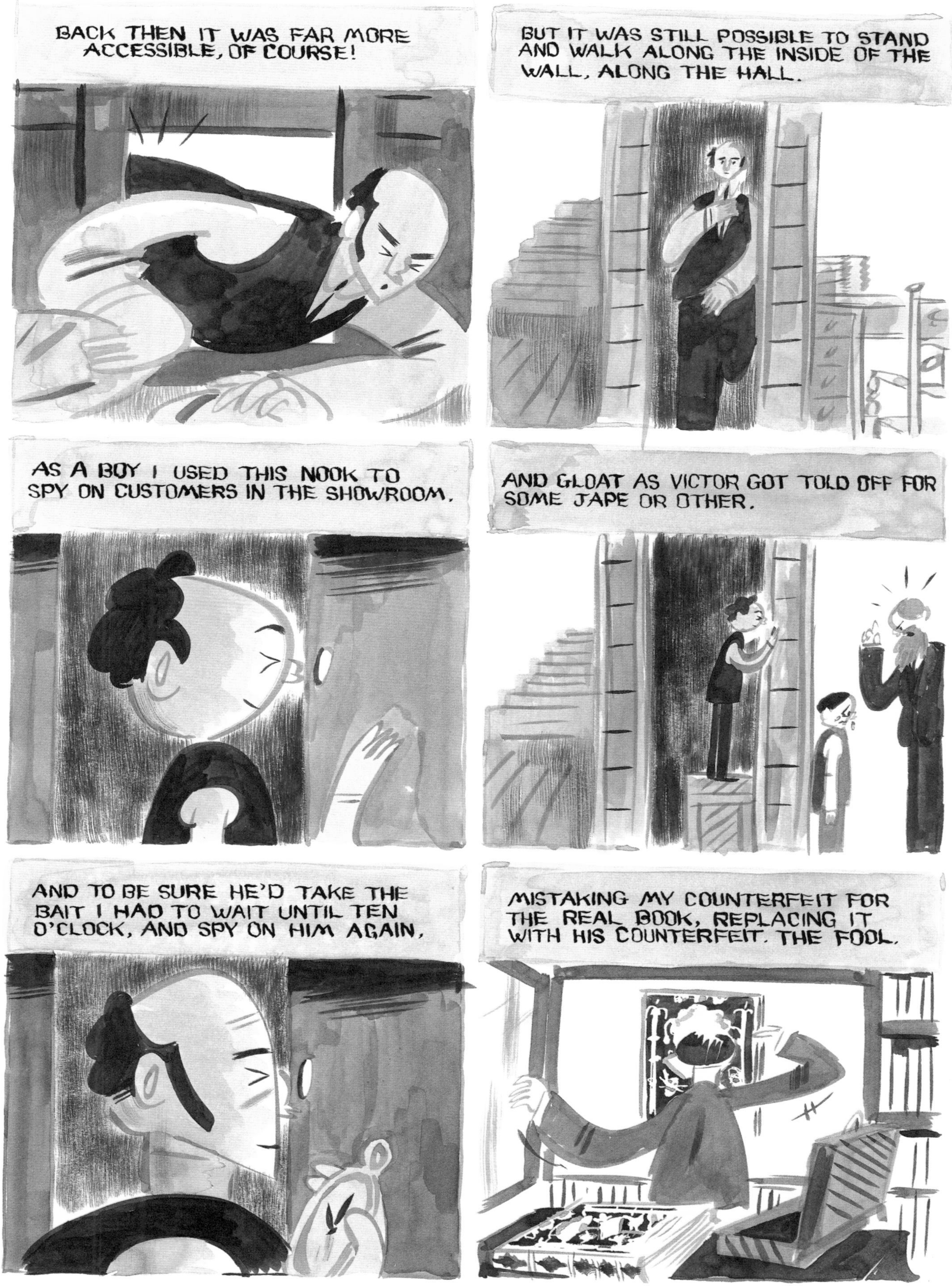
BACK THEN IT WAS FAR MORE ACCESSIBLE, OF COURSE!
BUT IT WAS STILL POSSIBLE TO STAND AND WALK ALONG THE INSIDE OF THE WALL, ALONG THE HALL.
AS A BOY I USED THIS NOOK TO SPY ON CUSTOMERS IN THE SHOWROOM.
AND GLOAT AS VICTOR GOT TOLD OFF FOR SOME JAPE OR OTHER.
AND TO BE SURE HE'D TAKE THE BAIT I HAD TO WAIT UNTIL TEN O'CLOCK, AND SPY ON HIM AGAIN,
MISTAKING MY COUNTERFEIT FOR THE REAL BOOK, REPLACING IT WITH HIS COUNTERFEIT. THE FOOL.

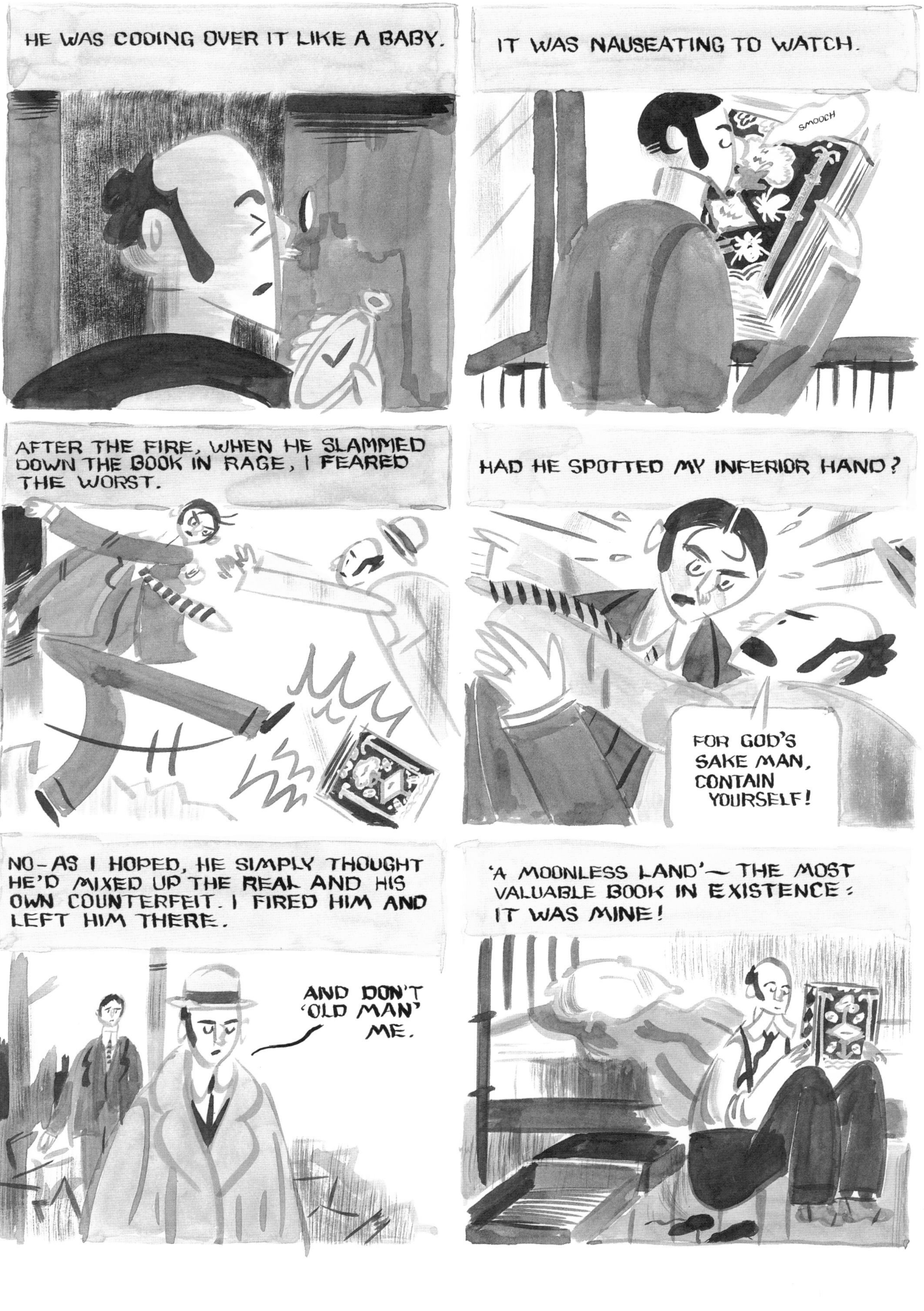
HE WAS COOING OVER IT LIKE A BABY.
IT WAS NAUSEATING TO WATCH.
SMOOCH
AFTER THE FIRE, WHEN HE SLAMMED DOWN THE BOOK IN RAGE, I FEARED THE WORST.
HAD HE SPOTTED MY INFERIOR HAND?
FOR GOD'S SAKE MAN, CONTAIN YOURSELF!
NO– AS I HOPED, HE SIMPLY THOUGHT HE'D MIXED UP THE REAL AND HIS OWN COUNTERFEIT. I FIRED HIM AND LEFT HIM THERE.
AND DON'T 'OLD MAN' ME.
'A MOONLESS LAND'— THE MOST VALUABLE BOOK IN EXISTENCE: IT WAS MINE!

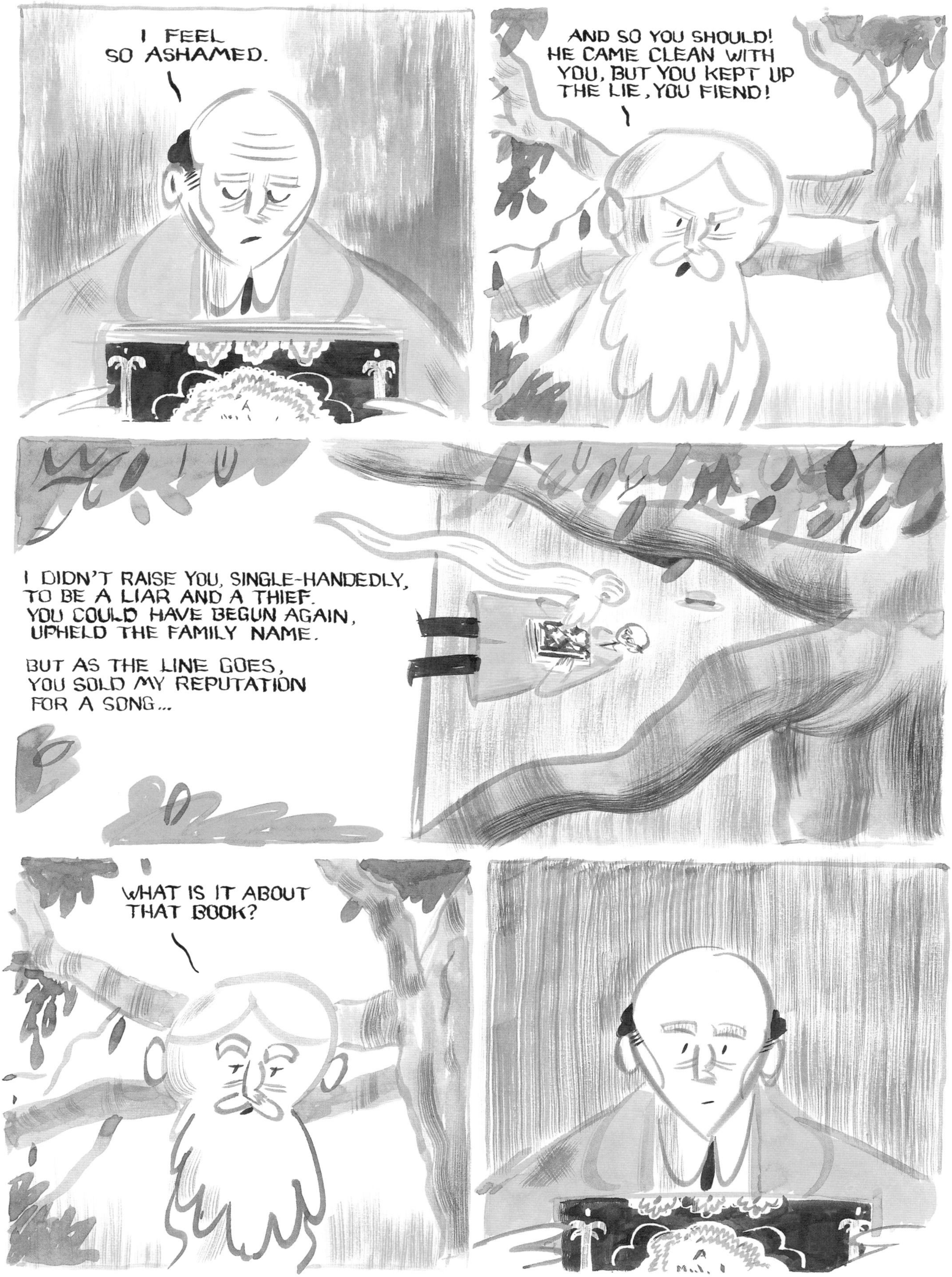
I FEEL SO ASHAMED.
AND SO YOU SHOULD! HE CAME CLEAN WITH YOU, BUT YOU KEPT UP THE LIE, YOU FIEND!
I DIDN'T RAISE YOU, SINGLE-HANDEDLY, TO BE A LIAR AND A THIEF. YOU COULD HAVE BEGUN AGAIN, UPHELD THE FAMILY NAME.
BUT AS THE LINE GOES, YOU SOLD MY REPUTATION FOR A SONG...
WHAT IS IT ABOUT THAT BOOK?

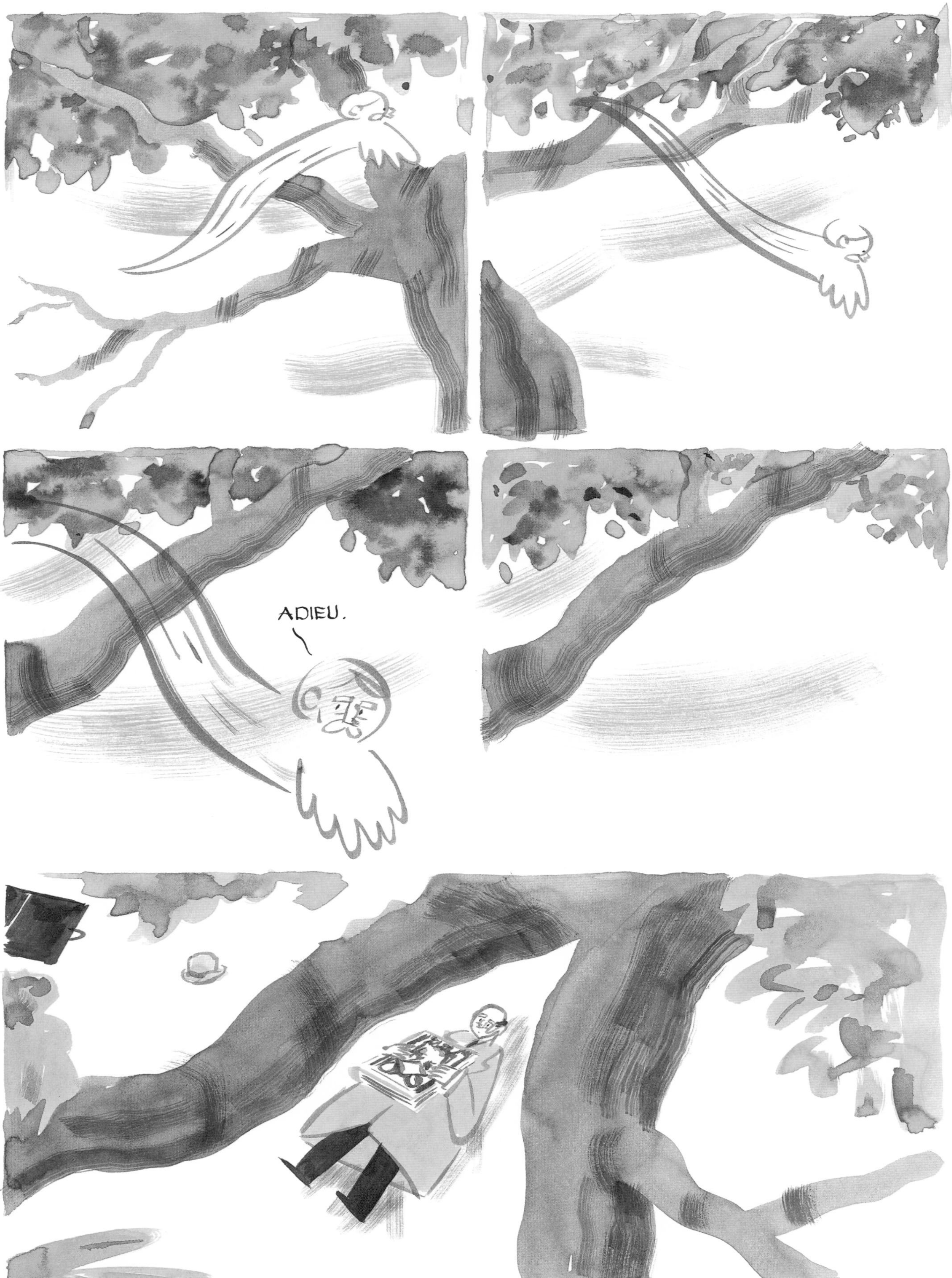
ADIEU.

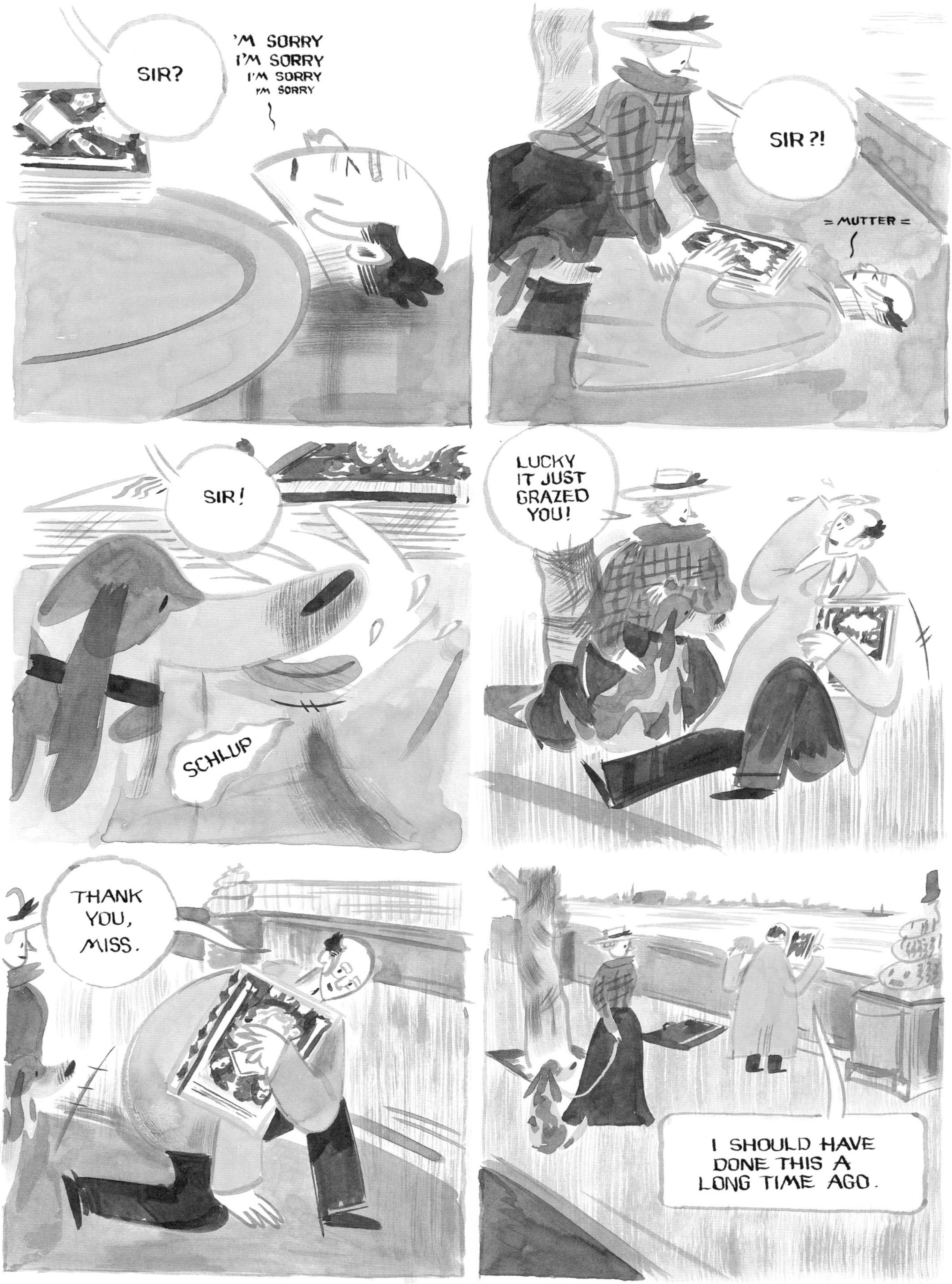
SIR?
'M SORRY I'M SORRY I'M SORRY I'M SORRY
SIR?!
= MUTTER =
SIR!
SCHLUP
LUCKY IT JUST GRAZED YOU!
THANK YOU, MISS.
I SHOULD HAVE DONE THIS A LONG TIME AGO.

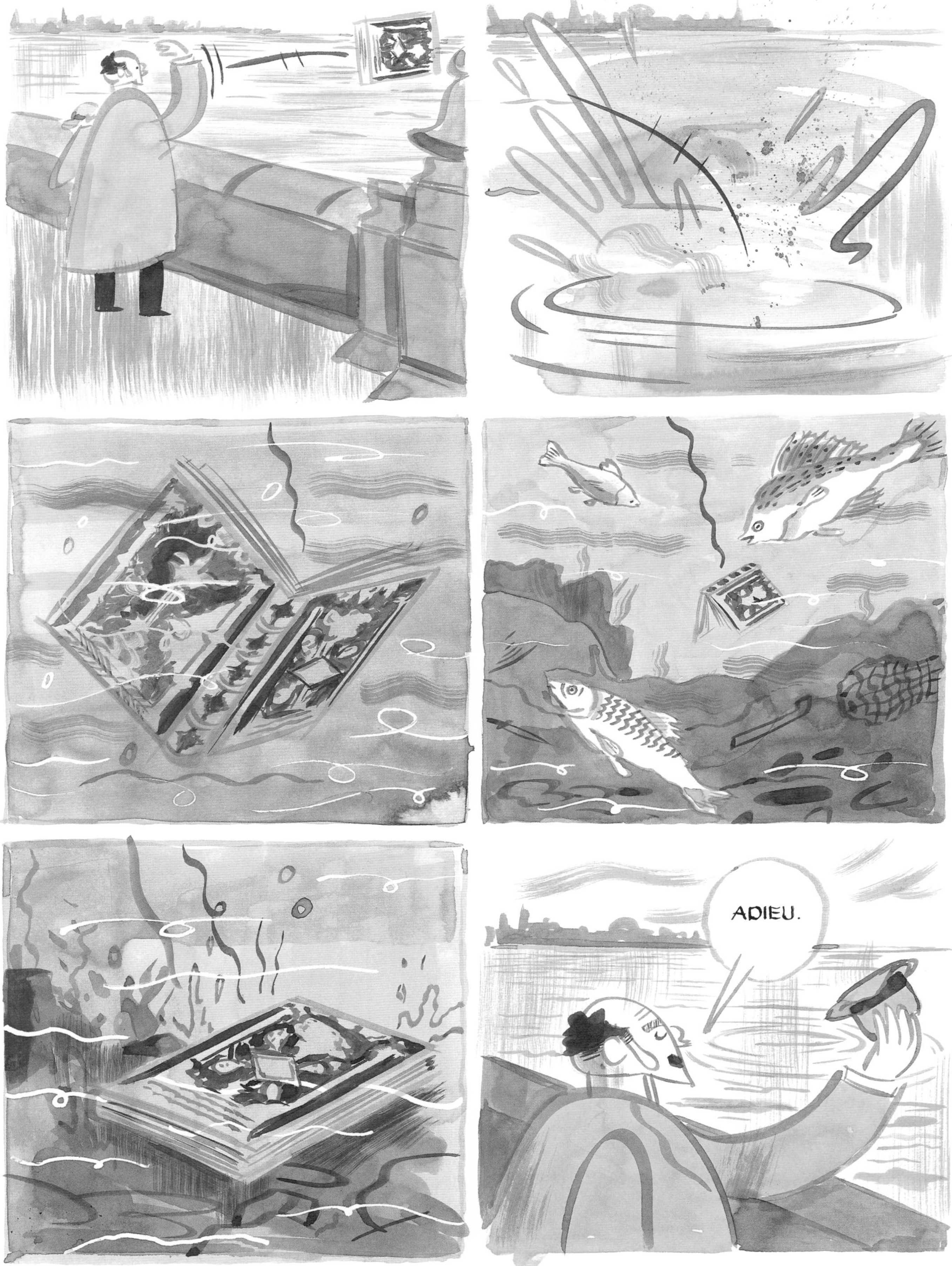
ADIEU.

PART FIVE

Carnation

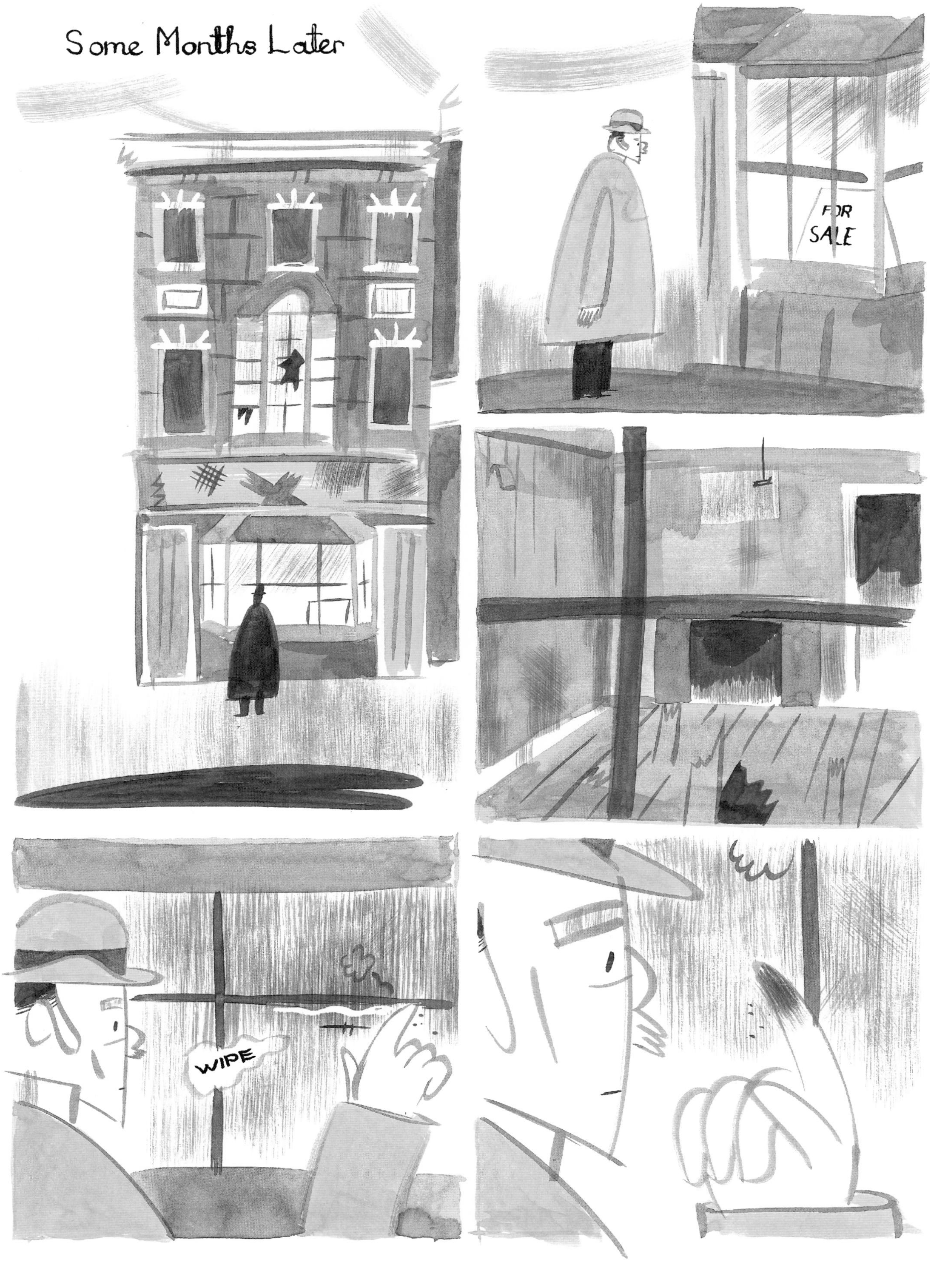
Some Months Later
FOR SALE
WIPE

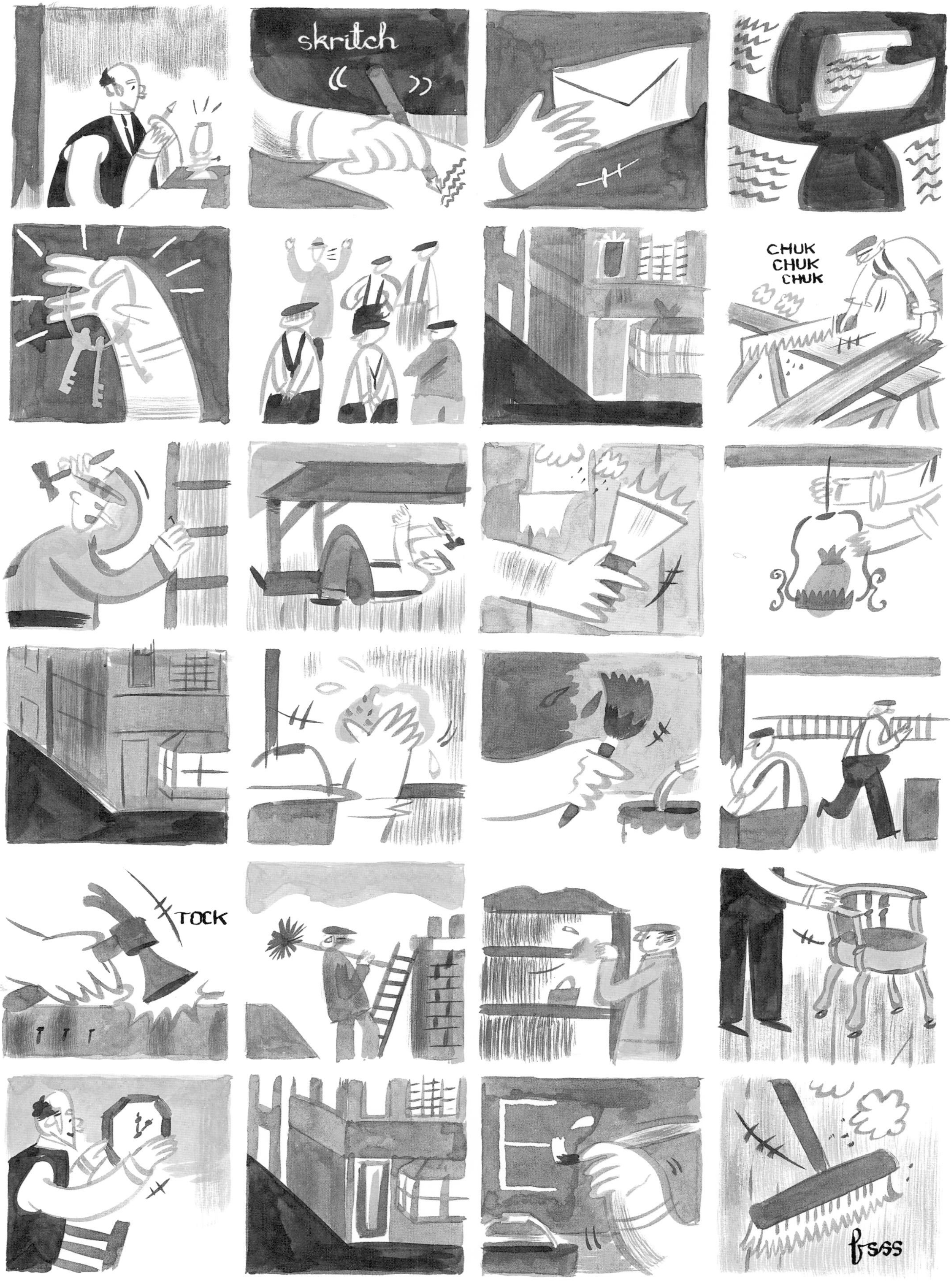
skritch
CHUK
CHUK
CHUK
TOCK
fsss

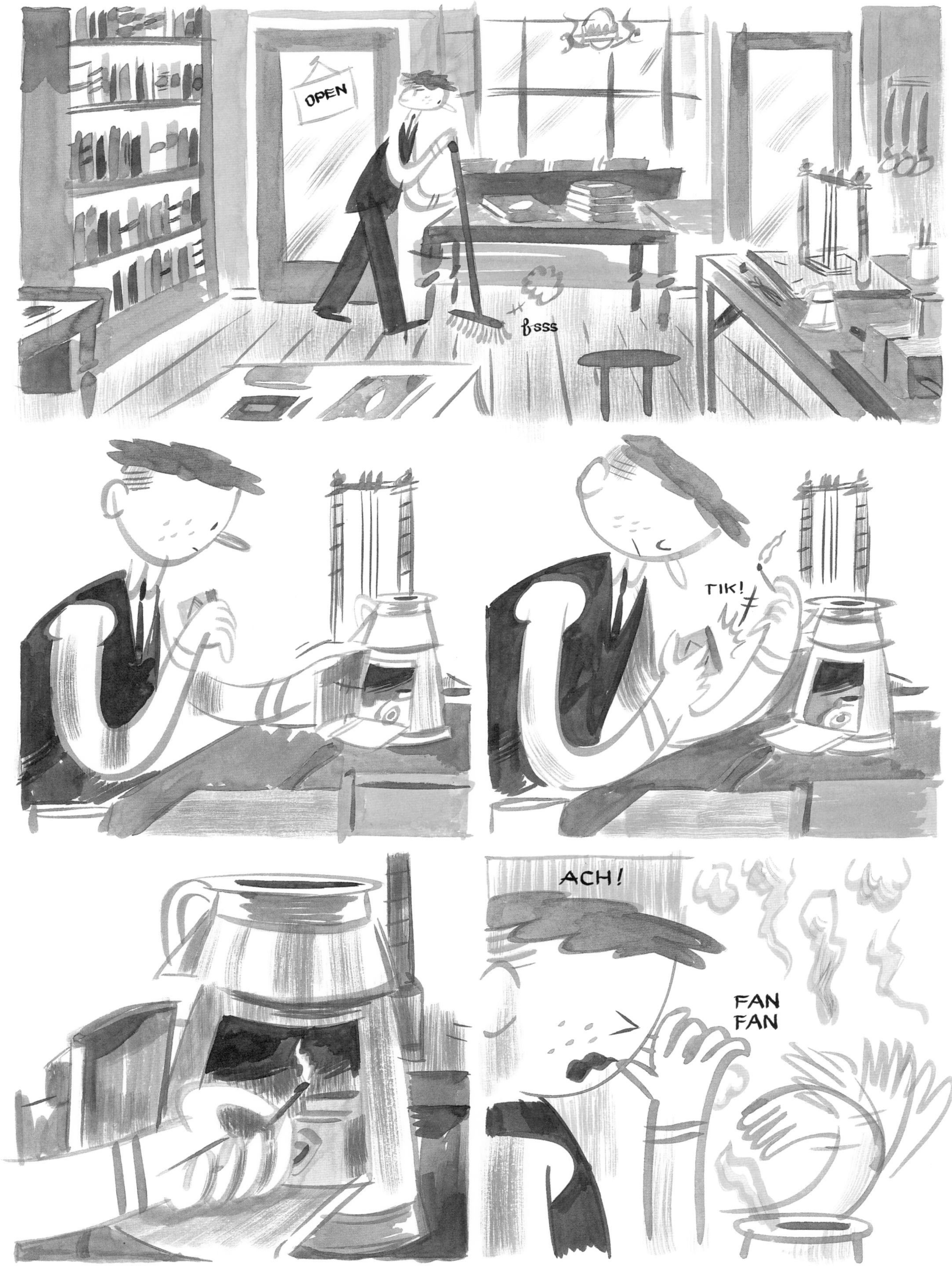
OPEN
fsss
TIK!
ACH!
FAN
FAN

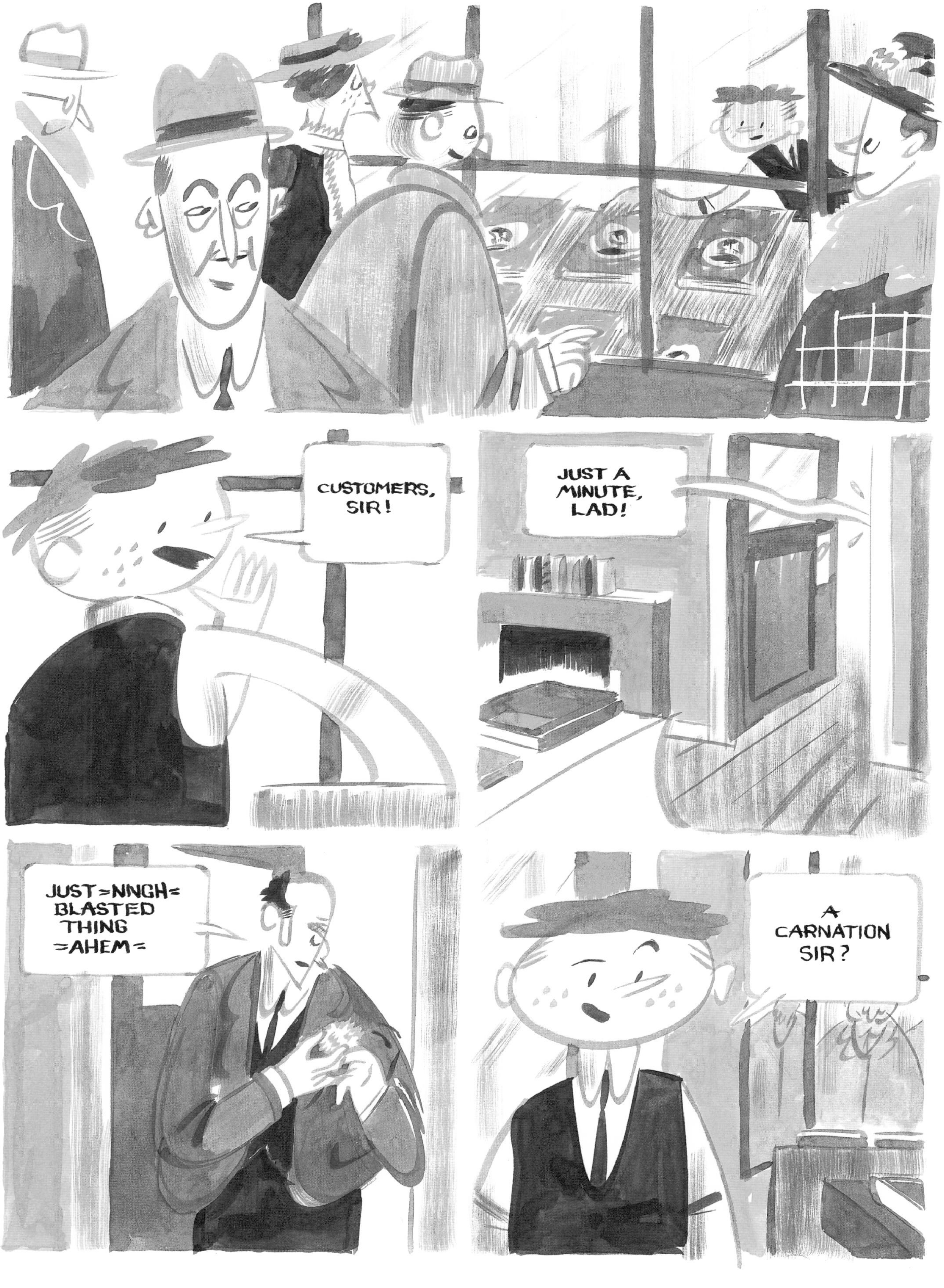
CUSTOMERS, SIR!
JUST A MINUTE, LAD!
JUST =NNGH= BLASTED THING =AHEM=
A CARNATION SIR?

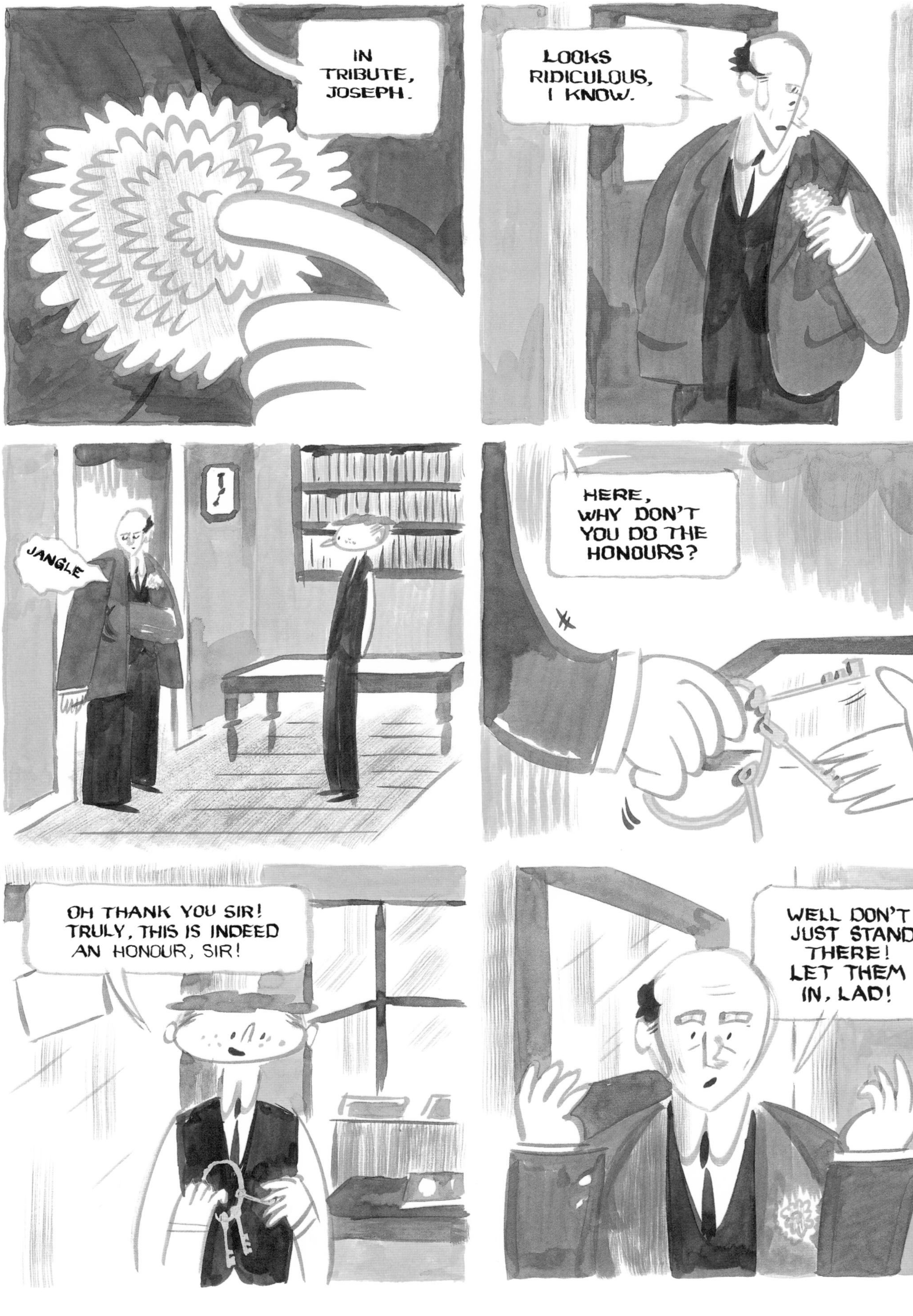
IN TRIBUTE, JOSEPH.
LOOKS RIDICULOUS, I KNOW.
JANGLE
HERE, WHY DON'T YOU DO THE HONOURS?
OH THANK YOU SIR! TRULY, THIS IS INDEED AN HONOUR, SIR!
WELL DON'T JUST STAND THERE! LET THEM IN, LAD!

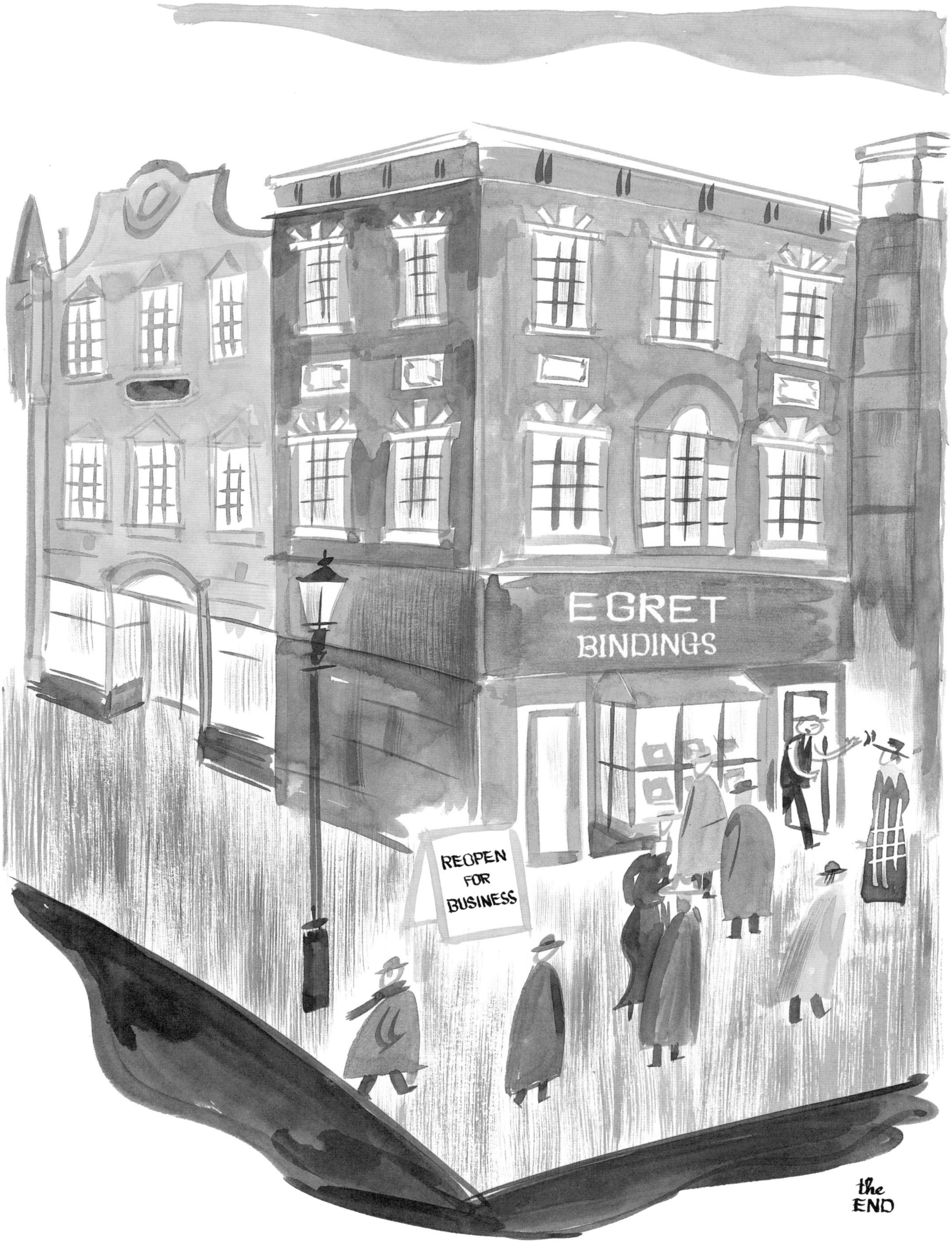
EGRET
BINDINGS
REOPEN
FOR
BUSINESS
the
END

WILLIAM GOLDSMITH IS THE AUTHOR
OF THE CRITICALLY ACCLAIMED
'VIGNETTES OF YSTOV',
ALSO PUBLISHED BY JONATHAN CAPE.
'THE BIND' IS HIS SECOND BOOK.
TO VIEW MORE SAMPLES OF
WILLIAM'S WORK, PLEASE VISIT
WWW.WILLIAMGOLDSMITH.CO.UK

)|17

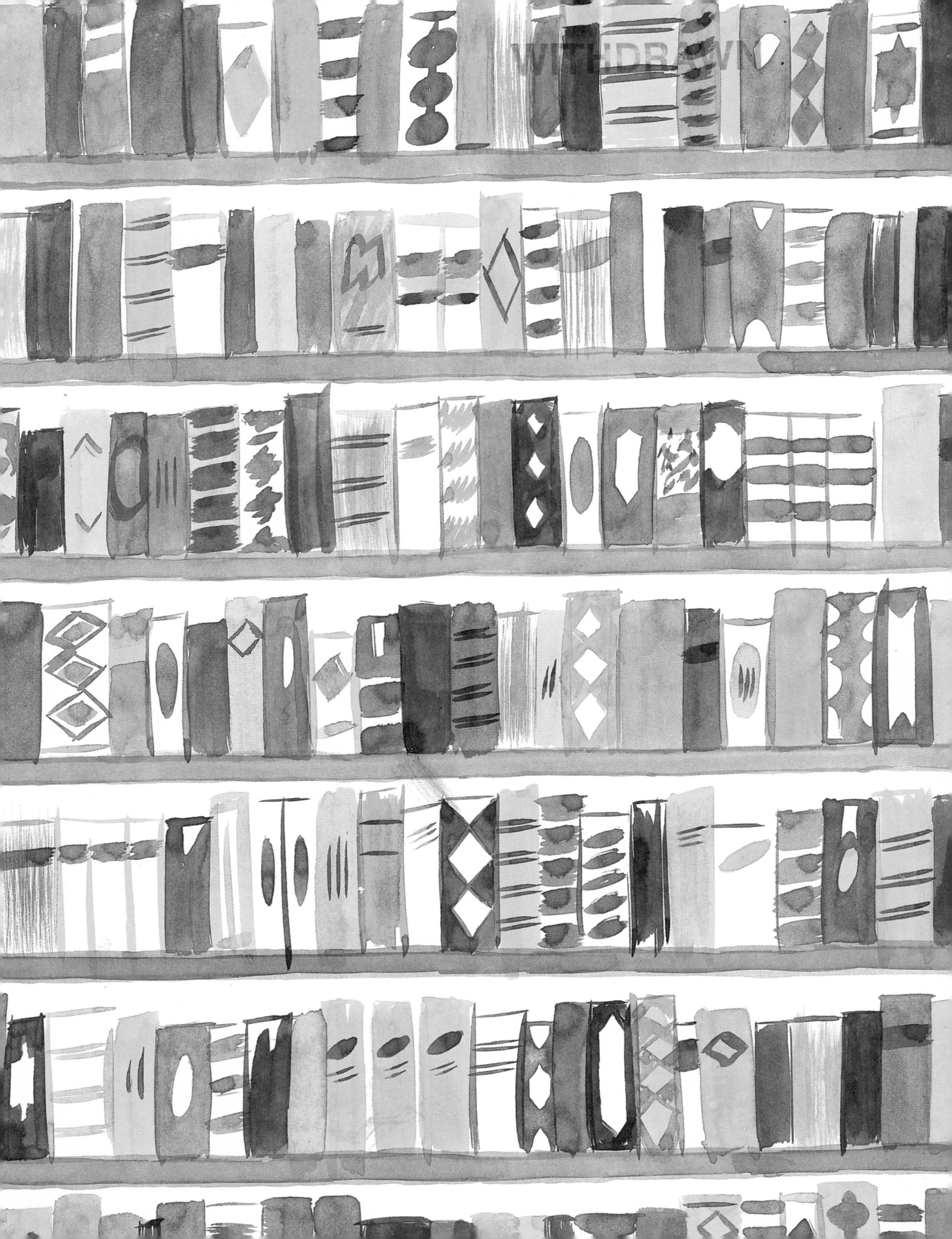